The
Secret Lives
of
Superhero
Wives

JOYNELL SCHULTZ

WET DOG PRESS

THANK YOU

Instead of a dedication, I always start with a thank you to you, the reader. I appreciate you selecting this story in an overwhelming sea of great books to read. I hope you enjoy the untold story of the wives behind the superheroes.

Also, a giant thank you to a few special beta readers who've stuck with me since the beginning and have helped with nearly everything I've published so far. Scott, Molly, Troy, and Heather, you guys are my superheroes!

BLURB

Nobody said being married was easy, but try being married to a superhero. Not only is there laundry, cooking, and a career to balance, but throw in a few supervillains and your day's booked.

Ariana, Victoria, and Emma's men spend more time saving the world than doing dishes. These wives want some semblance of a normal married life, but would settle for an uninterrupted meal together. Besides, how can they compete with saving the world?

When a catastrophic earthquake devastates Shadow Town and crime spirals out of control, it appears the city needs all the help it can get to clean it up. Everyone expected the resident superheroes to save the day, but didn't expect the wives help too…

Table of Contents

Meet the Wives

ARIANA
- Twenty-four years old
- Newly married to Adam (aka The Kite)
- Lives in Windy City
- Works as a personal banker

EMMA
- Thirty-two years old
- Married to Estevan for seven years (aka Capitán Rápido)
- Lives in Actionville
- Works as the chair of Actionville's City Council
- Has one sibling, a sister, and a niece who lives in Shadow Town

VICTORIA
- Twenty-nine years old
- Divorced six years ago from Vance (aka Icy Tundra)
- Lives in Shadow Town
- Works as an accountant at SynPharmaTek

Saturday, April 3rd

ARIANA
in Windy City

'Psst. I'm gonna be late.' Adam's hushed voice whispered in Ariana's mind, jolting her out of the present.

"Hold still," her mother said.

Ariana stiffened and ignored her mom, focusing on her future husband instead. How long would it take to get used to his telepathic superpower? She opened her mind to him and sent a reply, *'Why?'*

'I've been...detained.' Adam forced an image to flood her mind: his naked body with his manliness poorly covered by his hand. Her cheeks tingled and warmed as she looked at her mother's smile. She focused on the image in her head instead, noticing the scorch marks on Adam's skin. Black ash against his thighs and across the ripples of his abdomen. *What had happened?* She assessed his skin—unharmed as usual. Thank goodness for an invincible fiancé.

His voice continued, *'I may not make it in time.'*

'Like hell you won't!' She shifted her weight and the chair she stood on creaked. "Ouch!" Her hand jolted to her rump, swatting her aunt's hand away.

"Hey, you need to keep still." Her aunt gripped her hips to keep her in place.

Ariana sprang off the chair, the bustle of her white gown half-pinned and half-flowing behind her. "Um, I have to go."

Her mom's jaw fell open, but she righted it. "You need to go? Now's not the time for cold feet."

Finding her mom's purse, Ariana pulled out the minivan keys and gave her mom a kiss on the cheek. "Trust me, if I don't go now, there won't be a wedding."

"Won't be a wedding? What's going on?"

Her mom was on her heels as Ariana flew out of the bedroom and ran down the stairs, focusing on Adam.

Tingling filled her chest. *'Where are you?'*

'The alley behind Top Perks Coffee Shop.'

'Do you know what time it is?'

Adam sent an image of his bare wrist. *'I was going to look for my missing watch, but I couldn't find the time.'* He transmitted a chuckle.

'Of course, you have a joke. Come on! Our wedding starts in less than an hour.'

'I know.' Adam's words were clearly enunciated in her mind. *'That's why I'm telling you I'll be late.'*

'Don't move! I'm coming to get you.'

"Where are you going?" Her mother stood in front of the front door.

"No time to explain. Meet me at the church," Ariana panted.

She stopped in the study of her parents' house and snatched Adam's tux, flinging it over her shoulder. With a quick movement, she wrapped yards of her gown's white fabric around her arm and ran outside.

"You can't do—" Her mother's voice was drowned out by the purring V-6 of the sensible gold party machine.

With squealing tires, Ariana flew down the driveway and left her mother yelling in the front yard. "Sorry, Mom, but there's no way I'm being stood up on my wedding day."

More than one neighbor's necks turned to rubber as they watched the scene of the runaway bride. Ariana waved and blew them a kiss before she further pressed the accelerator and clenched the steering wheel.

The van lurched one way and then the other as she rounded the corners through the back streets of Windy City, rolling through red lights and ignoring the speed limits. Who had time for that crap, anyway?

Leaving black tracks on the pavement, she screeched to a halt in front of a rusted dumpster at the end of the alley, perfectly matching the image Adam had sent.

She clicked the button to open the side door, yelling into the empty ally, "This better be good."

With caution, Adam emerged from behind the dumpster with one hand covering his frontside and another covering his backside. The hair was singed off his chest. Hmm…was all his hair below his neck burned off? She looked down at his legs. Yup, that'd be interesting.

He crawled into the van.

Before the door slid shut, Ariana threw the vehicle into reverse and spun the tires out of the alley, heading for the church.

"Here," she huffed, handing her naked fiancé a small, foil-wrapped package. *He's okay, Ari. He's always okay.*

In the rearview mirror, Adam twirled the package in his hand. "Fingernail polish removing wipes?"

"If I were you, I wouldn't be complaining right now. Get the soot off and throw your tux on. Honestly, today, I don't care what you look like. I wouldn't even care if the hair on the top of your head had been burned off. You have a wedding to be at in thirty minutes."

Adam ran a hand through his short, light brown locks, ensuring himself that it was still there. "Don't you want to know what happened?"

"That's not important right now. *Focus.*" Ariana pointed at the tux, then to Adam.

Adam laughed. "Well, he got away."

"I said, get ready." She hid any amusement from her voice.

"Isn't it bad luck to see the bride in her wedding dress before the ceremony?"

Ariana glanced in the rearview mirror, then back to the road, holding up her index finger. "One day. All I ask is that you show up ON TIME this one day." Ariana's arm was shaking. She returned her hand to the wheel and tightened her grip. *Note to self: don't let Adam out of your sight on days with important events.*

Adam laughed. "Don't you ever worry about me?"

Ariana's heart raced and her palms sweated. "You're invincible. You assured me yourself that you'll always be fine. Come on, throw that tux on! I'm sure it'll be all over the Superhero News Network later today and monopolize our wedding reception anyway. I'll catch up then."

Pulling the van up to the church steps, she turned to her future husband. His lip curled up, and all her anger melted away. She took a deep breath as he leaned forward and placed a kiss on her temple, giving one of her blond ringlets a little tug. He whispered, "I love you, but, I think, *you'll* be late." In a flash, Adam was out of the van and disappeared into the church.

Out came Ariana's mother, her wavy gray hair wild in the wind. Ari stepped out of the van, took a deep breath, and smiled, letting it all sink in. She was gonna marry the man of her dreams today. This was truly the beginning of the rest of her life. A fabulous life with an amazing partner at her side.

Her mom took her hand and helped her out. "We have ten minutes to finish getting you ready."

Her dad stepped beside them. "You look beautiful, dear."

Ariana smiled. This was everything she'd ever wanted. Loving parents and marrying a man everyone drooled over—even if they only drooled when he was in costume, saving the world.

VICTORIA
in Shadow Town

Victoria swirled her straw in her Diet Coke. She hated Diet Coke, but being in a newer relationship, she needed to keep her figure in better shape than a Marshmallow Peep. That thought made her stomach growl. She enjoyed being "full bodied" and wanted to keep her curves. It was a fine line to not be too skinny, nor too heavy. The Diet Coke was her balance, but it reminded her how much it sucked to be pushing thirty and divorced.

Today, her mind was on everything except the man in front of her. Work, the book she was reading, and her grocery list.

"Vicky?"

Victoria shook her head and looked up at Mike. "Sorry, I was distracted. What did you say?"

"I had asked if you wanted to get away this week. You said you took a few days off of work. We could go to my cousin's lake cottage." He winked at her. "It would be romantic."

Should she tell him she hated winking? It was creepy and something a sleazebag would do. She bit her tongue and focused on his question. "This week? Um… I'll have Chew-Barka. Can I bring him?"

The smile on Mike's face dissolved as he rubbed his temple. "I can ask, but can't your ex take him?"

She sat back in her chair. "Ask him to do me a favor? I'd rather give up chocolate."

Mike tilted his chin. "You know Thursday's our anniversary."

"Anniversary?"

"We've been dating for three months."

Had it been that long already? "You're counting months? I thought only teenagers did that."

Mike's lips tightened. "Are you not into this

relationship?"

She swirled her straw, splashing soda over the edge of the glass. "Yeah, it's fine… I mean good. It's just—"

Mike looked over Victoria's shoulder, and his eyes bulged. "Speaking of the devil. How is it he always seems to interrupt us?"

She ground her teeth, not needing to spin around to know her ex-husband stood behind her. "Yes, *Vance*, how is it you always seem to know where I am?"

Her ex made his way to the side of their table. His voice was smooth, deep, and familiar. Victoria tried to forget how much it appealed to her. "Coincidence, I guess. I was on my way to the mayor's campaign headquarters, but saw you here."

"Come on. Campaign headquarters is across the city." Victoria took a drink of her soda to prevent her thoughts from escaping.

"You're a supporter?" Mike asked. "I thought nobody liked the mayor. How he won, I'll never know."

"Obviously, more than half the city liked him enough to vote for him, otherwise he wouldn't be mayor. Besides, I always root for the underdog."

Mike leaned forward. "I read that they are trying to have a recall election. Nobody believes he won."

Victoria turned to Vance and didn't hide the annoyance in her voice. "So, why are you here?"

Vance's smile said I'm-hiding-something-I'm-not-going-to-tell-you. "I was simply taking a walk for a little exercise. You know, being healthy and all." He rubbed his neatly trimmed, dark beard while turning toward Victoria's date. "So, how've ya been?" He gave Mike a small punch on his shoulder.

"Ow—" Mike jerked away, rubbing his bicep. He straightened and recovered his pride.

Vance motioned to the table. "Were you done here?"

"No. We hadn't ordered yet." Victoria ground her teeth together.

"Great! I'm starving." Vance grabbed a chair from the neighboring table, turned it backward, and straddled it.

"Join us," Mike said to the already sitting down Vance. "I think Victoria has a question for you, anyway."

Vance picked up the menu that lay in front of Mike. "Were you done with this?" He tipped down his sunglasses and stared at Mike's hot coffee for a moment.

He better not use his power.

He tipped his sunglasses back in place and smiled again. A smile that made Victoria sweat. "A question for me? How sweet of you to think about me."

Victoria shook her head and sputtered out the lies. "I don't have a question, and I never think about you."

Mike interjected. "What she means is would you take Chew-Barka until the weekend?"

"This weekend?"

"Yeah, I'd like to take Victoria away for our anniversary this week." Mike picked up his coffee.

"Anniversary? What's it been? A few months? I thought only kids counted months." Vance shook his head and focused on the menu. "Nah. That won't work. I'm busy."

Victoria set her menu down and glared at her ex. "You're busy? If you've got so much going on, how do you always find the time to hunt me down and torment me?"

"Well, I didn't have plans, but I do *now*." Vance turned away from Mike, toward Victoria, and curled the corner of his lip up into a sly smile. Of course he had plans. They involved keeping her and Mike apart. Now throw in a little irritating Victoria, and Vance's week was full. Did he really hate her that much? Well, she *had* broken his heart.

Victoria choked down a sip of her Diet Coke. "That's okay. I think it's time I found a kennel here for Chew-Barka." She turned to Mike, who had lifted his coffee mug to his lips.

"No—" Victoria tried to stop him, but it was too late. He had tipped the coffee cup back and taken a sip. The icy cold liquid sprayed out of his mouth, all over the table.

Mike set the cup down. "What the hell! It's freezing."

Victoria wiped her face and glared at Vance.

Vance's cocky smile appeared again, then a little chuckle. "I don't know why you're looking at me."

Victoria shook her head at him, trying to tell him she was on to him—on to the fact he used his freeze vision.

Vance set the menu down and changed the subject. "No kennel for Chew-Barka. That's like doggie jail. It's bad enough you put him in one of those things when you moved out west. Let me see what I can do. I'll get back to you."

Mike frantically wiped the coffee off the table. "That would be great if you took him for the whole week." He reached over to reciprocate the punch Vance gave him.

"No!" Victoria tried to warn him again, but it was too late. Mike shook out his fist after slugging Vance's shoulder. Vance hadn't budged. Like a rock as always.

Mike opened and closed his hand. "Wow, man, you must spend a lot of time at the gym."

Victoria stood up. "I've lost my appetite. You two enjoy each other. Mike, call me with details. Vance, I'll see you tomorrow when you pick up Chewy." Victoria left the men alone for their romantic lunch.

EMMA
visiting Shadow Town

The first thing Emma saw when Becky opened her front door was her sister's beautiful, bright white smile. "Hey, sis! I'm so glad you could come over at the last minute. I hope I'm not pulling you away from quality time with your hubby."

Emma bit her lip, holding back a smile of her own. Quality time? Ha. She purposefully didn't leave out his costume when she left. Would Estevan be able to find his black leather supersuit without her? Fight supervillains without her guidance? "It's really no problem. Besides, I want to hear your news."

A little curly-haired, pig-tailed girl, wearing a black sweat suit and black mask, pranced across the room like a gazelle, finally stopping in front of Emma. Swooping her niece up in her arms, Emma kissed her chubby cheek. "How's the little princess today?"

Samantha lisped, "I'm not a princess. I'm a superhero."

"Oh, my mistake. What are your secret powers?"

"I'm just like Capitán Rápido. I can move super-duper fast and can see into the future…a whole day into the future."

"Instead of only ten seconds? You'll be unstoppable!"

Samantha slid from Emma's arms and ran as fast as she could around the living room.

Emma laughed, "She's so cute!"

Becky took her purse from the shelf beside the door. "Ever since she saw Capitán Rápido on the Superhero News Network today, she's been racing around the house."

"Capitán Rápido was on SNN? What happened?" Was her husband okay?

Becky pulled her keys from her purse. "I guess that

supervillain he had been chasing took off out of Actionville and made an appearance in Windy City. Smoke everywhere, but I'm sure The Kite has him under control."

Estevan would be so disappointed that he didn't make the capture. Emma shoved a hand in her pocket, thinking of the bright side. Estevan drove Smoke Shield out of Actionville and Emma might finally get some quality time with her husband. Of course this happened now when she had a pile of proposals to work on at the City Council.

Becky continued, "I'll be home in about two hours. Do you want to hear the news now or later?"

"Now, of course."

Becky's smile brightened, if that was possible, swallowing all her other features. "I'm pregnant!"

"Really?" Emma hefted her sister into her arms. "That's fantastic!"

"Hopefully, you'll have success soon, too."

Emma shook her head, refusing to think of that possibility. "This isn't about me right now. I can't wait for another niece...or maybe a nephew this time."

Becky looked down at her watch. "I gotta go. Josh is meeting me at the doctor's office. I have my first ultrasound today, three months along already." Becky gave Emma another hug before heading out the door.

"Watch this, Auntie Ems!" Samantha crawled up on the couch and jumped off the back with her arms outstretched. "Did you see that? I can fly!"

"Wow, you're even better than Capitán Rápido. He can't fly. Not like The Kite."

"Mommy says I'm going to have a brother or a sister, but I need to be patient."

"Your mommy's wise. You'll need to be very patient."

Samantha ran around the sofa, crawling back up and jumping off again. Emma smiled. Oh, how she wanted a child of her own.

Was that even possible in her life?
Someday, I hope.

Sunday, April 4th

ARIANA
Honeymoon in San Pedro

"Phew. We made it." Ariana faced the hotel room door, brushed her hair out of her eyes, and attempted to comb her fingers through her wind-blown knots. A gentle tug. "Ouch!" She tried again, and again, but gave up. *Note to self: tie hair back when flying with Adam.* Had she packed enough conditioner to return her hair to normal? Being married to a superhero that could fly had practical complications that people didn't think about. "I don't know why we couldn't just do this like normal newlyweds."

Adam grabbed her wrist and spun her around to face him. "Hey, we did *most* of it like a normal couple. We took an airplane to Belize City." A spark grew in his eyes and his lip turned up in a half-smile. His voice dropped into a seductive whisper. "If we would've waited for a connecting flight to San Pedro, we would've had to wait to do this." Adam lifted Ariana up in his arms and kissed her deeply before opening the resort door to carry his new bride over the threshold.

Ariana pulled away enough to whisper, "Well, then. I fully support your decision to use your special skills." She kissed him again.

Adam kicked the door closed as he carried his bride to the canopy bed and laid her down on the soft white sheets. The balcony doors were already open, and a fresh ocean breeze filled the room with a fragrance that was pure heaven. He grabbed her hand, rubbing his thumb over the diamond ring upon her finger. "Since you're Irish, how do you feel about that diamond?"

"What does being Irish have to do with anything?"

Adam crawled on top of her with a menacing, hungry look. "I was hoping you didn't think it was a sham rock." He laughed slightly at his joke while Ariana groaned. "Seriously now, I've been waiting too long for this, Missus Turano."

Mrs. Turano? Ariana didn't like the sound of that and her playfulness disappeared. "That won't do. It reminds me of your mother. Maybe I should have kept my last name or go by *Miz.*"

He didn't back away. "Are you trying to kill the mood talking about my mother?" He shook his head and laughed, then buried his face in her neck. He mumbled into her skin, "Nope. Didn't work. I'm still interested." He smoothed her frazzled hair from her face.

"It doesn't take much to get you excited, does it?" Ariana's giggle was interrupted by Adam's lips. She shifted in bed and wrapped her arms around her husband. In the silence, the sounds from the TV in the other room caught Ariana's attention, specifically two words made her stop: *The Kite.* She cursed the hotel management for leaving the TV on.

Adam stiffened, turning toward the other room.

"No, no, no," Ariana said, wiggling out from underneath her husband. Once free, she rushed to the other room, flicked the TV off, and ran back to the bedroom, flinging herself on top of Adam. In between kisses, she breathlessly forced out the words, "No need...to worry...about that. You're allowed a...vacation...or at least a honeymoon. After all, we're only doing this once."

Adam moaned and flipped her over. Ariana wanted to enjoy it, but her mind was on the news report. Images of past heroic rescues Adam had made flooded her mind. What if there was something big going on? What if people would die if The Kite didn't make an appearance?

"Urgh." She threw her head into the mattress. "Why don't you turn that back on. Hopefully, it's nothing."

"No, that's okay. I'm quite entertained here." He trailed a line of kisses down her arm, then stopped and looked at her.

Ariana shook her head. "Those creases on your

forehead tell me something different."

Giving her a peck on the cheek, he sprang off the bed. "Thanks. You're the best." In moments, he had settled on the wicker sofa in the other room and Ariana sat next to him. The news report caused Ariana's heart to sink.

"Smoke Shield strikes again! A black cloud of smoke hovers over Windy City. It's been over twenty-four hours since anyone has spotted The Kite. Where are you? You're needed."

"Great," Ariana said, pulling her feet up on the couch and wrapping her arms around her knees.

Adam looked at her with expectant eyes. "Why would Smoke Shield move to Windy City? He's the one who burned all my clothes, and hair, off on our wedding day. I didn't know he'd cause this." Adam returned his eyes to the images of the heavy smoke that lined the streets of their hometown.

She dismissed him with her hand. "Fine. Go. You have a job to do."

Adam repeated his words. "Thanks, you're the best." He dug his costume out of his small backpack and soon was dressed from head to toe in light gray complete with a black cape with elaborately stitched, silver feathers to resemble the Swallow-Tailed Kite—Adam's favorite bird. He kissed Ariana again and secured the white hooded mask over his eyes. "I'll be back as soon as I can. Check out the beach while you wait."

He ran across the room and jumped off their third story balcony, flying off into the sky and leaving Arianna alone in the honeymoon suite.

In her mind, her husband's voice whispered, '*Don't forget, I love you.*'

She sighed. '*I love you too. Hurry back.*'

~ ~ ~

Hours had passed since Adam flew off the balcony, and he hadn't returned yet. Ariana left a note, directing him to the beach, even though he could find her by using his telepathy.

She relaxed into a lawn chair and inhaled the gentle ocean breeze, enjoying the warm sun on her skin and noting the light taste of salt in her mouth. The beach was mostly empty, since it was almost the off-season, but she still had to fight for her chair. It was sandwiched between a middle-aged woman and a hairy man that overflowed the edges. Ariana attempted to scoot away, but the chair was tied to the others by a thick, silver cable. *Note to self: bring your own chair next time.* She giggled, imagining Adam flying her a lawn chair through the sky.

The woman to her right tipped up her wide-brimmed hat and eyed Ariana. "You must be from somewhere way north."

Ariana tilted her chin. "Why?"

"First, there's a cold spell here, being only seventy degrees, and you're in a bikini. Cute, by the way. I like the yellow polka-dots. Secondly, you're as white as a ghost. Just look at those legs. You could blind someone with them."

Ariana crossed her legs to make them less conspicuous as she fought the desire to cover them with her towel.

"Don't worry, honey. I'm from Minnesota. I'll keep my sunglasses on and won't go blind. Speaking of blinding, wow, that's some diamond on your finger."

"You don't think it's a sham rock?" Ariana finally chuckled at Adam's joke. She took a deep breath. She hated missing him.

"Shamrock? I don't get it."

"Oh, never mind. It's an inside joke."

The woman adjusted her hat and shifted in her chair. "Are you here on a girls' weekend?"

"No, I'm here with my husband."

The woman sat forward. "Not getting along?

23

Vacations will do that. All that time together, you're bound to get on each other's nerves."

"That's not at all what happened. In fact, this is our honeymoon."

"Honeymoon? And you left your room?" She chuckled. "I see. He must be resting—if you know what I mean."

What was this woman insinuating? "He's not resting…he had business to attend to."

"Hmm. Well, hon, stick with me. I'll keep you busy. If he can't see what a catch he's got, well, that's too bad."

Ariana rolled away, but when she faced the hairy man, she turned up to the sky, attempting to tune out the lady's life story while she fell sleep.

By the time she woke up, the sky was on fire with oranges, reds, and pinks and the sun was dipping toward the horizon. Clicking on her phone, she counted hours. How had eight hours flown by?

'Adam?' She reached out to him with her mind. Nothing. Something else must be pulling his attention. Sometimes she could grab his thoughts if he kept their connection open. From what Adam explained, this drained a bit of his energy and sometimes he had to close it. Was he okay? *Stop thinking about him. It'll only drive you nuts.*

Arianna sat up and cringed in pain. Her legs were the color of a cooked lobster. She pressed her hand to her abdomen and her fingers left white impressions on the burnt skin.

Retreating to her room, she showered and slipped into the red lace lingerie her aunt had given her at her bachelorette party. Her skin, at least on her front half, was red enough to blend in with the lace. Urgh! *Note to self: wear sunscreen!*

She walked around the bed, swinging her hips in as sexy a way as she was capable of, picturing Adam lying in bed. Her chuckle filled the room, but soon she grew tired of pretending.

As she settled in bed, she cringed when she pulled the sheet over her sunburned body.

Where are you, Adam?

Grabbing her phone, she pulled up the Superhero News Network.

She scrolled past the news from Shadow Town: *Attempt on the Mayor's Life Thwarted by Icy Tundra.* Directly below the headline was an image of a regal man, dressed in soft blue with a royal blue cape flowing in the wind and standing on a pad of ice.

She also breezed through the news from Actionville: *Bank Robbery Stopped by Capitán Rápido.* This photo was of a man dressed in black leather standing in front of Federal Financial Bank.

She searched for something from Windy City, any report about The Kite, but there was nothing yet, only reports of the black cloud still hovering. *There's nothing you can do, Ari. He's got this.*

She and Adam had dated for two years before they were married. The first year and a half, she had no idea he had a secret identity. The last six months, she worried nonstop about his safety. It wasn't until he took her for a hike up in the bluffs and then jumped off—refusing to use his ability to fly—that she finally realized he was truly invincible. He plummeted to the ground and smashed nearly flat…well, he didn't smash flat. He made a nice little indentation into the earth and brushed his clothes off like nothing had happened. "There are better things to worry about than me," he had said. Did she still worry? Of course, how could she not? But she buried it deep inside.

She yawned.

Stay awake. He'll be back soon.

Despite her nap, the sun and fresh air had made her tired, and she quickly fell asleep.

VICTORIA
in Shadow Town

Victoria opened her apartment door to Vance's calculating smile. Her ex was up to something, and it made her skin crawl. "What do you want?"

Chew-Barka's tail wagged, and his nose explored as much of Vance as he could. At least one of them was excited. Victoria had to snicker when Chewy's nose nudged Vance in a sensitive spot. Too bad he was nearly impervious to pain.

Squatting down, Vance rubbed the fur behind Chewy's ears. "You know I'm just here to pick him up."

Victoria shook her head. "You're earlier than I expected. Don't lie to me. I know you too well. You have that look on your face that says you have other plans."

His face went falsely blank. "What look?"

"That twisted up lip look. Your Elvis impersonation—minus the charm."

Vance lifted his eyes, focusing on her shirt. "No, not up to something, just checking out the view."

Had she dropped guacamole on her clothing? She glanced down. Grrr. She had taken her bra off and her t-shirt wasn't thick. That focused expression he got when using his powers spread across his face and the room suddenly turned cold. *Vance!* She folded her arms over her chest. "You had your chance six years ago."

"Why didn't that work out again?"

"Because you're an ass."

"How about giving me another chance? I'll be gone before you wake up in the morning." He chuckled.

"Yup. Still an ass."

Vance gave Chew-Barka a kiss on the top of his head. "Yeah, that's what you say, but I don't believe you mean it."

Victoria turned away from him and got Chewy's

leash. "I'll pick him up at your place next week."

After hooking the leash to Chewy's collar, Vance stood, towering over Victoria. She pulled her long, chestnut hair over her shoulders, shielding her chest. Stepping back, she wrapped her arms tightly around her body.

Vance took a step closer, making Victoria wrap her arms tighter. She held her breath in the silence. Why couldn't he just leave? "Okay, you can go now."

He shook his head. "What are you doing with Mike? He's a bit of a dud. I mean, he's unemployed...been unemployed for months."

"Well, you weren't the best at holding down a job either."

"Hey, I have a job and have always had a job. It just doesn't pay anything. You know I don't need the money, anyway."

To break Vance's eye contact, Victoria squatted down, motioned for Chewy, and rubbed his head, smoothing the gray hairs that were now prominent on his black muzzle. The almost human wisdom from Chewy's eyes made Victoria's heart grow heavy. "He's getting old."

Vance rubbed his hand along Chew-Barka's back and all the cockiness left his voice. "Someday, I'll need another excuse to come and see you."

"I still don't buy this one. You really can't live without seeing him every week?" Of course he'd survive without Chewy, he had before, but Victoria couldn't help feeling guilty about what had happened.

"Maybe I want to see you."

"I don't think so. It's not an excuse to *see* me. It's an excuse to *punish* me. To make my life miserable."

Vance smiled again and gave his shoulder a little shrug. "Maybe, but I don't see you refusing me."

Victoria had thought about it, over and over, but there was something inside of her that needed to know he was okay. Was she a sucker for punishment? She stood up and shoved Vance out the door. As she was swinging it shut, his hand stopped it.

"Vicky, there's been some bad stuff going down in town lately. I need you to stay away from the East Side."

The hair on her arms rose. "You have no right to tell me what to do."

"I may no longer be your husband, but I'm warning you as Icy Tundra. With the last election being a major political upset, there are plenty of people angry that the mayor's in office. Some are saying the election results were tampered with. I've been watching him closely because there have been multiple attempts on his life now. Nothing a little brute force can't handle, but who knows what will happen? Until I can track down whoever is orchestrating this, I don't want you near him."

"Any idea who's behind it?"

Vance rubbed a hand through his beard. "Montgomery Marchant has been on the news lately opposing him. He says he supports that radical anti-mayor group."

"Doctor Marchant? I don't think so."

"I know you work for him, but I don't trust him."

"Why? Because he has superpowers too? You never believed he doesn't use them."

"How could you not use them? Powers are tempting. Especially his. Time manipulation is something nobody would even notice."

Victoria rubbed her temple, realizing she would stay away from the East Side...but she wouldn't let Vance know she listened to him.

"Just be careful, okay?" Vance's eyes flashed a tenderness Victoria didn't wish to remember, so she pushed his hand away and shut the door. She leaned against the wall, remembering why she couldn't stay away from Vance completely. Every once in a while, a moment like this happened. A moment when he showed he actually cared.

EMMA
in Actionville

Emma blew out the candle in the center of her small dining room table. She'd spent the past two hours simmering the soup she prepared earlier today and had finally given up waiting for Estevan. Smoke Shield had left Actionville and all the news reports of Capitán Rápido sightings on the SNN ended an hour ago. The threat was stopped, the bad guys apprehended, yadda yadda yadda. Now where was her husband? Sundays were their special day.

She turned the stove off and filled her bowl with soup. All alone at the kitchen table, she blew on the contents and thought back to all the commotion at her sister's house. Things were too quiet here and she loved excitement. She caught herself smiling while thinking of her niece.

The door latch clicked and a gentle breeze blew her wild black hair over her eyes. Hot breath caressed her ear as a soft whisper surrounded her. *"Tienes una sonrisa hermosa.* Mind if I join you?"

Emma couldn't hold back her smile. She stood up and wrapped her arms around her husband's lean, leather-clad body. "I had given up on you."

Estevan pulled his black Zorro-like mask off and kissed her. "Why do you always give up on me? You know I'll always come home to you."

What did one say to that? With a gentle stroke, she brushed Estevan's too-long, nearly-black bangs off his forehead, then headed for the stove to get him a bowl of soup.

A rustle of wind, and he was in front of her. "Sit down. I got it." He zipped away and returned moments later with a steaming bowl of cheeseburger chowder.

Emma picked up the matches and relit the candle. "I

forgot to tell you that I went to my sister's house yesterday. Guess what her good news is?"

"She's pregnant again."

"How'd you know? Oh. After seven years of marriage, I still forget sometimes. Stop using your power on me."

Estevan laughed. "I can't help it when you make me guess."

"It takes all the fun away from me."

"Okay. I'll try, but I'm not promising anything."

"What would you think about us trying to have a baby again?"

"I didn't see that one coming." Estevan shook his head. "We've tried for years. It's not possible... I think my DNA is too different."

"Maybe if we saw a fertility doctor, they'd be able to help."

"I can't risk going to a doctor. What if they discover who I really am?"

"What if it's not you and it's me instead? Maybe I can go. It'd be nice to have you along."

Estevan was still shaking his head.

"What's wrong?"

"I'd gotten used to the thought that we weren't meant to have kids. What if something were to happen to me?"

"You can't go on thinking that way. What if something happens to me? I could get in a car accident on my way to work."

"I think my job's a little more high risk."

Emma took another slurp of soup, but her stomach turned. She pushed the bowl away from her. "Just think about it, okay? I'm tired and am heading to bed. Would you mind cleaning up?"

"Hey, *mi gatita*, I'm sorry. I'll think about it, okay?"

Emma nodded as she slipped behind the bedroom door. Crawling into her cool sheets, she wondered how she could feel so lonely when her husband was right in the other room. Maybe she was crazy for wanting a child. Who ever heard of a superhero with a kid? But who ever heard of a superhero with a wife?

A tear slid down her cheek and pooled on her pillow. Samantha running around in her homemade mask and black jogging suit, trying to replicate Estevan's leather outfit, had rekindled a suppressed desire for her own children. Besides that, how excited would Samantha be to know her uncle was Capitán Rápido? Just another secret for Emma to keep.

The mattress sunk, and soon a strong arm wrapped around her. Estevan pulled her springy curls away from her face and kissed her cheek. "If you really want to try again, I'll do it. All I want in life is to make you happy."

Emma turned over and snuggled against his chest. "I don't know what I want, but thank you." She inhaled his clean outdoorsy scent and soon fell asleep in his arms.

Monday, April 5th

ARIANA
in San Pedro

Ariana awoke to the sound of Adam's voice. She moaned and ran her hand down her sides and over the lacy fabric of the lingerie against her hips.

She smiled. "Good morning, honey." She rolled over and reached her arm out to hug her husband…only to grip the cold pillow. Her eyes flicked open. "Adam?"

Silence.

She looked toward the bathroom and raised her voice. "Adam?"

Still nothing.

She closed her eyes and reached out for him with her thoughts. *'Adam?'*

His voice then echoed in her mind. *'I'm here. Well, I'm not there. I've been…detained.'*

Detained seemed to be his favorite word these days. Cringing from her sunburn, she sat up in bed. *'What do you mean, detained?'*

*'A man assaulted me with **milk, cream,** and **butter.'***

'What?'

*'How **dairy.'*** Adam's deep chuckle filled her head.

'Come on. Seriously. This is our honeymoon!'

'I…um, The Kite nearly captured Smoke Shield. You know, that guy that played in Actionville and now had Windy City covered in a cloud of smoke, but I…um…The Kite needs to work with the police on this. We're going to get him before he implements whatever master plan he has. I'm so sorry. I'll make it up to you, I promise.'

'You better.' Urgh! She didn't mean to send that last thought to Adam. *'Just hurry back as quick as you can.'* She pulled the sheets tight, twisting a corner around her hand and shifting positions. Failing to find a comfortable spot, since her skin was on fire and felt like alligator leather, she sighed.

Adam's words stopped her. '*I love you, and all the people of Windy City would love you if they knew your sacrifice.*'

She blew out a breath and managed to send him, '*I love you, too,*' before their connection closed.

After breakfast, Ariana slathered herself with sunscreen and went back down to the beach. Under the shade of a palm tree, she lay one way, then another, but she couldn't get comfortable as her mind churned. This was supposed to be her honeymoon. *Damn him.*

She sat up and looked down the long line of tied together beach chairs. Couple after couple lay next to each other in the warm sunlight. She wrapped her arms around her stomach. Being alone was such a disappointment.

Ariana retreated to her room, booked herself a flight home, and packed her stuff. Out of instinct, she dialed her parents' number.

"Hi, Mom. I need to come home early. Could you pick me up at the airport tomorrow?"

"What's wrong?"

She wished she could tell them everything, but keeping Adam's identity a secret was something she had promised him. "Oh, we'll talk about it tomorrow. Will you be there for me?" She held back tears. She'd have to come up with an excuse by then.

"Yes, of course. What time?"

"Three."

"Okay. I love you."

"Love ya too, Mom."

She stood out on her balcony, overlooking the ocean. In this romantic location, she felt so out of place. She needed to be with Adam, no matter where that was. It was her honeymoon, and a honeymoon should be spent with your spouse. She could do that anywhere…be it here in paradise or home in Windy City.

EMMA
in Actionville

After a busy day down at City Hall, Emma spent the evening researching fertility centers. She had decided to go herself—at least then she could determine if it was Estevan's issue or her own. She wished it was easier to find out if superpowers and children were compatible.

There had to be other superheroes that were married. She spent hours on the Superhero News Network researching other city's heroes and scouring news articles, mostly from tabloids. All she found was speculation.

> *Icy Tundra seen kissing a curvy brunette.*
> *Has The Kite hooked up with Scarlet Macaw?*

But no stories of children. Didn't the news find kids scandalous enough? What a shame. If only the superheroes worked together, she could ask them...but everyone was quite protective of their territories. Stupid egos, but she was guilty of stroking Estevan's on a daily basis. Besides, superheroes were a newish thing. It wasn't until fourteen years ago, when a solar flare sucked two comets into the sun, that a few people began to develop superpowers.

With the emergence of superheroes also came supervillains. A nearby city, Shadow Town, had a special, maximum security prison that harbored a few of these. Of course, they wouldn't discuss if they had a family or not.

Emma rubbed her head. Maybe Estevan was right. What if something happened to him? It was one thing leaving Emma widowed...it was another to leave a child without a father.

She turned away from this foolishness and focused on work. Shadow Town's mayor was coming to visit Actionville this week and speak to the City Council. There was quite a debate regarding the construction of a high-speed train connecting their towns. Shadow Town was not happy about it, and many people in Actionville were not either. Emma liked the idea, because it would cut forty-five minutes off her trip to visit her sister and create jobs for the people of Actionville. No matter what decision was made, some people would still be unhappy. This debate was exhausting, but fulfilling.

Rubbing her eyes, she glanced at the time; it was after 10PM and past her bedtime. Where was Estevan? She bit her lip, convincing herself he was off somewhere, saving someone. As images of him waving to the news cameras and shaking the police commissioner's hand filled her mind, a smile slipped out. She wouldn't tell him, but he couldn't do it without her. The whole thing had been her idea. After meeting him in high school, right when his powers began to develop, she was beside him every step of the way.

Closing the laptop's lid, she stood up for a snack before bed. When she twisted around, she ran smack dab into an iron chest. "Oh, don't do that!" She clutched her hand over her racing heart.

Estevan chuckled. "I forget you can't see the future."

Reaching up, she pulled her husband's black mask off from over his eyes. "Well, Mister Rodríguez, do you know what I'm going to do next?" She thought real hard about getting a sandwich from the fridge. It was a game she played: could she make him see a different future?

He smiled slyly. "You're going to take me to bed."

"Dang you!" she said, slapping his biceps.
His arms wrapped around her and he carried her to their room. Someday, she'd get the sandwich trick to work.

Tuesday, April 6th

ARIANA
Back home in Windy City

Ariana cursed herself during the flight home. Why had she called her parents? It had been instinct, and she needed to get over it, but twenty-four years of relying on them to always come to her rescue was a hard habit to break—especially for an only child. *You're married now, Ari. You have your own life.*

She attempted to formulate possible excuses, but her mind drew blanks. *Note to self: create a book of excuses. You'll need them, being married to a superhero.*

What possible reason was there for leaving your honeymoon? She hadn't thought of it then, but she could have called a taxi when she'd returned to Windy City. Deep down she wanted the support from the two people she knew would always be there for her. Her parents loved her, no matter what, and she craved that love. Despite Adam telling her he loved her, she couldn't help feeling hurt every time he abruptly left her...even if it was for a good cause.

Ari, you told him to go save the world.

"Hey, honey," her mom said, greeting her at the baggage claim. "What happened? That look on your face could scare a pack of hungry tigers away."

Ariana forced a smile and attempted to brighten her eyes. The worst part of all of this was that Ariana couldn't tell them everything... Actually, she couldn't tell them *anything*. In fact, she'd have to flat out lie. "Adam wasn't feeling well. I sent him home on an earlier flight, and his parents picked him up. There was only one seat on that plane, so I couldn't go along." Ariana fidgeted with the end of her blond ponytail, telling herself to stop talking. Any more information and an already weak story would sound fabricated.

Her dad raised an eyebrow.

She turned her focus to the luggage carousel. As suitcases began to make their way around in circles, her words flowed out. "I know. It was our honeymoon, but you know how that foreign water is. No matter how hard you try to avoid it, it still sneaks its way into something. Ice. Fruit. Who knows what? He had stuff coming out of both ends. I was glad I wasn't on his flight. Can you imagine?" *Okay, Ari, bite your tongue. Don't dig a hole.*

"I hope he's okay." Her mom rubbed her shoulder, and Ari leaned into her.

She spotted her lime green suitcase and fetched it from the carousel. "Yeah, he's fine. He called me a little bit ago and gave me the update." *Crap.*

"A little bit ago? Like when you were on the airplane?" Her dad saw through her lie, she felt it. He always was the first to spot a fib.

She didn't turn for fear he'd get confirmation from the look on her face. "I mean, after we landed, but before they let us off the plane yet. It's okay, guys. I know you love me, but I'm married now. It's time you let go a little."

If only Ariana took her own advice. She spun around and pulled her suitcase toward the door. Damn. A wheel broke during traveling. How did that happen? Every single time she traveled, something happened to her luggage. Why did she bother getting pretty ones? Did the baggage handlers hunt hers down and play Whack-A-Bag with it?

Her parents stared at her, probably waiting for her to continue to ramble on. They were on to her lie, she knew it. *Note to self: don't call your parents for help next time. Write that in your book of excuses and circle it in red.*

Ariana dropped the suitcase and put an arm around each of her parent's shoulders. "Come on. Let's get some chow. I'm famished."

She gave her bag a little nudge toward her father and smiled, silently asking for help. Once he reached out for the handle, she dropped her arms and led her parents out of the airport.

VICTORIA
in Shadow Town

"Refills anyone?" Dora stood at the end of the table, holding up the bottle of merlot for all to see.

"Aye, aye, Captain!" Victoria and four other women chanted in unison while holding up their nearly empty glasses.

"Keep it coming. Isn't that the reason we all meet, anyway?" Megan held back a laugh.

Steadying her glass, Victoria held it out for Dora to fill. "Did anyone actually read the book this month?" She swirled the wine under her nose. A hint of floral. Delicious. Definitely not low-calorie.

Megan's laugh escaped while she held her glass out to Dora. "I didn't even download it."

"I think you may have already had too much." Dora tipped the wine bottle away from Megan's glass, but a pouty lip easily scored her a refill.

Once everyone's glasses were refilled, Dora sat at the head of the table. Her eyes widened and an I'm-thinking-naughty-thoughts smile danced on her lips. She leaned forward and her voice dropped an octave. "Has anyone watched the Superhero News Network today?"

"How could we miss it?" Faye said, setting down her copy of the novel and seductively tracing her finger along the rim of her glass.

Victoria glanced around the table, taking in everyone's smiles. They seemed to share a secret. "What happened? Whatever it is seems really good, and I want to know all about it!"

Clutching the stem of her glass, Dora leaned forward. "Icy Tundra saved the mayor again today. This time, he stopped a bullet by freezing it, but as he leapt forward, his costume malfunctioned." Her eyes shifted between the other women, and they all burst out in an amused laugh.

Victoria bit her lip. How would she react if she hadn't been married to him…and currently annoyed-to-hell with him? She opted to stay silent.

"Mm mmm." Faye shook her head. "His blue belt came unbuckled…and the fabric ripped, showing off the muscles of his chest, his abs of steel, and maybe…a little lower. Too bad he wrapped his cape around himself before anyone took some good photos. Oh, what I'd give to rub my fingers against those ripples and trace those defined lines—"

"I wouldn't stop there." Megan erupted in laughter. "I'd love to thaw that Tundra."

Victoria's cheeks heated. "Okay, enough. Let's talk about the book." That nobody read.

Dora's wine glass clinked on the table. "What's wrong? Not your type? Don't tell me you don't like tall, dark, and handsome?"

Victoria gave her head an over-zealous shake. "I don't. There's nothing about him I like."

"I thought Icy Tundra was everyone's type. He's mysterious, got a hot bod, and runs around helping people all day. He's truly the complete package."

Leaning back into her chair, Victoria futzed with her shirt's hem. "Yeah, but we don't really *know* him, do we?"

"Oh, I'd like to get to *know* him," Megan giggled.

Victoria reached for her wine. Trying to seem relaxed. "I imagine he's full of himself. How can you not be, running around and being worshipped all day? I mean, just look at him, he looks like an ass."

"I wish I'd seen his ass." Megan winked, causing the room to laugh.

Victoria blew out a breath, then hid her frustration with a sip of wine. Had the room suddenly grown warm?

She pushed the wine away. "No matter where he goes, people tell him how wonderful he is. Imagine how that must go to his head? And running around all day, he'd never have time for you. Plus, he wears a mask, he probably looks goofy underneath or something." Though that last comment wasn't true. He was too good-looking, deep green eyes, dark eyebrows, square cheekbones, and full, soft lips. "I bet he slurps when he drinks, snores, gets too loud when he's excited, and keeps a lot of secrets." All of which were true.

"He could have yellow toenails and I wouldn't care," Faye said.

Victoria looked at the time on her phone. "I need to get going. I have to get up for work in…six hours. Have a nice night, ladies." She picked up her eReader, hugged them good-bye, and headed for the door.

"Oh, Victoria." Dora said. "Since none of us were prepared tonight, and the wine seemed to take over the book, how about we try this again next Friday? Same book?"

"Yeah, sure. I'll be there." She hoped the topic didn't focus on her ex's uniform malfunction again. She headed out the door, trying, but failing, to suppress the thoughts of her ex's chest, abs, and firm behind wrapped in his blue cape.

ARIANA
in Windy City

It was late when Ariana arrived home. The first thing she noticed wasn't the silent house, but the endless pile of dishes by the sink that told her Adam had been home. How much had that man eaten? Why did she think getting married would make him clean up after himself?

She struggled to wheel her broken suitcase to the laundry room. The thought of washing her stuff made her cringe. Traveling was exhausting. So was lying to your parents, over and over again.

In front of the washer lay a heap of clothes. Black, white, and gray. The Kite's costume. She picked it up with two fingers. *Blood?* What had happened? Her stomach did a flip.

Stop worrying, Ari. He's invincible. It's not his blood.

Despite this, she poured hydrogen peroxide on the blood, scrubbed, and threw the costume in the washer. Her clothes would wait.

When she stepped into her bedroom, she could barely keep her eyes open. She used her phone light to find her way, checking for Adam in bed first. He lay in his normal spot, sleeping soundly.

Something dark was over his eye. Ari flashed her flashlight in his direction. A gash on his head? Was that blood on his suit his? It was impossible, he was invincible, at least she thought he was.

She rubbed her hand down his shoulder. "Adam?"

He let out a soft snore.

She rubbed his face and brushed his light brown hair back. "Are you okay?"

He inhaled a deep breath and rubbed his eyes. "Hey, Ari."

"What's that?" Ariana pointed to the gash on his forehead.

"Oh, that. It smarts. Do cuts hurt this bad?" He smiled. "It's been so long that I don't remember. Too bad my whole left side didn't get cut off."

"What do you mean?"

"Well, I'd be all right then." Despite being half-asleep, he still let out a small chuckle.

Ariana put her hand on her hip. "You didn't answer me."

"This time, the bad guy was more invincible than me. Made me not-so-indestructible."

Ariana bit her lip, her eyes latched onto the cut on her husband's face.

"I need to sleep. Join me?" Adam moved over. "I caught Smoke Shield, though. He's behind bars over in Shadow Town." A huge grin emerged. "It took me less than a week…and Capitán Rápido had been trying for over a month. Aren't you proud of your hubby?"

Hubby? Ariana smiled. "Just give me a moment, and I'll crawl in."

She brushed her teeth and changed into PJs. Soon she lay beside her husband, debating if her whole life, married to a superhero, would be like this. Nearly missed his wedding and no honeymoon. How did she fit in? Then she thought about the gash on his head and realized she should be happy he wasn't hurt worse.

Wednesday, April 7th

ARIANA

in Windy City

The next morning, Ariana lingered in Adam's arms as long as possible before the weight of everything she had to do settled on her. She turned over and traced her finger along his newly healed cut from last night.
Invincible…mostly.

She slipped from his grasp and started getting things in order. If she had everything tidied when Adam woke up, they could spend the rest of the day together…it was still their honeymoon, after all. She tried to contain her smile, but she couldn't help beaming.

Ariana had done a few loads of laundry, picked up the house, and made Adam breakfast when he started to get restless. Arranging the food neatly on a tray, she brought the culinary masterpiece to him.

"Adam?"

He smiled. "What's that I smell?"

"I made you a cheese omelet and toast."

"Breakfast in bed?"

"Well, it is our honeymoon."

Adam shook his head. "Somehow, I think making breakfast in bed was my job, but you probably don't want me to do that. When I was younger, I was fired from my job as a chef."

"You were?"

"Yeah, I was caught stealing kitchen equipment. That was a *whisk* I was willing to take."

Ariana set the tray down on the nightstand and threw the pillow at her husband.

He sat up and pulled his breakfast onto his lap. "So, what's got into you?" Adam took a bite of toast and washed it down with the orange juice.

"I don't know. I guess I'm just enjoying being Miz Turano."

"Miz?"

"You know. So I don't picture your mother...and so you don't either."

Adam laughed. "I think my humor is rubbing off on you finally."

"Maybe a little."

Adam dug into the omelet, and Ariana sat on the bed, admiring her husband and listening to the details of the battle yesterday that had left him with the gash on his head.

He finished eating and handed the tray back to Ariana. She hesitated, but didn't know why as she took it from him.

"That was delicious. I need to get a little more sleep. Healing is taking a lot out of me." He turned over, leaving Ariana holding the empty try.

Breakfast in bed and all I get is a 'that was delicious' and a view of your back?

With a huff, she spun around and retreated to the kitchen. After another load of dishes and laundry, all she wanted to do is curl up on the couch and binge Netflix. So much for this magical married life. It was quickly going down the toilet. Why had she expected things to magically change once they said 'I do'?

As Ariana finished scrubbing the toilets, Adam peeked into the bathroom. She stood there, holding the toilet brush and smiling at how clean their apartment was. A perfect way to start out a marriage.

His voice was groggy. "Hey, wanna catch a movie with me?"

"Yeah. I think that's exactly what I need." Ariana's eyes dashed around the spotless house, then back to Adam's face. Did he even notice?

"Tonight, though," Adam said. "I have things I need to wrap up at the police station first."

Ariana followed him as he disappeared into the laundry room and came out dressed as The Kite.

"Thanks for washing my duds." Planting a kiss on her cheek, he flew out the window.

Was that all she got? It took half an hour of scrubbing to get the blood out of the costume.

She looked at the dirty clothes Adam dropped by the washing machine and sighed.

Note to self: put laundry back on your to-do list.

But not now. She needed some 'me time.' Curling up on the couch, she turned on Netflix.

EMMA
in Actionville

"I gotta run downtown tomorrow. Shadow Town's mayor is coming to meet with the City Council to discuss a high-speed railway between our cities," Emma said, scooping up some scrambled eggs.

"A rail to Shadow Town?" Estevan set down his fork. "That'll be nice when we go visit your sister, but why do they want to run a railway to that town?"

"SynPharmaTek Industries is rapidly growing over in Shadow Town and a high-speed rail would allow us to share professional workers."

"SynPharmaTek's run by Doctor Ma…Merrett, right? The guy that has superpowers but chooses not to use them?"

"Doctor Marchant, yes. He's the one protesting the outcome of the mayoral election."

"So, is the mayor coming here to support the railway or oppose it?"

"Support. It's good for his community. Otherwise, SynPharmaTek may move their research facility out of Shadow Town. Another thing that's interesting is that there've been some attacks on the mayor—attempts on his life. In fact, yesterday, someone pulled a gun, and last week, someone jumped from the crowd and punched him in the face. Turns out the guy had two knives strapped to his body. Icy Tundra stopped both attacks."

"Icy Tundra? Huh." Estevan took a bite of his scrambled eggs. "And The Kite caught Smoke Shield?"

Argh. She was hoping he didn't realize that so soon. "That's not important. You do a great job protecting this town. You may not have caught that villain, but you drove him out of town. Don't ever question your usefulness. We need to focus on the current situation, though." Was he not putting the pieces together? Emma urged further. "This past

Saturday, there was a shot taken at the mayor down at the acceptance office. Clearly missed, but we don't need any chaos in Actionville. You've done so great keeping things under control."

Estevan took his last bite of scrambled eggs, then dropped his empty fork. "I have an idea!" He raised one finger and pointed at the ceiling, eyes nearly as wide and bright as automobile headlights.

Finally. "And what's that?"

"What if I…um…Capitán Rápido watches the mayor when he's here in Actionville—make sure nothing bad goes down?"

"I think that's a brilliant idea. How'd you ever come up with that?" Emma kissed her husband on the cheek and picked up his empty plate, loading the dishwasher before heading out the door.

In the background, she heard her husband call, "*Te veré pronto, mi gatita! Te amo.*"

"Love ya, too," Emma called back.

VICTORIA
North of Shadow Town

"So…are you ready for my help yet?" Victoria sat in front of the cabin's fireplace, wrapped in an old yellow and blue quilt. Mike had firewood stacked on the rack, but fumbled with the lighter. The fire wouldn't start.

His hand jetted out, shaking his index finger, and his words were sharp. "No, I got it."

Sor-ry. "You've been saying that for fifteen minutes."

A little spark lit the bark, and Mike leaned in, giving it a gentle blow. The sparks multiplied, but when he ran out of air, it put itself out. "Shit."

Victoria threw the quilt aside, squatted down next to Mike, and took the lighter from him. "I got it. Go bring in a few more pieces of wood for later."

Mike hesitated, but when the entrance door closed behind him, Victoria pulled all the wood out of the fireplace. She restacked it with some newspaper and kindling underneath, leaving enough room for air to enter. Before Mike returned with the wood, she had the fire roaring. She sat on the stone hearth, warming her freezing fingers.

"You did it. You're amazing," Mike said, standing behind her.

Victoria laughed. "Yeah, I know."

"I'm sorry. I should have let you do that sooner."

"Yeah. I know."

He leaned down and brushed his lips on hers. "Happy anniversary."

"Three months, huh?"

Mike nodded and took her hand. "Wow, you're freezing." He pulled her into his arms. "I know a way I can warm you up."

"Yeah, me too." Victoria smiled. "Sitting closer to the fire."

Mike tucked her veil of chestnut hair behind her ear. "That's not what I had in mind." He leaned down and kissed her again. This time, it wasn't quick. In one motion, he sat down and pulled her onto his lap, wrapping his arms around her.

A noise caused Victoria to pull away. "What was that?"

They stiffened and listened for the noise again. A knock.

"Argh. Someone's at the door." Mike stood up.

Victoria sighed. "Ignore them, they'll go away."

"I can't do that." Mike was already at the door. He opened it to a familiar, brilliantly white smile. He groaned and turned toward Victoria. "I should have ignored it."

"Told you," Victoria said.

Vance stood on the porch, holding Chew-Barka's leash. "I need to talk to my wife."

"Ex-wife," Mike corrected.

"Okay...ex-*wife*." Vance said.

Mike wrinkled his eyebrows at Victoria. "You told him where we were going?"

"Um...not exactly." Oh, did she wish Vance didn't have the power to locate people and things. Victoria leaned into Mike, wrapping her arm around his waist and putting him between her and Vance. She nuzzled against him in a seductive way, just to piss off her ex. "What do you want?"

"Something came up, and I need you to watch Chew-Barka for the night."

"And you have no one else you can ask?"

Vance was silent.

"What's really up?"

Vance's eyes darted to the fire. "Can I come in?"

"No." Mike and Victoria said in unison.

Victoria continued, "What are you up to?"

"What do you think? Come on, Victoria. You know me *quite* well. I need a little help here."

"Fine." Victoria reached forward and took Chewy's leash. "Okay, go. Do whatever you have to do, and then come get him in the morning. I don't think I'm supposed to have dogs here." She pushed Vance out of the house and threw the door closed on those pearly whites.

Before the door slammed, he spoke fast, "I won't be back until the afternoon. I have to go to Actionville."

Actionville? What was going on there?

Victoria sighed and leaned into the closed door.

"That was weird. What's he got going on?" Mike asked.

"Vance's always weird." Victoria answered, avoiding the question. It was obviously superhero stuff.

"Why do you put up with him?"

"What do you mean?"

Mike shook his head. "He's...stalking you. He obviously still loves you."

Victoria rubbed her temple. She put up with him because he did a lot of good... Deep down, she knew his heart was in the right place. "He may be stalking me, but he doesn't still love me. Both his parents are gone and he has no one else." And no one else knew his secret.

"Believe what you want, but I can see it in his eyes."

Victoria was silent, thinking about the way Vance looked at her sometimes. Mike tipped her chin up. "He looks at you like this." Mike softened his eyes, leaning in and kissing her. She tried to kiss him back, but she still was thinking of Vance. "Grrr. I'm sorry. I need to clear my head. Would you mind if I took Chewy for a little walk outside, by myself?"

"That's fine." But the look on Mike's face said differently.

Victoria didn't stick around to process that. She lifted herself up on her tippy toes, kissed Mike's cheek, and headed out the door.

~ ~ ~

Victoria took off walking, and kept going, her mind focused on the nerve Vance had to show up and demand she take Chewy. He wanted to share responsibility for the dog, but that meant he should actually have some responsibility, too.

She turned his selfishness and, well, asshole-ness over and over in her mind before she reminded herself that he had an important job to do, and she never wanted to impede that, never wanted that kind of grief on her hands. Someone's life might truly be on the line... Or he might be just pushing her buttons. If he was any other man, she'd have filed a restraining order...but he was a hero, whether he behaved that way or not.

When her feet and legs grew tired, she realized she still had to make it back. Chewy's tail wagged, and he let out a little bark, wanting to keep walking forever. Victoria had left her cell phone at the cabin, but even if she had it, she didn't think she'd actually call Mike to pick her up. She did like him, but she had to confess to herself at least, that she kept him near to fill a gap...and perhaps to irritate Vance. It wasn't often that she felt she had the upper hand.

Arriving back at the cabin, she found Mike sound asleep on the sofa in front of the fire. Victoria tiptoed over to him and whispered, "Mike?"

He didn't move. She tucked the old quilt around him and made her way to the bedroom, thinking about what Mike must think. Vance was always popping up when she wanted him least. And lately, he was showing up more frequently. It must be his personal agenda to irritate her as much as possible.

Should she wake Mike up? It was their romantic anniversary away, but she didn't want to explain...and she was so tired from her walk home. She crawled into bed, and Chewy settled beside her on the mattress. She petted the fur on his neck.

"I don't know what I'd do without you." She took comfort in the warmth of her longtime friend. Chewy had been with her though the divorce, her returning to college, and these past years as she flew through numerous boyfriends. What was she looking for anyway? She'd had everything she wanted once before… It just all came at the wrong time. *He's an ass, Vicky. A complete asshole.*

Just as the heaviness of sleep fell upon her, Mike shuffled across the living room and entered the bedroom.

"Victoria? You made it back." Mike pushed Chewy off the bed.

"He can be up here." Chewy always slept on the bed. If he didn't, he paced and whined until she made room for him. She patted the spot next to her. "Chewy. Up here."

Mike's voice was firm. "I wish he wouldn't."

Chewy laid his head on the edge of the bed and whimpered.

"Fine," Victoria said, scooting out of bed. "This trip was a bad idea. I'll sleep on the couch."

"Hey, Vicky, that's not what I meant."

"No, it's okay. I'm just tired…and need time alone. I'm cold anyway and would enjoy the fire."

With that, Victoria scurried out of the room and curled up as small as she could on the sofa, leaving room for Chewy to settle at her feet. The warmth and the crackle of the fire didn't fill the void as she had hoped it would.

Consumed by thoughts of where her life was going, she attempted to fall asleep. She needed to do something about Vance, otherwise, she'd never move forward. It was time she took control.

Thursday, April 8th

EMMA
in Actionville

Emma tapped her pen against the desk in front of her and clicked her phone on. It was 1:13 PM. She sat in the first chair of double-depth row at the City Council meeting with an audience of at least a few hundred community members staring at her and the rest of the council.

As she scanned the room full of eyes, her tapping became faster. *Hurry up.* Joe Payne, the mayor of Shadow Town, was now thirteen minutes late. Feeling the weight of the audience's eyes, and the gentle increasing roar of the crowd, she flicked her phone on again and texted her husband.

He's late. Is he okay?

The reply was instantaneous.

He's right outside. Got stopped by a train. Kinda ironic.

K. Thanx.

A few minutes later, in walked a slightly overweight man with a full mustache, escorted by two bodyguards and followed discretely by her husband in his civilian clothes. Her husband settled into a seat at the back of the room, pulling a backpack containing his costume onto his lap. You could never be too prepared. Leather was hard to hide under clothing, which was why she always urged him to use spandex, but, according to Estevan, spandex wasn't a man's clothing. Besides, as fast as he was, he could throw his costume on in the blink of an eye—literally.

Emma clicked her microphone on and cleared her throat. "Hello, citizens of Actionville. As you know, today we have a special guest from Shadow Town. Mayor Payne, welcome."

The mayor scooted his way up to the front of the room, taking a spot behind the podium on Emma's right. The microphone squealed as Emma turned it on for him. The mayor gave it a little tap. "Thank you for having me."

Emma sat back down and spoke, "We've invited you here to discuss the proposal for the high-speed train that would connect our cities. We understand that Doctor Marchant is funding nearly half the project, but there will still be a small tax increase to cover the project's construction costs. We're curious about what this train means to Shadow Town."

The mayor adjusted his microphone. "Shadow Town's largest employer is SynPharmaTek Industries..."

Out of the corner of her eye, Emma caught her husband jumping out of his seat and disappearing into a blur. Crap. Something was going to happen in exactly ten seconds. The world slowed down.

Nine. Eight.

The mayor was still talking, but Emma didn't hear what he was saying. She was counting down in her head.

Seven.

She scanned the crowed, they were focused on the mayor. All of them.

Six. Five.

She turned to her left. The side door creaked open and someone was there.

Four. Three.

Emma dove toward the mayor, but was caught in strong arms instead.

Two.

The dizziness from high-speed movement disorientated her as the world blurred by.

One.

Emma, the mayor, and Capitán Rápido stood in the main lobby of the government building. Her world was spinning, but she righted herself in a few moments. She had been whisked away by Capitán Rápido many times in her years of marriage.

The mayor was swaying from what appeared to be a little motion sickness. "Wh-what was that?"

Capitán Rápido helped him stand. In a thick, overly-done, Spanish accent, Capitán Rápido's voice was smooth. "This beautiful *señorita* here will explain." He flashed a smile before zipping back into the council room. Emma struggled to keep from smiling. Oh, did she love how he played up his accent while in costume. Maybe he really did think he was Zorro.

Emma refocused on the Mayor. "Um… yes. You know how Capitán Rápido can see the future? He must have seen something." Emma pulled out her phone and dialed 911.

Moments later, Capitán Rápido was back in the lobby, holding a small contraption in his hands. "They got away. Call the police."

Emma held the phone up to her ear. "Already on it. What's that?"

"A smoke bomb. In my glimpse of the future, I saw it go off."

"A smoke bomb? What would that do?" the mayor asked.

"Your guess is as good as mine, *señor*," Capitán Rápido said. "Perhaps they are trying to kidnap you…or just hiding their identity before they… It could be anything, really."

Emma noticed something on the bomb. "Is that frost?" She swiped her finger on it. It had been frozen. "Icy Tundra?" The emergency operator picked up on the other end of the line. Emma gave them the lowdown on what had happened.

Capitán Rápido was questioning the mayor. "Any idea who's doing this?"

The mayor shook his head. "No. I was the underdog. There are a lot of people who don't like me. They were trying to orchestrate a recall election, but that was shot down. This train issue will not help matters. I'll be criticized no matter which side I support."

By now, there was a crowd around the three of them. Camera flashes began to blind her, and when she did get a glimpse of the crowd, almost everyone had their phones out, taking photos or video. Emma gave her husband the universal nod, and he flashed out of the building, disappearing from sight.

He always stayed close by in case he was needed, but preferred not to be the center of attention. Luckily, Emma was good at damage control. As Chair of the City Council, she could easily clean up the pieces without anyone being suspicious of her connection to the masked man. She had lots of experience smooth-talking her way out of things.

ARIANA
in Windy City

Ariana laid her head on a wet towel under the kitchen sink. A wrench snug against the pipe, twisting with all her might.

"Urgh!" A drop of filthy water dripped into her eye from the clogged, leaking trap. She readjusted the wrench and gave it another tug. "Come on!" She spat out the water that dripped into her mouth. "Enough!" *Note to self: Perhaps it's time to start working out. Your tiny arms are not useful for anything!*

All she succeeded in was making the leak worse. The sink was still full of dirty dish water.

Drip. Drip. Drip.

The water came faster. She pulled a pot out from the rack over her stove and put it under the sink. Where was Adam when she needed him? Oh, yeah. Out saving the world and all.

Drip. Drip. Drip.

It flowed faster now. She tried to keep busy, her laptop in front of her, paying the bills, but the plunk, plunk, plunk was driving her mad. The rhythm sped up as the drops filled the pot. She emptied it and replaced it.

If only she was stronger, she'd be able to tighten the bolt.

I need a man.

Her first thought was to call her dad. He'd fix it for her. *No, Ariana. You're married now.* After what happened on her honeymoon, she was determined not to ask her parents for help again—well, at least for the rest of this month. Who else did she know? Two doors down, she'd seen a guy move in. Didn't he work at the bank with her anyway?

Knocking on the man's apartment door, Ariana tried to remember his name. She had been introduced to him at work. Luke... Linus... Larry.

He flung the door open, shirtless in a pair of flannel bed pants. Ariana forced her eyes up. *It's okay, he'd look at you too if you didn't have a shirt on.* That thought made her smile. *You may be married, but you're not dead.* "Hi, I live right down there." Ariana pointed to the door at the end of the hall. "I have a leaky sink and was wondering if you could help?"

"Ariana, right?"

She nodded. "Larry?"

"Lenny."

"Oh, sorry."

"It's not a problem. I'm pretty forgettable." A smile on his face exposed two dimples on his left cheek.

"You're not forgettable. I just...forgot."

They both chuckled, and Ariana felt better.

"Well, you're lucky. I'm almost a plumber." Lenny closed his apartment door and headed toward Ariana's.

Hurrying behind him, she asked, "Almost a plumber? You work at a bank."

"Well, a plumber's son. That counts, right?"

"Um... Don't you want to put a shirt on or something?"

Lenny stopped and turned toward her. She almost bumped into him. He waved his hand toward his bare chest. "Does this make you nervous?"

Ariana took a step back. The words blurted from her lips. "I'm married."

"Well then, where is he when you need him?"

Ariana pushed in front of Lenny, opening her apartment door and leading him to the sink. "Here's the wrench."

He pulled the pot out and gave the pipe a little twist, pulling the trap out. The water rushed down, all over him like a waterfall. "Crap!" He jumped out and hit his head on the cabinet. "Frickin' A!"

Dirty water ran down his chest, soaking his flannel pants.

Ariana stepped back and laughed. "I'm so sorry." But another laugh escaped. "I got a mouthful of that before. It's delicious." Still laughing, she pulled a dish towel from the cabinet and handed it to Lenny.

Wiping his face, shoulders, and chest, he shook his head at her. "You owe me."

"You haven't done anything yet. *Almost a plumber*, huh?" She put her hand on her hip.

"I never said I was any *good*. I do work at a bank instead." Lenny threw the towel under the sink and crawled into the cabinet again. A grunt or two later and he climbed back out. "There, good as new."

Ariana peered underneath. Inside the bucket was a wad of food that had been clogging the drain, but the leak had stopped. "Well, thank you."

He winked at her and threw the towel into her hands. "There, maybe next time we meet, you'll remember my name."

Ariana willed herself not to blush. "I think I got it. Luke? No, Linus?"

He shook his head. "Well, I better be going before your husband catches you with a half-naked man." He gave her shoulder a pat and trotted out the door, saying, "Remember, you owe me one."

Ariana closed the door. *Note to self: Next time, let the sink drip until Adam's home.*

EMMA
in Actionville

Emma sat in her office at the government center. The whole smoke bomb thing with Mayor Payne had the entire building on lockdown. The police had swept the premises, but Emma knew they wouldn't find anything. Capitán Rápido would have already done that in a fraction of the time.

She pulled out her phone and sent Estevan a text.

Sorry, I'm not home yet. We're still on lockdown.

Instantly, came his reply.

No problem. I'm out taking care of little things. With law enforcement occupied, there's an increase in kitties needing rescuing.

Emma turned to her computer screen. She had already spent hours researching Mayor Payne and Shadow Town. The biggest thing that made her nervous was the activist group claiming that the mayor's election was rigged. Their website quote was, "We'll do whatever it takes to get him out of office." *Whatever it takes.* The leader of the group appeared to be none other than Montgomery Marchant, the Owner/CEO of SynPharmaTek. Interesting that Mayor Payne and Dr. Marchant were on the same side in the train proposal.

Emma pulled her phone out and texted her husband.

Wanna check out Montgomery Marchant? He's been boisterous about his dislike for Mayor Payne. Maybe your friend, Capitán Rápido, could pay him a visit over in Shadow Town?

Estevan's instant reply:

But that's Icy Tundra's territory.

Of course it was. This whole territory stuff was ridiculous. It was created by law enforcement to align their cities…so each government knew who their hero was.

Now, it was becoming more of a burden.

Just go anyway. He'll never know.

A knock sounded on her door.

"Yes?"

A uniformed officer stuck her head in. "Missus Rodríguez, the building is secure. You can go home now."

"Thanks." Emma stood up and grabbed her purse. She texted her husband.

Never mind, I'm on my way home.

With that, she took off out the door, nearly as fast as Capitán Rápido.

Friday, April 9th

ARIANA
in Windy City

'Ariana, meet me downstairs ASAP. Put something nice on. Maybe low cut?'

Ariana's stomach tingled, and she laughed. What did her husband have planned? She rummaged through her closet and threw on her standard little black dress and a pair of lime green pumps—her favorite color. She rushed to the bathroom, brushed out her hair, and applied a little mascara and a touch of pink lipstick.

'Aren't you ready yet?'

"Well, I guess this is what you get," Ariana said, staring into her reflection, noticing her pale, blotchy complexion. Her sunburn was fading and it wasn't pretty. Tough. If he wanted her dolled up, he should have contacted her earlier. *'I'm coming.'*

When the elevator doors opened, Adam stood in the apartment complex's lobby, dressed in a lime green shirt and black tie. She bit her lip trying to hold in her smile. He knew her well.

"These are for you," he said, handing over a bouquet of yellow and blue wildflowers. He knew she thought roses were too cliché. Her cheeks tingled as she interlaced her arm with his and headed toward the entryway, ignoring the people staring in the lobby. They were married. Love could fill the air.

"What do you have going on?" she said, leaning into him.

He patted her hand. "You'll just have to wait and see."

Outside, her chariot awaited…literally. A massive dark brown Clydesdale stood in front of a white carriage. Ariana felt like Cinderella. Adam helped her into the backseat and took the spot beside her.

"You planned all this?" Ariana rubbed her hand across the smooth red leather seats that dimly reflected the row of twinkling white Christmas lights that outlined the walls.

"I figured our honeymoon was kinda a disaster. Maybe we could have just this one night."

"Thank you. It's wonderful." All the hostility that had been building throughout the day disappeared. The coach glided forward, and Ariana took a deep breath. "It's all so beautiful."

Adam's eyes were not on the horse or the carriage, they were on his wife. "Nothing is as gorgeous as you are."

"Oh, stop it." Ariana buried her nose in the wildflowers, smelling the fragrance and hiding the humble smile on her lips. "But thank you."

The horse stopped outside a small Italian restaurant. Adam hopped out, almost like he was lighter than air. Well, he could fly and all.

"Be careful," Ariana warned.

"Ah, it's all good." He took her hand and helped her down the few steps, leading her inside to a table decked out with a white tablecloth, cloth napkins, wine glasses, and a candle. It was beautiful, even compared to the horse-drawn carriage.

Together, as man and wife, they enjoyed a delectable meal. When they finished, Ariana felt as stuffed as the manicotti she'd just devoured. She didn't know if she'd be able to peel the little black dress off when she got home. *Note to self: eat less next time…or wear a bigger dress.* Seeing the bright smile on Adam's lips, she knew he'd figure out how to get her out of the dress. She snickered.

"What's so funny?" Adam asked.

"Oh, nothing."

Adam's mind reached out to hers, and she let a small glimpse of him pulling off her black dress escape.

"Nothing, huh?" Adam's eyes sparkled.

They had one glass of wine after another, and Ariana couldn't contain her happiness. It was there in the way she laughed at Adam's jokes, the way she couldn't take her eyes off him, how she leaned in on the table, and tried to seduce him by licking the rim of her wineglass. Did he even notice that one?

"Ariana, having you makes me the luckiest man alive. Care to dance?"

She looked around. She hadn't even noticed the small dance floor. Soft music played from a violinist.

His hand was soft and warm when it wrapped around hers. "Of course."

"Now that you have such a nice tan from Belize, you'll be able to do a new dance."

Ariana stared at him. She didn't have a tan. All her sunburned skin had already peeled away. "What do you mean?"

"You'll be able to dance the Tan-Go." Adam chuckled.

Ariana shook her head.

Adam led her to the center of the floor, wrapped his arm around her waist, and gripped her hand with his other one.

Unable to take her eyes off their intertwined fingers, Ariana felt lighter than air. "It's so weird you can dance now."

"I figure I better take advantage of those dance lessons you made me take before the wedding." Adam swirled her and pulled her back into his arms. As the music played, they danced and the night slipped away.

As much as she didn't want it to end, she leaned in and whispered, "I think it's time we go. They're starting to clean up."

"I don't care. I don't want to let you go."

Ariana leaned in and deepened her voice. "The night doesn't have to end yet." She gave his earlobe a tiny lick, grazing the edge with her teeth.

Adam grabbed her hand, rushed her back into the carriage, then instructed the driver to take them directly home.

While Adam fumbled with the apartment keys, Ariana rubbed the hem of her dress, almost nervous. "Thank you for everything—it's been so perfect."

Adam smiled slyly at her. "Well, *Miz* Turano. You said it doesn't have to be over yet. I was still hoping for a little dessert."

"Hmm." Ariana laughed. "I hope it's cheesecake."

"That's not quite what I had in mind."

"Hot fudge sundaes?"

"Something with fewer calories."

Ariana reached up and kissed him.

Adam swooped her up in his arms. "I haven't had the chance to do this into our own home." He opened the door and carried her over the threshold.

VICTORIA
in Shadow Town

Victoria cringed as she opened her apartment door to Vance once again. It was time she took control. Enough avoiding the inevitable. She clipped on Chewy's leash and handed him over. Vance leaned down and ruffled his fur.

"I missed you, boy." Vance looked up at Victoria. "I'm sorry I had to spring him on you Wednesday night."

"Sorry?"

Vance stood up and turned serious. "Yes. Sorry. Why?"

"You always show up at the exact wrong moment. I know you can sense where I am, but can you now sense who I'm with too?"

Vance shook his head and held his hands out to her. "No. Not at all."

"Then why are you insisting on ruining my life?"

"Ruining your life?"

"Yes! Ruining my life. My future. My happiness."

"It looks like you've got it all together. You have a great job, an apartment of your own, and a college education. You've got everything you ever wanted... Everything I couldn't give you."

Victoria shrugged it off. "We need to stop meeting like that. I really need you to let me get on with my life, and you need to get on with yours."

Vance scratched his chin. "No, I don't think so."

"Why?"

His evil, lopsided smile painted itself slowly across his face. "You broke my heart, Victoria. I will be a pain in your ass as long as possible."

Vance tugged on the dog's leash and headed out the door, calling over his shoulder. "Actually, Wednesday night, I had a date...with Mary, that curvy blonde you don't like." He stopped a moment. "No city to save, no good deed to do...unless you call Mary a good deed."

Victoria slammed the door.

That self-centered asshole!

How could she have ever married him?

Saturday, April 10th

ARIANA
in Windy City

Ariana lay in her husband's arms, inhaling his fresh scent and dwelling on their night together—smiling on the inside as much as she was on the outside. They'd been married a week now and this was the first time she felt comfortable. He stirred behind her, then kissed the back of her neck.

His voice was heavy with sleep. "Hey. What time is it?"

Ariana rubbed her stinging eyes, then stretched her legs out. She squinted at the clock. "It's quarter after eight."

"Eight?"

Ariana squinted again. "Yeah, eight."

"Crap." Adam sat up and flung his legs over the edge of the bed.

"What's wrong?" Ariana scooted beside him, straightening out the t-shirt she was wearing—Adam's t-shirt.

"Give me a sec. I need to tell her I'll be late."

Her? Adam stared at a crack in the drywall, appearing to be in a faraway place. "Who are you communicating with?"

He stayed focused on the wall, his expression unchanging. Ariana rubbed the shirt's hem. In that moment, it felt like her life had swung 180 degrees. He was using his powers to communicate with a woman…and it was a woman who knew he had these powers. Had Adam's romantic evening been at all connected to *her*? A way to break the news? She stared down at her hands and straightened the hem out.

"Honey?"

Ariana balled the fabric in her hand and looked up. "Yeah?"

In front of the closet, Adam pulled out his costume. "I have to fly."

"Who was that?" Ariana scooted to the foot of the bed.

"You've heard of Scarlet Macaw? Well, I've agreed to help her out and mentor her. She just came into her powers and is struggling to balance her life, her powers, and her duty." Adam was now throwing his legs into his light gray suit, the black cape getting in his way.

"Why you?"

"Her powers are similar to mine. I mean, she can fly and use telepathy too. She's stronger, though, and struggles with using those skills. Enormopolis is her home base and they could use a hero to watch over them. Last week, she went up against a villain and lost control. I'm helping her with that balance. I think it'll be fun."

"How long—"

"We can talk about this later. I need to get going." Adam leaned down and kissed her, then flung his hooded mask over his face and rushed to the window. He jumped, leaving Ariana alone.

She wrapped her arms around her hurting stomach. How could she go from a peaceful high to a violent low in only a matter of moments? She'd seen photos of Scarlet Macaw on the news. She was curvy…exotic…bold. All the things Ariana wasn't. She saw Adam telling her a cheesy pun and her laughing, then them holding hands as they soared through the sky.

Stop it, Ari. You're the one he married. You're working yourself up for no reason.

She took a long, hot shower before making herself breakfast. When she finished, she was left with nothing more than the dishes, the laundry, and memories from the night before while Adam was out having "fun."

Sunday, April 11th

ARIANA
in Windy City

The bank Ariana worked at was closed on Sundays and she wanted to do nothing except enjoy her day off. Instead, the time had flown by with chores. Laundry. Dishes. Dusting. Picking up Adam's pile of home improvement magazines. Home improvement! Really? Who fixed the sink this past week? Ariana shook her head. Never mind. She didn't want to think of that cocky neighbor, Lenny, or whatever his name was.

All these chores made Ariana hungry. She pulled a head of lettuce from the fridge before a soft knock on the door interrupted her.

She sighed and opened the door, coming eye-to-eye with the big green orbs of a giant, overweight feline. "Go away," she moaned. Where had that rudeness come from?

"Hey, that's no way to treat the man who saved your apartment from flooding." Lenny held the cat tightly to his chest.

"Hardly." Ariana couldn't take her eyes off the feline.

"You seem ungrateful. Did I do something wrong?"

She took a step away. "I just had a rough past few days."

"Can I help?"

"No, you've done enough already." Ariana placed her hand on her hip. "So why are you here?"

"I've actually come for a favor. Remember, you owe me one."

Ariana ground her teeth once again and looked up at his soft eyes.

"You're pretty when you pout." His smile was...charming.

Ariana's cheeks warmed and she tensed. This guy made her uncomfortable. "I'm waiting to hear what you need from me."

"I'm going out of town for a few nights and need someone to check on Sir Fluffypants here."

"That's *your* cat?"

"That surprises you?"

"Well, you look more like someone who'd have a snake." Ariana had to hold back a smile.

Lenny didn't hold his. "Yeah, I have one of those too."

For the second time, her cheeks heated. "I can't watch your cat. I'm allergic." A small lie.

"You didn't seem allergic when you stopped over and asked for my help."

"I wasn't there long enough."

Lenny lifted the cat up to his cheek, so both their eyes stared at Ariana. "Please. Sir Fluffypants needs you." Lenny stuck out a pouty lip.

Ariana sighed. "Fine."

"Stop over after work tomorrow, and I'll give you instructions."

"Maybe my husband can help too. I'll bring him along."

Lenny looked around the apartment. "Hmm... It doesn't seem like there's much masculine stuff here."

Ariana looked around. She had cleaned up so much, all signs of him were gone. Plus, they didn't have many things. Maybe it was out of fear that they'd have to leave quickly if their cover got blown. Plus, Adam was extra careful with anything personal. He couldn't accidentally leave something lying around that would give his identity away. "We enjoy the simple life."

He looked down at Ariana's left hand, and she quickly moved it behind her back, hiding her bare ring finger. "Husband, huh? I'd like to meet him."

"My ring's being sized, and the wedding band is being fused to the engagement ring. We were just married."

"Hey, I believe you. No worries. You say you have a husband, I'll take your word for it."

"I'll see you tomorrow." With a nod, Ariana shut the door and headed back to the kitchen, ignoring the sound of Lenny's chuckle from the hallway.

She pulled out a giant knife from her kitchen drawer and began chopping the lettuce, even though she had lost her appetite. What was it about that man that got on her nerves?

She had literally shredded the lettuce when she jumped at the opening apartment door. Didn't she lock it? Lenny would have to have a lot of nerve to just walk in here.

She gripped the knife handle and waited. Adam walked into the kitchen.

Ariana's fingers tightened further; her knuckles turned white. "Why are you home now?" Why couldn't he have showed up when Lenny was still there? Ariana could have proven his existence to that overconfident neighbor.

"Um. I have bad news."

"Bad news?" She further pulverized the lettuce.

"Maybe you should put the knife down."

"Seriously?" Ariana waved the knife in the air. "You think I'd use this on you?"

Adam shook his head and laughed. "I guess I'm trying to use a little humor to soften the news."

Ariana put the knife down. "Just spit it out. I hate suspense, especially today."

"I lost my job." Adam cringed away.

"What?"

"I got fired."

"What happened?"

"It's kinda hard to keep coming up with excuses about where I've been all day instead of at work.

Obviously, I can't tell them I'm The Kite and out saving the city."

Ariana's fists tensed and her shoulders tightened, thinking about the wedding bills that had started to arrive. "So you don't have a job?"

"Not right now. Balancing a job and being a hero is impossible. I don't know if I have it in me to try again."

Ariana cocked her head and glared.

Adam looked away. "This is the fourth time I've been fired. The second one since you've known me."

"I thought you quit the last one."

"I did. It was instead of being fired." Adam shook his head. "I'm sorry. I need to just find the right job. In the meantime, I need you to understand. I didn't want to start our marriage out this way."

Ariana picked up the knife and squeezed the handle.

"We'll be fine, Ari. You make plenty of money for us to live on. Many people live on less."

"Yeah, but we're still paying for the wedding…and our attempt at a honeymoon." Was this what married life was like? Partnership? Ha. Ariana bit her lip. She'd need to support him, and that was a lot of pressure on her. It wasn't what she planned on. Adam sat on a stool at the island in silence.

Ariana pulled out a tomato and violently chopped it into mush. "We'll get through this. You have a lot more responsibility than I do…and I knew what I was getting into… I just expected…I don't know." A knight in shining armor? He was a superhero, after all.

After making her lunch and eating it without saying a word, she listened to Adam apologize, over and over. Maybe having him home would be a good thing. He could help with chores. In fact, he should do them all, since he had nothing else to do. Ariana sighed.

Adam put his hand on her upper arm. "Relax. Keep in mind what's important. We have each other."

She glared at him when she put the empty salad
bowl in the sink, thought about washing it, but didn't. Hell,
that was what she had an unemployed husband for, right?
She then crawled onto the couch, wanting nothing more
than to watch Netflix all day. Adam joined her for one
episode, then said, "I'm gonna get going. Scarlet is free
now for a lesson, and I need some superheroing to take my
mind off my day."

She stared straight ahead at the TV. "Fine. Go.
Have *fun*."

EMMA
in Shadow Town

"Where did your superhero costume go?" Emma sat across the kitchen table from her niece.

Samantha held a giant-sized puzzle piece and stared at the images laid out on the table. "Mom says not today. It's laundry day."

Emma leaned in and whispered, "I bet Capitán Rápido even has laundry day." Cleaning a leather suit was a chore. Especially since you couldn't just drop off a secret identity costume at a dry-cleaner. Luckily, his suit was black and hid a lot of things.

"Really?" A toothless smile filled Samantha's face. Emma had to stop herself from giggling, oh, how she loved this little girl.

Becky draped a wet dishrag over the stove handle. "Okay, my little superhero, it's time to go to bed."

"But, Mommy!"

"It's seven o'clock. Your bedtime."

Big, brown, puppy-dog eyes turned to Emma. "I wish I could stay up as late as you, Auntie Ems."

"Hey, kiddo. I can't help you with this one." Emma motioned her thumb toward Becky. "I'm afraid of her too. She's my big sister and all."

Out jetted Samantha's pouty lip.

Emma melted. "Oh…how about I tell you a story first? About Capitán Rápido, and how he saved the mayor of Shadow Town this week."

Samantha's pouty lip disappeared, and her eyes lit up. "Were you there?"

"You bet I was." She lifted Samantha in her arms and carried her upstairs, telling her an embellished tale of the icy smoke bomb Capitán Rápido found and her suspicions about what the owner's intention was. Once

Samantha was all snuggled in, Emma joined her sister at the kitchen table.

On the table sat two cups of tea. "Sugar or honey?" Becky asked.

"Sugar today." She looked up at her sister. "Can I ask you a question?"

"As long as I can ask you one when you're done."

Emma smiled. "Sounds like a deal. What do you think of this high-speed train proposal?"

"I think it makes visiting you a lot easier."

"Yeah, but what about for the town?"

"On one hand, it's bad. It keeps people from moving to this city. They can just take the train in. These are professionals. The kind of people we want to settle here."

"And on the other hand?"

"I don't want SynPharmaTek to move somewhere else. It'd devastate us. Doctor Marchant does a lot to keep this city clean. He brings a lot of resources here, like Montgomery Park, the dog run, and he funds the community pool." Becky pulled her cup closer to her and added a scoop of sugar. "Okay, my turn?"

"Yeah, you bet."

Becky leaned forward and whispered, her eyes big and a sly smile tugging at her lips. "You've met Capitán Rápido a few times now, haven't you?"

Emma jetted her eyes toward her cup, reaching for the sugar to keep busy. "Being on that City Council always seems to put me in the right spot." Before she dropped in the teaspoon of sugar, she saw a ripple flow across the surface. Emma cocked her head and then the whole room began to shake. The stacked dishes Becky just washed fell over, some tumbling to the floor and shattering.

"Earthquake!" Becky screamed.

Samantha's cry carried downstairs. Emma flew out of her chair and up the steps nearly as fast as her husband could move. She had Samantha scooped up in her arms as her toys tumbled from the shelves.

"Get in the doorways," Becky commanded, prying Samantha out of Emma's arms.

Emma's world stopped as she watched Samantha being cradled by her mother. Oh, did she want to protect that little girl. *Stop it. It's Becky's job. She's her mother.*

Samantha's sobs made Emma's chest constrict.

The family photos on the wall crashed to the floor.

Emma couldn't focus on the world surrounding her—a similar feeling to when Capitán Rápido rushed her around in his arms.

She felt queasy and closed her eyes, listening to Samantha cry and Becky trying to soothe her daughter.

Then, as fast as it started, the earth stopped shaking. The only noise was Samantha.

"It's okay, honey. It's okay," Becky kept repeating, smoothing Samantha's frizzy hair.

Emma made her way to the other doorway and hugged her family. "How'd you know what to do? There's never earthquakes on this side of the country."

Samantha had calmed and hugged her mom tight. "When I was in college, out west, we had drills. Never had to live through one, thank God."

Emma pulled her phone out of her pocket and swiped into her contacts. "I need to call Estevan." The phone beeped fast and then went dead. "Let me text him." She typed in:

R U okay?

Clutching the phone to her chest, she smiled at Samantha. "Well, I guess you get your wish."

Samantha smiled. "My wish?"

"Yeah, didn't you say that you wished you could stay up late? Well tonight, we've got some cleaning to do."

Emma turned the phone over in her hand, still nothing.
Estevan was lightning fast at replies. Either he was
extremely busy…or the phones were out. She took a deep
breath. *It'll be okay. He has superpowers.*

VICTORIA
in Shadow Town

Victoria had spent the past two hours putting her house back together after the earthquake. Two hours of the news reporting complete devastation on the East Side of Shadow Town. She couldn't watch it anymore and had flicked it off.

Despite being tired, her mind rolled, so she retreated to her couch for some downtime before bed. Cuddling up in a blanket, she held the newest edition of her sinful indulgence—book eight in *The Charmed Nymph* series.

Before the earthquake tonight, she was supposed to go to a movie with Mike, but didn't feel like celebrating. The newness of the relationship was fading. The butterflies were disappearing. Fleeing, actually. Fast. She had used the earthquake as an excuse to stay home. There had never been an earthquake so vibrant here in the southern states. The news stations were saying it was a fluke of nature. Victoria was always skeptical. When strange things happened in Shadow Town, they never seemed by accident.

Victoria closed her mouth. She had been so into the book that she hadn't known it was hanging open. Her belly tingled as Edgar discovered Reglana was a Nymph...but said he loved her anyway. A passionate kiss made her earmark the page and set the book down, thinking about the excitement of new love. She loved that feeling...a feeling completely gone with Mike.

Real world, Victoria. The butterflies always go away. That's when real love begins to happen.

What was love anyway? Did anyone even know?

Victoria played the scene out in her mind, over and over until it grew old, then picked the novel up once again. She had made it to the end of the page when there was a knock on her door.

Once again, she set the book down, then glided to the door with warm tingles still in her stomach. Through the peephole, she saw Vance. All her calmness crashed to the floor.

What the hell is he doing returning Chewy so soon? Another date with the blonde?

She grit her teeth.

Stay strong. Don't take Chewy.

The images from the news of the destructed city flashed through her mind. She moaned. The city needed him, how could she turn him away? But what if he was using her?

She looked down at her thin t-shirt. "Hold on," she yelled, pulling a zip-up sweatshirt from the rack and wrapping it around herself.

Opening the door, Chewy bounded in, tail rapidly wagging. Grrr. She may be able to refuse Vance, but not Chewy. She let out a sigh.

"Okay, fine, turn him over." She held her hand out for the leash.

Vance cocked his head. "So, he's your dog?"

"Knock it off. Fine. *Our* dog." Chewy pranced around and Victoria unhooked his leash. "Okay, see ya around." Victoria slammed the door. As she was turning around, there was another knock. She cracked the door open. "What do you want?"

"It's obvious that I don't live here…and you don't like me, but do you know where I live?"

"Knock it off." Victoria leaned into the door, opening it further, and examined Vance for clues on what he was planning. Something was off. His confident posture gone.

"I'm sorry. But I don't seem to remember where I live, or who I am."

Victoria opened the door the rest of the way and put a hand on her hip. "What's your game?"

Vance shook his head, then wiped his forehead. Behind him, in the hallway, lay a trail of frost. *What was going on?*

"It's happening again!" Vance reached forward and slammed the door on himself. A spot of frost appeared on the inside of the door and grew, engulfing the entire thing. When the ice stopped growing, Victoria took the corner of her sweatshirt in her hand and opened the freezing door.

Vance shook his head. "I'm so sorry. I don't know what's going on."

"Get in here." Victoria pulled Vance inside and shut the defrosting door. "You know you can't do that in public. What's up?"

"I told you, I don't remember."

Victoria raised an eyebrow at her ex-husband, searching his face for a clue about what he was planning. His cocky smile was gone, and his eyes looked lost. She placed her hands on his head, rubbing for a bump of some type. "What happened to you? Did you get hurt in the Earthquake?"

"Earthquake? Is that what happened here?" Vance tipped his head. "Oh no… Get away!"

Victoria jumped away, and Vance froze her couch.

"Close your eyes!" Victoria yelled. "They need light to recharge. Keep them closed."

Vance stood in front of her apartment door with his eyes tightly closed.

"I got something for you. Don't move." Victoria rushed to her bedroom and pulled out a purple frilled eye mask. She helped Vance put it on. "There. This will help keep your eyes closed so you don't accidentally freeze anything. Here, have a seat." Victoria led him to the chair in the living room. She picked up her romance novel and shoved it under a couch cushion, shaking the cold out of her hands from the frozen cushion. She didn't need Vance's taunts if he found the book. Even with his eyes covered, she knew she was asking for harassment. He'd figure it out, somehow, sometime.

"So who are you?" Vance asked. "How do you know what to do?"

"Come on. I'm not liking this game." She twisted her hands, hoping he'd give in. Admit he was fooling her, though deep down, she didn't think that was the case.

"It's not a game. I swear that I remember nothing. My life before a few hours ago is dark. I keep trying to turn the light on, but it remains black. I can only go back as far as remembering myself kneeling on the sidewalk with that dog licking my face. Then I started freezing stuff." Vance sunk his head in his hands and played with the mask straps at his temples.

He might be a childish ass at times...well, most of the time, but he wasn't careless. He wouldn't risk anyone knowing about his secret identity, no matter what. There was no way he'd freeze something in public just to play some elaborate game. Even if it was a game, what would the purpose be? Victoria rubbed her temple.

The last thing he remembered was a few hours ago...that was when the earthquake hit...an earthquake that shouldn't be even close to this side of the country. Something fishy was going on.

Vance rested his elbows on his knees and lifted his head in his hands. "Why don't I remember anything? Then this freeze vision thing. That's not normal. I at least know that."

Did she need to take him to the hospital? They didn't know the first thing about managing a superhero...and Vance would never forgive her for exposing his identity. "How did you find me? Do you have control over your ability to locate someone or something specific?"

"My ability? I asked for directions to the address on the dog's tag. Chewy, is it?" He rubbed the dog's head that had weaseled its way onto his lap.

Victoria touched the couch. It had warmed up, so she sat down. "Chew-Barka actually. Named after our...your favorite movie."

"Why did I have your dog, and why was it named after my favorite movie?"

"It's actually our dog."

Vance sat up straight. "So, I live here?"

Victoria laughed, "Of course not!"

He cocked his chin. "But he's our dog."

"It's a long story." Victoria yawned. She couldn't shove Vance out her door in this condition, could she? "Do you think we can try it with the mask off again? You never told me how you control your powers. It all seemed so easy for you, but I know you struggled with it before we met. I think if you focus on it, knowing what will happen, maybe you can get it under control?"

Vance nodded. He slipped the mask up and squinted open one eye, then the other, looking right at Victoria. "You're beautiful, by the way. There's something about you I'm drawn to." He smiled—not sneaky, nor sly, but awkward and sincere.

Victoria looked away.

Vance held his palms out to her. "Hey, sorry. I didn't know that was the wrong thing to say." When Victoria looked up, he was shaking his head, then flipped the mask down. "Oh no. Not again."

The purple eye mask turned light lavender with frost, and Vance flung it off his face, squishing his eyelids closed and rubbing his face with his hands. "I'm so sorry to bother you, ma'am, but I should get home. Um..." He scratched his head. "Do you know where that is?"

"It's Victoria," she said, standing up and making her way to her bedroom. She pulled down a spare blanket and pillow, joining him again in the living room. "You'll need to stay here tonight. Maybe tomorrow you'll remember things."

Victoria laid the blanket out and helped Vance to the couch. "Is there anything I can get you?"

Vance grabbed Victoria's hand. "Thank you."

The softness of his touch made Victoria's stomach jump. She yanked her hand away. "Yeah. No problem. Don't make me regret this."

Vance tipped his head. "I'm sorry. I'll keep the mask on and not freeze anything again."

"That's not what I meant." Victoria sighed. "Never mind, it's a long, complicated story. Get a good night's sleep, and hopefully, we can get this under control tomorrow."

Victoria retreated to her bedroom. When she turned to close the door, Vance was situating himself on the couch. She shook her head, never expecting to have him stay with her again in her lifetime.

EMMA
in Actionville

After an exhausting hour or so of putting Becky's house back together, and being unable to get in touch with her husband, Emma headed home for the two-hour drive. Her brother-in-law, Josh, had made it home. The majority of the destruction had been on the East Side of town. They had nothing but some broken dishes and knickknacks, and the house was as good as new.

The cell phones may have been out, but the news was still broadcasted. The earthquake was specific to Shadow Town, though ripples were felt in the neighboring cities.

Emma should have been exhausted when she walked through the door at 11:30 PM, but all she could think about was ensuring Estevan was okay. Pins and needles danced in her stomach, and she couldn't fly up the stairs fast enough. There in bed, tucked soundly under the covers, was her husband's body. She crawled beside him. How could he sleep? Had he not heard the news?

She whispered and rubbed her hand down his bare shoulder, giving him a gentle squeeze. "Hey, Estevan."

Nothing.

"Estevan?"

He rolled over and smiled. "*Mi gatita.* You're home?"

Emma crawled on top of him and hugged him. "I'm glad you're okay."

"What time is it?"

"The middle of the night. Didn't you get my text? There was an earthquake."

"Earthquake?" Estevan sat up—slowly, cradling Emma in his arms. "I've been in bed for hours. I didn't hear my phone going off."

"Yeah, an earthquake hit Shadow Town."

His eyes widened as the pieces seemed to click into place. He rubbed her cheeks. "Are you okay?"

Emma crawled off his lap and changed into her pajamas. She should be tired, but all the stimulation had her mind racing. "Yeah, I'm fine. I was worried about you. The phones didn't work. They said that some towers went down and the few that still worked had overloaded circuits."

Estevan swung his feet off the bed. "Does Shadow Town need me?" He moved his feet back and repeated the motion. He shook his head.

"No, they should be okay. Icy Tundra's there and all."

Estevan repeatedly moved his legs off and on the bed. His eyebrows furrowed.

Emma put her hands on his knees and stopped him. "What's going on?"

"I don't know. Maybe I'm tired. I can't seem to use my superspeed." He jerked his head up. "Tell me what you ate for dinner."

"Grilled Cheese."

Estevan sprang from the bed, at normal human speed. "I didn't see that coming." He was rummaging through the items on top of their dresser. He lifted a pen. "Hold this behind your back and toss it somewhere in the room."

"Are you saying your powers aren't working?"

"I don't know. Try it."

She took the pen and tossed it into the bathroom. Estevan dashed forward…no faster than anyone else.

"Crap, crap, crap!" Estevan was running his hands through his hair, holding his bangs off his forehead. He fisted a handful of the strands between his fingers.

Emma made her way around the bed and grabbed his hand. "What were you doing tonight? How'd this happen?"

He was back to shaking his head. Emma grabbed his cheeks and forced him to look at her. "I...I don't know. Nothing different. I did my rounds of the city and came back here. I was so tired."

Fifteen minutes later, Estevan was confidant his powers were gone. He had passed the denial stage and now felt guilt.

"Who'll protect Actionville?"

Now, Emma was tired. This conversation wasn't going to get anywhere. Her entire family was safe, and that was good enough for her right now. She went for a different approach.

"It's late. We've been up since four-thirty this morning. How about we get some sleep and address this tomorrow?" Emma yawned.

"I don't think I'll be able to get my mind off it."

Emma gave her husband a sly smile. "Do you know what day it is?"

"Is it Monday already?"

"No, it's still Sunday." She stepped right in front of her husband and traced her finger down his bare chest. "And you know what day Sunday is?"

The focused look on Estevan's face melted. A smile tugged at the corner of his lips, and he tilted his head to one side. "As I said, I don't know if I can get my mind off this. I'd need something really convincing."

"I may be able to convince you. At least it'll be fun to try... Besides, I bet you'll have to go really slow. Usually, you bring a whole new definition to the term *quickie*." Emma lifted the corner of her t-shirt up, showing the skin on her hip bone. "Sunday is our day to be adventurous...and slow would sure be an adventure. Unless you're too preoccupied?"

Estevan stepped forward and pressed his body against Emma's. He gave a deep laugh. "Okay, you win. I'll let you try to take my mind off it."

Emma took Estevan's hand and led him back to the bedroom.

Monday, April 12th

VICTORIA
in Shadow Town

Victoria rubbed her eyes and stretched as she woke up. Was everything that happened last night a dream? Vance couldn't have lost his memory and control of his powers, could he? She threw a bathrobe on over her t-shirt and shorts before opening the bedroom door.

There he was, sitting on her couch and fumbling with something in his hand. Victoria's eyes darted down to the familiar, half-naked man on the book's cover.

Shit.

Victoria flew out of her bedroom and lunged forward to snatch *The Charmed Nymph* from Vance's hand. He had it opened to her earmarked page.

Shit. Shit. Shit.

Victoria's cheeks heated as she reached for the book, but then the book grew covered in frost. Vance flung it onto the coffee table and replaced the purple eye mask over his eyes, sinking back on the sofa. It hadn't all been a dream. Her ex-husband had truly lost his memory and control of his powers.

She cleared her throat and shuffled to the kitchen to make a pot of coffee. "Not better today, huh?"

He rubbed his beard. "Um…sorry about your book."

"Don't worry about it." Victoria didn't want to talk about that book. Hopefully, he read nothing. She prepared the coffee filter and grounds.

Vance twisted over the back of the couch in her direction, which was ridiculous because of the mask over his eyes. "Any thoughts yet on what happened?"

"How much do you remember today?"

"Everything since meeting you."

Victoria filled the pot with water and clicked it on, joining Vance in the living room. "The first time or the second time?"

"The second time, I guess. How long have we known each other?"

Sitting down, she counted the years: divorced for six, married for four, and dated since high school. "Over thirteen years now."

"You're a close friend?"

"Not anymore."

"Did I do something?"

"We both did." She sprang out of her seat. "Would you like coffee?" There was no way it was ready yet, but she didn't care.

"Yeah, sure. That'd be great."

Victoria filled a glass with her hazelnut creamer and the second with just milk, the way Vance had always liked it. She leaned against the counter and watched the coffee drip into the carafe.

When it was halfway full, she filled the mugs and carried them to the living room. "Here." Vance lifted his hands and Victoria centered the mug of heavenly liquid in his palm.

"Thank you. I mean that. I feel bad you're taking care of me. Somehow, I feel it should be the other way around."

"Okay, stop that. You're being kinda creepy. You're way too polite."

"Too polite? Wasn't I polite before?"

Victoria couldn't hold back the laugh. "No. You weren't. You were a lot of things, but polite wasn't one of them."

"I'm sorry. I'm seeing why we're no longer friends." Vance smelled the creamy liquid.

"That...and other reasons." Victoria sank back in the chair beside Vance and flipped on the news, wanting to avoid talking about their relationship...or lack thereof.

Vance took a sip of his coffee. "It's perfect. I

imagine you know a lot about me after thirteen years."

Victoria stayed silent, hugging her warm mug with her hands.

Vance continued, "I think you should take me home after this. I get the feeling I'm not welcome here."

He wasn't, but this man in front of her wasn't the Vance she despised. He was unsure of himself and worried about her comfort. "Stop worrying about it. It's not—"

The news reporter captured her attention, when she flicked her eyes to the screen, and old footage of Icy Tundra wearing a white suit with a royal blue belt, boots, and cape made her tense. "Last night, the mayor sent a request to Icy Tundra, but so far, there hasn't been a reply." The screen cut over to the mayor, standing in front of a pile of rubble. Wind blew over the microphone, muffling his words.

A sling cradled one of the mayor's arms while the other gripped the microphone. "Icy Tundra, if you're hearing this, the city needs you. Even though the heroic firefighters and police officers of Shadow Town worked all night, rescuing everyone they could from the rubble, secondary problems are developing all over the city."

The news screen flashed images of a man in a black hoodie throwing a rock through a store window. The mayor continued, "Looting and petty crime is out of control and intensifying. Our law enforcement cannot keep up."

Victoria sat back in the chair and took a sip of her coffee, taking comfort in the velvety goodness that coated her scratchy morning throat.

On the screen, the mayor looked over to a blond, preteen boy beside him and gave his shoulder a rub with his good arm. A man in a suit leaned over and whispered something to the mayor.

The mayor continued, "Icy Tundra, it looks like the penitentiary had a security breach. Two superhuman prisoners escaped during the earthquake. You're needed now, more than ever."

The report flicked back over to the news anchor. "Amidst the earthquake, missing Icy Tundra, and the escaped prisoners, the talk on Shadow Town's social media is the mayor's heroic rescue of his nephew. Nobody caught this on camera, but it was reported that Mayor Payne and his nephew were about to enter campaign headquarters on the East Side when the earthquake began. The mayor pulled the boy out of the way of a falling beam, saving the boy's life, but injuring his own arm. Social media is calling the mayor a hero. Not quite Icy Tundra, but a hero on his own. Citizens of Shadow Town, let the mayor be your role model. With Icy Tundra missing, everyone needs to do whatever they can to help in this time of crisis."

Victoria looked at Vance.

He took a sip of his coffee and clutched it in front of him. "I hope they locate Icy Tundra soon."

She let out a sigh. "Come on...think about it. When you open your eyes, you freeze things."

Vance rubbed his temples, then trailed his hands down his beard before straightening on the sofa. "What... Me? Holy crap!"

Victoria sat back and crossed her legs, taking another sip of coffee. "Yeah. That's why this is a big deal."

Vance felt for the end table, set his coffee down, and then stood up. "I need to do something. If the city's this bad off...and I have these powers..."

"Do what? Even setting a mug down on a table is a challenge for you."

Vance rubbed his hands through his hair, pulling some out from under the lacy purple straps. "I need to get my memory back...or at least get control of my powers." He flipped up his mask and focused on the cup of coffee on the table. He picked it up and brought it closer to his face. Frost grew, and he dropped the mug on the floor. "Shit! I'm sorry."

Victoria flew from her chair and rushed to the kitchen for a towel. Luckily, the coffee was frozen in a solid block. She scooped the cup and the block up into a dish rag and dropped it into the sink.

She glanced at the time on the microwave, then over her shoulder at Vance. "Grrr! I need to go to work." What the hell was she going to do with him? She couldn't send him on his way. Could she let him stay here? Again, she glanced at the digital clock. There was no time to escort him to his home, and honestly, she'd never been there, though she should be able to figure out where it was.

"I need to get going. I'm still new at work and can't call in sick. What can I get you before I leave?" Victoria made her way toward her bedroom to get ready.

His voice was soft. "You're going to let me stay in your home?"

Victoria nodded, but then realized he couldn't see her movement. "We have little choice."

Once Victoria had showered and gotten ready, she walked Vance around her home as a quick introduction in case he needed anything. She then rushed out the door, realizing that there was no hope of being on time.

Before she shut the door, Vance called to her, "Thank you. I'm a fool for not being your friend. A fool for whatever I've done to you. You've been so kind."

Victoria rubbed her temple, then closed the door.

EMMA
in Actionville

Emma woke up in Estevan's arms, squinting at the painfully bright morning sun. How long had they slept? "What are you smiling about?" she teased, thinking back to their night.

"I knew you would wake up at this exact moment."

"Your powers are back?"

"It appears so." Estevan leaned in and kissed her, then blurred out of bed at superspeed. Emma's eyes followed wads of clothing as they flew across the room into the hamper before the sound of the shower filled the room.

Emma joined her husband in the bathroom, calling through the shower door. "Don't you think it's strange you lost your powers?"

Estevan peered over the top of the glass door. "It happened off and on when I was a child and first coming into my powers. It was a lot worse when I was tired. Considering how I passed out last night, maybe I had just run myself down. Yes, it's odd…but not impossible."

Emma made her way to the kitchen, deep in thought. How was it that there was both an earthquake and a temporary loss of Estevan's powers in the same day? Was that too much of a coincidence?

There was nobody to ask. Nobody understood superhuman physiology well enough. A few superhuman prisoners had agreed to be studied in exchange for a shorter sentence, but the scientists couldn't find a physiological difference that explained their powers.

No sooner had Emma stuck the bagels in the toaster, Estevan finished his shower and dressed. He made them both a cup of black tea—despite caffeine being the last thing he needed. There was nothing like a hyper husband with the gift of superspeed.

He looked the same. His eyes were still as crystal

103

blue, hair as dark brown as ever—though there were a few more grays showing through. Was he certain he was feeling fine? "Are you—"

"—back to normal? Yes."

"Argh! I wish you'd stop glimpsing into the future."

"Hey, I was just testing my powers." The toaster popped up and in a rush of air, there were two bagels, slathered in cream cheese on the table. "Are you going to join me?"

"Okay, fine. You're back to normal. I almost think that whole thing last night was a ploy to get me into bed so late at night."

A deep, masculine chuckle rolled from Estevan's chest. "If I was only that clever, *mi gatita*."

With a laugh, Emma pulled out her phone and scrolled through the news reports. "It says here the earthquake was a 7.2 magnitude. Seismic geologists are perplexed at what caused it since there hasn't been an earthquake on this side of the country—ever. I'm serious, Estevan. Do you think the two things are connected?"

Estevan zipped across the room and retrieved his phone. He had his fingers flying at lightning speed and then stopped. "It says here there was an old, inactive fault line under the city. The scientists are studying what caused the sudden display." He looked up to catch Emma's icy stare. "Yes, they could be connected…or maybe they're not. I'll check it out. I gotta get to work. We're doing a big advertising push tomorrow, and I need to make sure things are set up correctly."

"Then afterwards?"

He laughed. "I suppose I'll do what I always do on Mondays. Make a swing through the city as Capitán Rápido and then bring pizza home."

Moments later, Estevan's bagel had disappeared and his mug was empty too. "*Te quiero, mi gatita.* I'll be home soon." He gave Emma a kiss on her cheek.

As soon as the door swung shut, Emma booted up the computer. She had research to do about what could cause an earthquake, beside Mother Nature. Once she figured this out, perhaps she could figure out how something could interfere with superpowers.

VICTORIA
in Shadow Town

In between number crunching in the accounting department at SynPharmaTek's towers, Victoria spent as much time as possible researching amnesia… not that any of her research would apply to superheroes with amnesia.

What she found was that many cases of amnesia resolved without intervention. Which was good because there was no way she could take an out-of-control superhero to the doctor, spoiling his hard-earned secret identity. Vance hadn't even told Victoria he was Icy Tundra until after they were married. She should have known back then what a jerk he was.

Her research also said that there was no guarantee that amnesia would recover, and even if it did, it may not resolve fully. That many people with amnesia needed to come up with alternate methods for remembering things. Alternate ways to return to functioning.

Or Vance could be making this all up. Trying to piss her off for leaving him. Victoria rubbed her temple. He may be deceptive and evil to her, but this was over the top. Vance would never appear to be helpless. He was always strong and in control. She dropped her head in her hands. Vance had truly lost his memory.

Victoria rubbed her eyes, trying to ease her throbbing head. She needed a super-sized giant coffee.

For her afternoon break, she slipped outside for a trip to the coffee shop on the corner a few blocks away. She flung her purse over her shoulder and leaned into the cubicle next to her.

"Want anything from Perky Joe's?"

The head accountant looked up, pushing her glasses up her nose. "No, thanks. I'm good."

Victoria strolled outside, following the walking path off of SynPharmaTek property. A man came running down the sidewalk toward her. He wore a surgical mask over his face. Victoria hesitated. What was he doing? Even with the dust that had been in the air from the earthquake, the air quality wasn't that bad.

Victoria gripped her purse tighter and moved over on the sidewalk. Her racing heart told her something was wrong. She held her breath until the man passed, but as soon as he was out of her field of vision, she was jerked backward.

She twisted around, and her eyes darted down. The man had her purse with one hand and a gun in the other.

OMG, I'm being robbed. Give him the purse, Victoria. That's all he wants.

"Hand it over," came the gruff voice from behind the mask.

Yup, that was all. Where's Vance? His superability to detect her also alerted him when she was in trouble.

Her heart sunk realizing that he wasn't coming to her rescue. He was at her house, wearing her frilly purple mask. Helpless.

Her hands shook as she removed her purse and handed it over. She didn't see the other man run up behind the gunman—and luckily, neither did he.

What happened next was a blur. The man behind the gunman swept his arm over the robber's and grabbed the gun from the assailant's fingers. With a twist of his arm, the man had the gun pointed at the robber.

"I'll take that," Victoria said, twisting her purse from the robber's hands. Perhaps she was too bold, but with her years being a superhero's wife, she'd had more brushes with crime than she wanted to remember.

"You okay?" her rescuer asked.

She focused on his familiar face. It was Dr. Marchant, the big head-honcho at SynPharmaTek. "Yeah, thank you."

With the distraction, the gunman took off running.

"Crap!" Dr. Marchant exclaimed as they watched the last of the man disappear into the small forest beside them. Her rescuer hesitated and conflicted thoughts flashed across his face.

Victoria patted his shoulder. "Hey, thank you."

"No problem. I can't let my prize accountant get into trouble."

"No really. That was fabulous."

Victoria swung her purse over her shoulder, clutching the strap to stop her shaking hands.

"Be careful. Ever since the earthquake, crime is at an all-time high, especially with Icy Tundra being missing."

Victoria tried to swallow, but her mouth was dry.

"You look worried, and after what happened, I don't blame you. Take the rest of the day off. I'll see you back at work tomorrow."

Victoria nodded, no longer needing the cup of coffee to keep her awake.

Victoria set off for home with one focus. Vance had to regain control of his powers. Not only did she need him out of her house, the city needed him. Hopefully, in the process, his memories would return.

Victoria felt like an idiot, knocking on her own door, but she didn't want to enter if Vance had taken his clothes off or something worse.

"Vance?"

"Come in."

A shiver shot down her spine as a memory of their married life knocked on her consciousness from his familiar voice...then her memory fizzled when she saw a cascade of thick, wavy blonde hair, disappearing completely at the cleavage overflowing the woman's V-neck top. Victoria fisted a hand, but forced it back open. "What's going on here?"

"Oh, hi." The blonde's voice was low and breathy.

She stood up. Her butt cheeks hung from the bottom of her shorts. "I'm your neighbor, from the end of the hall. I moved in last month and have seen you walk this little bugger here." She ruffled the fur on Chewy's head.

Victoria patted her leg, but Chewy didn't come. She looked at Vance still wearing the frilly eye mask. Did he even know how beautiful this woman was?

Vance stood up, fumbling with the table. "Chewy needed to go outside, and obviously, with my *surgery*, I couldn't find my way. I knocked on doors until I found someone who was willing to escort me downstairs and up and down the street. Lindsay here was very willing."

I'm sure she was. "Chewy doesn't need to go out during the day. He does just fine while I'm at work." She forced her fists to unclench.

Vance shook his head. "He was whining, and I didn't know what else to do."

I'm sure he was.

"Alrighty then, I'm going to go," the blonde said. "Vance, you've got my number." She shook her ass all the way out the door.

Vance faced Victoria, clueless of what was going on. Had he snuck a peek at her at some point throughout the day? Was he frolicking with this woman while Victoria was busy working and researching how to help him? Then she had been nearly robbed, and where was Vance? Flirting with a curvy blond.

She set her jaw, keeping her thoughts to herself. This wasn't her problem. There was no reason for jealousy. She had Mike and never wanted to be married to Vance again. *Remember, he's a jerk. A complete asshole.*

Once the door clicked shut, Victoria let out a sigh and refocused on her problem. She needed him out of there and had no choice but to help him. The city depended on her...um...on him.

She sat down across from Vance. "I have a plan.

We need to work together on getting your powers back. That way you can go home and become Icy Tundra again."

When Vance reached out to feel for her hand, she pulled her hands off the table. He recovered by rubbing his hand along his chin instead. "Did we used to date?"

Victoria nearly choked on her own saliva.

"I heard you sigh at Lindsay. Did I break your heart?"

This would only complicate her situation. "Never mind that. Us working together will be so much easier if we don't talk about it. We need to keep this a business arrangement. Let's go somewhere where we can practice your powers. We need you to get control of them."

While ideas flowed through her mind, Victoria let her guard down and Vance snatched her hand. His fingers were ironically always extra warm. His voice was sincere. "I'm sorry."

Victoria pulled away and sprang out of the chair. Vance was right behind her when she hooked Chewy's leash up. "Okay, let's go."

"Wait a sec, I have something to show you." A proud smile spread on his lips. He fumbled his way to the sofa and lifted it completely off the ground with one hand.

Victoria's chest tingled. "Do you have control of your powers again?"

Setting the sofa down, Vance's smile disappeared. "Just that one, it appears. I still can't control the freeze vision nor the ability to locate stuff. I focused on you all day, but didn't feel connected at all."

Obviously, he missed her being robbed. "This is promising. Maybe with a little work, we'll get it all back." Gripping Vance's shoulder, Victoria guided him outside. "There's a place up in the mountains we can practice. It's private. You can take the mask off, though you look kinda pretty in all that lace." For the first time, a sincere smile spread on her face, and her body relaxed.

A deep, almost beautiful laugh rolled out of
Vance's chest, and Victoria was glad he had the blindfold
on, because he didn't see her moment of happiness.

ARIANA
in Windy City

Ariana's day had been chaos at the bank; everyone flocked to pull their money out because of the events happening in Shadow Town. In fact, some of them claimed they felt the earth rumble here in Windy City.

Happy to be home, she flung the apartment door open with a tired arm only to see Adam sleeping on the couch with the TV on. Was that Netflix he was watching?

"I'm home," she announced. Her eyes focused on the dishes piled in the sink. "Adam?"

Nothing. She searched for their mind connection. *'Adam!'*

He startled on the couch.

"Nothing good to do today?" She didn't care that contempt laced her voice.

He cleared his throat. "Hey, is it five already?"

"Actually, it's six. I see you've been busy today." She darted her eyes to the full sink. There was her salad bowl from yesterday. She wouldn't wash it. Adam had nothing else to do during the day now that he didn't have a job. He should have the common decency to do a few household chores.

Turning toward her, Adam smiled. "You know how I feel. Doing dishes can be *draining…*"

Ariana crossed her arms. She wouldn't give him the satisfaction of knowing she caught his joke.

"Hey, Ari, dishes can wait until we need them."

"Wait for what? The magical dish fairy to clean them? Well, I hate to break it to you, but that fairy's me! I'm the magical dish fairy, and I'm not happy."

Adam laughed.

"It's not funny. Why do you make everything a joke?"

Adam flew over the couch and stood right in front

of Ariana before she formed her next words. He reached out and took her hand. "You know I love you."

Her entire body tensed, and her arms shook. Her vision clouded when tears rolled down her face. She spun around and retreated to the bathroom. When the door slammed shut and lock clicked, she paced.

Adam's voice came through the door. "Hey, what's wrong? This is more than the dishes, I think."

"Nothing. I'm fine." She wiped her eyes with a tissue, then blinked until she could see straight again. *What was wrong?* Was it the chores, the pressure of being the only one making money, the feeling of loneliness, or simply the fact her dream of what marriage was like fizzled?

Through the door, Adam called again. "Something's wrong."

"I don't want to talk about it."

"Really?"

"Yes." She waited for him to say something, but there was only silence. She opened the door, and Adam almost fell on top of her. She bit her lip, but the words flowed out with the tears she had just gotten under control. "This isn't what I expected married life to be like."

"What did you expect? This is how it was before we got married. Did you expect it to change? Something magical to happen?"

Ariana's hands fisted. Yeah. That was what she was hoping for. It was unrealistic. She sighed. "I need space. Some air."

After exiting her apartment, she circled the block three times before she was ready to return home. More than an hour had passed. *Note to self: Adam won't come looking for you...even if you really want him to.*

She opened her apartment to silence.

"Adam?"

Nothing.

She searched all the rooms and stopped in front of the open bedroom window. Adam had taken off. How long had he been gone?

Ariana didn't care. She took a deep breath and sat in front of the TV, getting ready to binge-watch Netflix. It was what single life was like, and she missed it.

EMMA
in Actionville

Emma rubbed her neck. While managing City Council emails, she'd spent hours searching the internet about the devastating earthquake in Shadow Town. Beside the twenty-one people that died from falling debris, there were more that were injured. The hospitals were full, and they had diverted patients to neighboring cities, including Actionville.

Not only was Shadow Town in a state of crisis from the injuries, but two supervillains had escaped the SuperMax prison.

Were the earthquake and the escaped prisoners connected? Emma skimmed the news and found that it didn't appear the villains had caused any trouble...yet. Luckily, the other eighteen supervillains remained secure in the facility.

The door swooshed open, and Emma jumped. "*¿Que te preocupa?*"

The smell of pizza filled the air, and Emma smiled at her masked man. She moved away from the computer monitor to show her husband the screen. "Things look pretty bad in Shadow Town. Lots of people injured. A lot of damage to clean up."

"Luckily, they have Icy Tundra." Estevan pulled his black mask off, then disappeared a moment before two plates appeared on the kitchen table, each holding a slice of pizza

Emma sat down. "That's the thing. They don't have Icy Tundra. He hasn't been seen since the earthquake."

"Do you think something happened to him?"

"Do you think your power loss was a coincidence?"

Estevan rubbed his hand down his face. "If they are connected, Icy Tundra would have been the closest superhero to the earthquake. It can't be a coincidence."

Emma prodded Estevan with her idea. "Did Capitán Rápido intervene here in Actionville today?"

Estevan shook his head. "This city is so clean and put together, rarely does anything bad happen anymore. That smoke bomb with Shadow Town's Mayor was an exception."

Emma wanted to say more, but instead, she silently urged her husband to continue.

Suddenly, Estevan's eyes lit up and grew as wide as quarters. His finger pointed up to the ceiling. "I have an idea!"

Emma struggled to keep a straight face. "And what's that?"

"What if I...um...Capitán Rápido visits Shadow Town and helps out?"

"I think that's an excellent idea. How'd you ever come up with that? I could arrange to be there too. I'm sure Actionville will be happy to send the Chair of the City Council as a goodwill gesture."

"Oh..." Estevan wrinkled a brow. "I still have my project at work."

"Aren't you fast enough to handle both?"

Estevan smiled and gave her a wink. "I am fast." His pizza disappeared before Emma even took her first bite. "I'll pack," he said as he disappeared from the room.

VICTORIA
in Shadow Town

On their way to the private spot in the mountains, Vance gave Victoria as much of a description as he could of where he woke up, holding Chewy's leash, a day ago. They swung over to the East Side, pulling the car as close as possible to the devastation. Police tape surrounded a crumbling building that flooded Victoria with memories.

"Hmm, remember that place?"

Vance lifted up his mask for only a moment before replacing it. "No."

Victoria pushed the memories away. "It's not important, anyway."

"Tell me. Maybe it'll trigger something."

Victoria sucked in a deep breath as images of brightly decorated cupcakes filled her mind. She had come over to Vance's apartment one day, thinking they were going to catch a movie, and arrived to a table full of cupcakes, spelling out 'MARRY ME.' Oh, how in love they used to be. The cupcakes had been from this shop, their favorite bakery. "We used to come here every Saturday afternoon and grab a cupcake before heading toward the movie theater or up the mountains for a hike."

Vance stared at the building, then shook his head. "I'm sorry. I don't remember."

"It's not a very good memory trigger. It looks different now with all the fallen concrete and without the bright pink sign." Victoria rubbed her hands against the steering wheel. "When you woke up yesterday, do you remember any debris around you? All I can think that happened is that you hit your head." She reached over and rubbed Vance's head again, more thoroughly this time. His hair was soft, and her fingers moved carefully through it, massaging his scalp.

"That feels good."

She ignored him. "Any tender spots?" Why would there be? He was invincible...at least he had been.

"No, it's all fine. Nothing hurts. You already did this, and I checked, too."

Victoria pulled her hands away. "What if your memory loss was caused by something else...like whatever triggered the earthquake?"

"Then we need to find out exactly what happened. Maybe it'll give me my memory back."

"In the meantime, we'll keep trying the traditional ways." Victoria started the car again and pulled away.

~ ~ ~

Night had fallen when Victoria guided Vance out of the car. She guided him down the trail. Her insides tingled from the feeling of his hand in hers. The memories it brought were not something she wished to relive, so she pushed them away. His hand in hers was nothing more than a hand. A necessity. She needed him to gain control of his powers. She needed him out of her life.

You're losing it, Victoria.

The path opened up to a clearing with a swell in a river forming a small lake. Victoria positioned Vance in front of her, placing her hands on his shoulders. "Close your eyes."

He nodded.

She lifted the lacy mask from his face. "The sunlight charges your freeze power. It's dark now, so it takes more time to *re*charge. In fact, you have to look at the moon to speed the process up. The darkness should help us with taking this slowly. When you open your eyes, you'll see a pond. I want you to try to freeze it."

Vance nodded. "Okay. I'm ready. Are you?"

Victoria stepped next to him, out of his line of sight. "Give it the best you've got."

They stood there for a bit. "I don't know how to turn it on," Vance said.

"Try to focus on your eyes. Focus on that sensation you have right before it happens, or while it's happening, and try to grab that feeling and use it. You always made it seem so easy."

Vance squinted his eyes and stared at the small lake. Eventually, he laughed. "It's not easy. How long have I had this power?"

"Since puberty. You said that when your scraggly facial hair came in, so did your powers."

Vance continued to focus on the lake. "Puberty, huh. I imagine I lived with my parents then. Maybe they can help? Do they know how I controlled it?"

Victoria's stomach felt like a bag of rocks suddenly filled it. She took a deep breath while shaking her head. Taking Vance's hand, she turned him toward her. "I'm sorry, but they're both dead."

Vance arched an eyebrow at her. "Why do you look at me like there is more to that story? What happened to them?"

"There is more, but I don't want to burden you with it now. We need to focus here and get you back to normal."

Vance brushed a strand of hair out of Victoria's face, and she looked away. He squeezed her hand. "You're so beautiful, and it's a shame I need to wear that mask around you. You've been nothing but kind to me, despite some kind of history we have. Thank you."

Victoria was happy the darkness kept her blushing cheeks from showing. The tingling sensation still made her want to slip away and hide. Instead, she focused on their current situation. "You're doing good. You're holding the power in just fine right now."

Vance smiled, but then his nose wrinkled and he looked like he was going to sneeze. "Oh no!"

Victoria tried to get out of the way, but Vance gave her a shove...a strong shove. She flew through the air and stopped when her rump smacked a pine tree.

"Urgmphf." Victoria couldn't breathe.

Vance rushed up to her. "I'm so sorry." He squished his eyes closed. "You okay?"

Victoria couldn't find the breath to speak.

"It's okay," Vance helped her up. "Can you move your toes? Fingers?"

Victoria gave them a little wiggle, then nodded. Vance's eyes were still closed, so she found the breath to squeeze out in a croak. "Yes."

Vance was shaking his head. "I'm so sorry."

"It's okay." Victoria rubbed her back and caught her breath. "We'll just have to start with something less dangerous. Maybe your power to locate people. A little game of hide and seek may be safer."

The glistening of the surface of the lake captured Victoria's vision. "It looks like you froze the whole thing."

"I almost froze you. What happens if I would have got you instead?"

"Um… I'd die."

"And you still try to help me?"

"Yeah. Pretty stupid, huh?" She laughed a small, painful laugh, but stopped when she noticed Vance wasn't laughing with her. "What's wrong?"

"Have I ever done that? Killed someone?"

Victoria shook her head, not wanting to answer that question. "It's been a long night, Vance. Let's go home. We'll talk about this later."

"I have, haven't I?"

Victoria stood up and took Vance's hand. "Yeah, Vance. You fight evil. Sometimes you freeze people. It's all part of the job. It's for the greater good."

"But I killed *people*? Like, more than one?"

"That's a demon you have to face yourself, and without your memories, it will be hard to come to terms with that. Just know, you've saved people too. A lot of people. Good people."

"I don't know if these superpowers are a blessing or a curse." With his lips pressed tightly together, Vance replaced the purple mask and pulled some hair out from under the straps.

Victoria reached up and took his hand. "I'd love to tell you it's a blessing, but it's both. Attitude is everything and at some point, you learn that you need to focus on the good, realizing what would happen if you weren't around. Just look at what's happening here in Shadow Town with your absence." She gave his hand a little tug. "Let's get home and try again tomorrow."

With a hesitant nod, Vance followed Victoria down the path and out of the forest.

ARIANA
in Windy City

Ariana took a deep breath before knocking on Lenny's apartment door for instructions about his cat. *Don't let him get to you, Ari. Why does he pull your strings, anyway?* Ariana was just on edge. Adjusting to married life and his comments on her husband being MIA aggravated her. In reality, she'd probably take her frustrations out on whoever pushed the right buttons.

Lenny opened the door, holding a book, *Peter Pan and Wendy.* Of course it was *that* book, Ariana's favorite. Had he asked around at work? Purposefully trying to aggravate her further?

Ariana's insides clenched. "Let's make this quick." Urgh! Why was she so rude? "I mean, I don't want to make you late."

Lenny raised an eyebrow. "Well come along. Sir Fluffypants is looking forward to meeting you."

I'm sure he is.

Lenny led Ariana into his living room. Curled up on the back of his couch was that fluffy calico cat with too-big eyes. "Sir Fluffypants looks just like a cat I had as a kid." *Huh, a calico cat and most calicos are girls. Did Lenny not know?*

Ariana petted the cat's head, tracing her finger on the white patch of fur right in the center of the cat's forehead.

Lenny stood beside her. "I thought you were allergic."

"Oh... I meant Adam, my husband, is allergic."

"That husband I have yet to meet."

"Yeah, that one."

Lenny showed Ariana where Sir Fluffypants's food dish and litter box were, along with giving detailed instructions on the wet to dry food ratio and when to feed him…um…her. He also instructed her on the fur ball medicine.

"Any questions?" Lenny asked.

"Just one. Where did Sir Fluffypants's name come from? I mean, most calicos are female."

Lenny rubbed the fur along the cat's spine, then laughed. "I know Sir Fluffypants is a girl."

"Yet you call her *Sir*—it's kinda over the top, don't you think?"

"What? Didn't you expect over the top from me?"

"Yes, but not the soft side."

Lenny rubbed his hand on the back of his neck. "She was my girlfriend's."

"And you got her in the breakup?"

"Yeah. Something like that." He looked away and laced both hands behind his neck. "Um… She actually died."

Ariana's heart dropped. "I'm sorry."

"Don't worry about it. There's nothing that can be done now. Who knows if it would have ever amounted to anything, anyway?" Lenny looked at Ariana with soft blue eyes. "It's kinda morbid, but I knew you'd take good care of Sir Fluffy because…well…you remind me of her."

All the mean things Ariana had said rushed through her mind, and she pushed them away. She hadn't known. Instead, she repeated, "I'm sorry."

Lenny clapped his hands together once. "Okay. I gotta get going, and you need to…get back home to that husband of yours." Lenny flashed a sly smile.

"Yes, of course. I'm sure he'll be waiting for me." If he ever came home. *Stop it, Ari.*

Ariana took Lenny's spare key before rushing home to her empty apartment. For some reason, she preferred when Lenny was a jerk. Now, she was developing a soft spot for him that only frustrated her further.

Tuesday, April 13th

ARIANA
in Windy City

Ariana sat across the table from her parents, clutching three playing cards and enjoying playing thirty-one for quarters. It was their Tuesday morning ritual since it was typically her regular day off of work. Adam hated card games, so he never came. Besides, he had an additional city of crime to clean up, instead of a house, and *fun* to be had with some woman named Scarlet.

"Hey, honey. What's wrong?" Ariana's mom peered over her cards.

Was her aggravation with Adam that apparent? Both her parents stared at her, waiting for her to say something. She'd always been honest with them, but did she want to admit her troubles?

"Ariana?" Her dad snapped his fingers.

"Oh, sorry. I was just thinking. What did you say?"

"You seem distracted. What's wrong?"

"Wrong?" Everything. "What do you mean?"

"It's written all over your face." Her mom picked up a card from the deck, then discarded it.

No sense in denying the inevitable. They'd find out one way or another. "Adam lost his job." She took her turn with the cards.

Her mom laid her cards face down on the table. "Oh no, what happened?"

She couldn't tell them the truth...and it killed her. "They downsized. He was next on the list." Ouch. A flat-out lie. Who was she becoming? The other thing eating at her was she couldn't tell them how difficult being married was. She couldn't look like she failed. When she told them Adam had proposed, she had gotten the "make sure he's the right one" lecture.

"I'm sorry, kiddo." Her dad said, reaching across the table and giving her shoulder a gentle rub.

She forced a smile. "Thanks, but it's okay."

"He'll find another job." Her mom picked her cards back up.

Yeah, but he'd have to look for one. She shrugged. "Hopefully."

Her dad picked up a card and placed it in his hand.

"Look at the bright side." Her mom perked up. She always saw the silver lining; it was one of the many things Ariana loved about her.

"Huh, what's that?"

"He'll be around more for you to enjoy. You're newlyweds and all." Her mom winked, and Ariana internally cringed. "How's married life treating you?"

The honeymoon was over, that was certain. Hey, it never even began. "Great. I'm lucky to have him." Those words were also true. They used to have such fun together: explored the world, laughed at the same movies, and even the long nights they spent playing Monopoly. Ariana needed to figure out a balance and a way to get that back. Figure out how this whole being married thing worked.

"Ha!" her dad exclaimed. "Thirty-one!" He laid down a king, queen, and ace of spades. He reached over and grabbed the little dish of quarters. "I'm rich." He winked at Ariana, too. What was up with the winking all of a sudden?

Ariana's mom tossed her cards down. "Seriously, honey. Everything will be fine. It may be a little early for you, but every marriage has rough times. You just need to talk about them and wait them out. They'll pass."

Her dad dumped the quarters out and replaced the change dish in the middle of the table. "Here's a little secret your mom tells me about men. We sometimes have a hard time expressing our feelings...our wants and desires, and sometimes, our women know what we need before we do. Sometimes you need to whack us upside our heads for us to notice."

Ariana never thought she'd say this, but she missed living at home with them. She had always been close to her dad, but grew closer to her mom the older she got. If she lived with them now, she'd appreciate the time together and all the work they did to make her life easy, instead of trying to sneak out, being upset about the rules, and counting down the time until she could move out on her own.

Her mom gave her a sweet smile. "When I'm struggling, I talk to your dad about things. That's one key of being married: communication. Tell Adam how you feel. See what he's feeling."

"Yeah, sweetie. Men don't take subtle hints. Remember what I said? They need to be whacked across the head with things. If he doesn't know what's going on, he can't change."

"I've tried talking to him. It ended up in disaster." With him flying out the window. Maybe Ariana hadn't been trying hard enough.

Her mom reached across the table and grabbed her hand. "They need to hear things more than once to sink in. Try a different approach. I'm sure he missed the point. A lot of times, emotions get in the way of the message."

Ariana took a deep breath. She sure hoped that was the case. Glancing down at her watch, she realized the time. "I have to go. I'm taking care of the neighbor's cat, and it's Sir Fluffypants's dinner time."

With that, Ariana kissed her parents good-bye and took off.

VICTORIA
in Shadow Town

Victoria and Vance stood outside Vance's house. It wasn't much. A small one-story in need of either new siding or a good coat of paint. When they were married, they had a nicer home, but Vance, being a superhero, couldn't hold down a real job and lived off a small trust fund left to him by his parents. When they divorced, they sold their home and split the small proceeds. Victoria put it toward the college education she'd been craving, and Vance bought this shit-hole.

Vance flipped his mask up and took a quick look. He reached out and pulled a piece of peeling paint from the doorframe. "I live here?"

"Yeah. I guess you do. I haven't been here before."

He flipped his mask down again. "You haven't?"

"No, you always pick the dog up at my place. We're not exactly friends." Victoria shifted her weight to the other foot. "Do you have the keys?"

Vance dug in his pocket and handed over a few keys. Victoria flipped through them and on her second try, the key slipped into the lock and she turned it open. "Ready?"

Vance nodded.

The inside of the home shocked her. It wasn't at all like the outside. Everything had been remodeled. New drywall, beautiful fresh paint in mellow hues of blue and green, clean and organized furniture, and a few abstract wall paintings. Vance was full of surprises.

Victoria laced her arm through Vance's, realizing she was getting used to touching and guiding him along. They weaved in and out of rooms until she found the master bedroom. The bed was even made.

"I'm going to dig through your things." Victoria released Vance's arm. What would she find? What would

Vance think of this when he regained his memory?

"Go ahead." He flipped his eye covering up, looked around, then replaced it. "It's like I'm in a stranger's house. None of this is familiar."

Victoria rummaged through the closet, pulled out a shirt, and tossed it at Vance. He jerked in surprise, but pulled the shirt that stuck to his shoulder into his hands. She repeated this with some jeans and finally a pair of boxers, which landed right on top of Vance's head. She laughed.

Vance gripped the corner of his boxers and pulled them down. His face was serious as he fiddled the fabric in his hand. "I guess it's only fitting. Seems my head's been up my ass."

Victoria laced her arm through his. "Perhaps it had been. This Vance here--" She elbowed him with her interlaced arm. "--is an okay guy, though." He formed a soft smile as she guided him into the bathroom and got the shower started.

"Get cleaned up and I'll wait for you. You'll have to keep your eyes closed, otherwise, I'll find you naked in a block of ice."

"A shower sounds wonderful." Vance pulled his shirt off.

"Whoa, boy. Wait until I'm outta here." She slipped out the door and settled on the sofa, listening to the sounds of Vance moving around in the bathroom. She folded her hands on her lap. *Hurry up.*

A photo on the windowsill drew her eyes in. She picked it up, vividly remembering the day it was taken.

She and Vance were standing on the deck of a sailboat, surrounded by the most brilliant turquoise water she had ever seen in her life. It was their honeymoon trip to the Caribbean. Victoria had a copy of that photo too…well, used to have a copy. She threw it away along with everything else that reminded her of him. Her eyes clouded and she put the photo back, face down. *Think of something else. Think of how mean he is to you.* But that seemed so distant now. He was different from that man that harassed her and Mike last week. He reminded her of the man she fell in love with.

She wiped her eyes and flipped on the TV for a distraction, putting on the Superhero News Network.

The banner on the top of the screen read, *Two Days After the Earthquake.* Victoria only caught the tail-end of the report on the status of the city clean up. The screen flipped to a reporter standing on a street, in front of the city jail. People were passing in the background.

"One of the two escaped supervillain prisoners was captured today, thanks to The Kite and his new sidekick, Scarlet Macaw. One prisoner is still free. I'm here with Mayor Payne, who would like to give a few words to the city." The anchor turned toward the mayor. "Thank you for joining us. I know you're a busy man."

The mayor nodded, then lifted his microphone. "Not too busy to address our citizens. I wanted to thank everyone who has pitched in in this time of crisis. The news has focused on The Kite and Capitán Rápido coming to our rescue, but really, every citizen has helped. From cleanup in their own neighborhoods, to clothing and food donations for the thousands without a home. Even the simple task of having patience with the increased traffic has been helpful. Every day, things are getting better."

The anchor spoke, "So true. I think everyone was worried about these escaped villains, but now, with one caught, there's hope."

"You bet. I know we'll find the other one as well."

"On behalf of Shadow Town, I wanted to extend everyone's appreciation for your leadership. I understand your approval ratings have shot through the roof."

The mayor smiled. "That's not what's important right now. We need to get our city back. There's still a lot of petty crime that needs to be contained."

Vance stepped into the room, his hair still wet from the shower. She helped him back into the bedroom, where she packed a bag of his things. Then they were out the door, on their way up the mountains to continue to retrain Vance on his power to locate anyone or anything, anywhere.

ARIANA
in Windy City

A pacing Sir Fluffypants greeted Ariana at Lenny's apartment. "Meow. Rohw." The cat rubbed against Ariana's leg.

"You can tell I'm a couple hours late, can't you?" Making her way to the kitchen, Fluffypants jumped on the countertop and pushed against her hands. "You make this impossible," Ari said, futzing to pull the lid off the canned cat food in between the cat rubbing against her fingers.

"Meow."

Once she fed the royal cat, Ariana thought of returning to her lonely apartment. All that was there for her was her dirty salad bowl, which she refused to wash. It drove her nuts, so she curled up on Lenny's couch instead, opening his *Peter Pan and Wendy* book from the coffee table and stroking the cat on her lap. It was perfect. She laughed. *Purr-fect.*

Adam was allergic to cats, and she had to give hers up when she moved in with him. He'd been worth it, she told herself. Now, while the warm feline was purring on her chest, she wasn't so sure. "At least you're here for me."

The cat was one of the friendliest cats Ariana had encountered. Fluffypants came running to her, rubbed against her arm, and settled comfortably on her lap when she sat down.

"Either Lenny takes good care of you, or you're attention-deprived."

Flipping through Lenny's book, Ariana noticed some earmarked pages. She opened and started reading. Oh, they were some of her favorite scenes in this book. Maybe Lenny had actually read this book and wasn't simply trying to aggravate her?

As Ariana reread the marked passages, she was carried away for hours, absorbed in the emotion in the writing.

Ariana's stomach groaned. Wiping a stray tear away, she set the book down, still wanting to read the last few earmarked passages. "Stay here," she said to Sir Fluffypants, wanting to stop at her apartment for a granola bar. On her way out of Lenny's door, Sir Fluffypants took off, right between her legs.

"Stop!" What the heck was she yelling for? The cat wouldn't listen. She slammed the door behind her and ran after the feline. *Note to self: watch where the cat is next time!*

It'll be okay. She'll stop at the front door. Ariana stumbled down the steps to catch that cat. If only she had superpowers.

The cat stopped right in front of the main entrance. Ariana stepped off the last step.

I gotcha.

But the door creaked open and out zipped Sir Fluffypants, around the mail carrier.

"Stop that cat!" Ariana yelled as she pushed her way through the partially open door.

Cars rushed in both directions on the four-lane street in front of the apartment complex. How would she explain a flat cat to Lenny? He had already been through so much and couldn't lose his beloved feline, too. She slowed down, trying use different psychology. "Here, kitty, kitty," she called in her sweetest voice.

Sir Fluffypants stopped, then beelined for the road.

"*No!*" Ari yelled, lunging forward.

It was as if the cat understood, because at the last possible moment, she turned slightly and climbed up a giant oak tree that overhung the highway, climbing and climbing to a flimsy outstretched branch near the top. She pranced her way out on the limb that dangled above the racing traffic.

"Meow." The cat's big eyes looked right at Ariana

standing below the tree.

"Sure. Now you want me, knowing your life's in danger."

"Moouw…merwooow!" Sir Fluffypants was not happy.

Ariana put her hand on her hip. "Serves you right."

"Is that your cat up in the tree?"

Spinning around, Ariana found a uniformed officer on a bicycle behind her. "Um, not exactly, but she's a…friend of mine's."

"What's her name?"

"Sir Fluffypants."

"Sir?" The officer arched an eyebrow.

"It's a long story."

The man pulled a walkie talkie from his waistband. "I'll get some help."

Ariana shielded her face from passersby as the officer radioed for help. She needed this to end quickly. *'Adam? Are you there? I kinda got myself in a jam.'*

'I'm here. What's up, Ari?'

'Um, the neighbor's cat got stuck up a tree.' Ariana sent an image of the cat, dangling over the road.

'I'll be right there.'

Ariana filled with pride. Not every girl got to call a superhero husband to save them. She looked to the officer, still on his radio, trying to explain what was going on. "Oh, you can stop. I don't need help anymore."

The officer shook his head.

How would Ariana explain that? "Never mind. I'll take whatever help gets here."

Before the officer clicked the radio off, a caped superhero appeared in the sky. Ariana squinted to see her husband, but it wasn't him. The person was wearing red… Oh no, he wouldn't do that.

He had.

Scarlet Macaw touched down right beside Ariana.

"I heard on the police scanner that there was a cat caught in a tree." Scarlet's vivid green eyes radiated from under her yellow mask. "The Kite thought this would be good training."

Ariana gritted her teeth, but swallowed her pride. Adam had sent her, without a doubt. "Sir Fluffypants is right over there."

In a moment, Scarlet Macaw, wearing her form-fitting red dress and yellow tights, handed Ariana Lenny's cat. Ariana wrapped her arms tightly around the feline, biting her bottom lip and wishing it was Adam there instead.

"No thanks needed. I gotta fly," was all that red bird said before she disappeared into the sky.

"Wow, weren't you lucky?" the officer said.

"Yeah, lucky." Ariana's chest tightened. She thanked the officer and headed back into Lenny's apartment with Sir Fluffypants tucked tightly under her arm.

She was about to set the naughty cat down on the fur-covered worn spot on the back of the couch when the doorknob jingled.

"Ariana?"

She jumped and nearly threw the cat across the room.

Lenny continued, "I didn't expect you here."

"Um, I thought I'd keep Sir Fluffypants company. She seemed lonely." She wouldn't tell him about how his cat almost died today.

"That was sweet of you. I have chocolate cake." He lifted up a grocery bag. "I want to pay you back. Want to split it with me?" He pulled the most delectable looking, multi-layered slice of chocolate cake from the bag. "It's bigger than I can eat."

"No, I need to get home."

"To that husband of yours?"

"Yes." Why hadn't Adam come when she called him today? And he had the nerve to send *her*. *Get over it, Ari.* "No. Honestly, I don't know when he'll be home."

"Come on. You don't want me to eat this whole thing by myself, do you? I'll get a stomachache. Plus, I'm not going to pay you any other way for the extra care you gave Fluffy."

She coughed, choking on her own saliva. "Extra care? Yeah. Right, of course. I don't want to eat your cake, though."

Lenny cocked his head and gave a little pout.

"Fine. You win. Chocolate cake is my weakness."

Soon, they sat side by side on the sofa, each with a fork in their hands.

Lenny's eyes darted to the book beside Ariana. "That's not my favorite one by that author."

"It's not?"

"No, I like the earlier work better. It's rougher, but the emotions seem more real."

"I have a confession. I've never read the original *Peter Pan*."

"Well then, I won't let you leave without borrowing it from me." Lenny got up and pulled a worn book from the shelf beside the TV. "So tell me about this husband of yours. Why would he avoid coming home to his beautiful wife?"

Beautiful now? Ariana's cheeks heated as Lenny handed her the book. "He works odd hours and is gone a lot."

"I don't know an easy way to say this, so I'm just going to blurt it out. It sounds like he has another woman."

"He does not." The words came out, but deep down, all Ariana saw was Scarlet Macaw, flying around in her red dress, yellow tights, and lush red hair. If only Ariana was more like her. She realized she was biting her lip and looked up at Lenny with rage in her eye.

Lenny held up his hands. "I don't wanna piss you off, but it's something to think about."

"It's okay. I should get going, though." She gave Sir Fluffypants's head a stroke, tucked the book beneath her arm, and took off out the apartment door, ignoring whatever Lenny was saying about being sorry.

VICTORIA
in Shadow Town

Victoria had played hide-and-seek with Vance a hundred times. They even were brave and attempted the freeze power again, but it was still out of control. His powers were useless. On top of this, Vance showed no signs of his memory coming back, and that wasn't the worst part. The worst part was that Victoria was forgetting all the reasons she hated him.

Back at Victoria's home, they sat on the sofa next to each other, eating a sausage and pineapple pizza. The news was on and they watched as their city slowly fell into destruction. Communication was still spotty with many cell phone towers out, and people were still looting stores. Sick people couldn't make it to the hospital…couldn't call 911.

The news reporter's voice overlaid images of the city in shambles, then finally an image of a man in a blue cape, running off into the distance. "Citizens keep asking, where is Icy Tundra? Has our hero abandoned us?"

Victoria flicked the news off. "I'm so sorry." She reached over and squeezed his knee.

Vance reached a blind hand out and grabbed her shoulder, then slid his arm around her back, tugging her to his chest for a half-hug. His voice was soft and quiet. "I can't sit back and do nothing anymore. We need to put me on the accelerated program. Maybe trying to get control of my powers isn't the important part. Maybe I need my memory jogged first."

"What are you suggesting?"

"Let's switch our focus to returning my memory instead of my powers. Maybe if I visited some sentimental spots? Perhaps my house to go through my things? Maybe you could tell me more about us…"

Victoria pulled away, but his hand slid up to her cheek. She was used to his touches, as they were constant now, a way for him to notice her silent movements while wearing his blindfold.

With a tight-lipped smile, Vance felt for the remote and turned the TV back on.

"Shadow Town is receiving help from neighboring superheroes." Images of a man in a gray and black costume and a woman dressed in red, both wearing masks, filled the screen. "The Kite and his new sidekick, Scarlet Macaw, along with Capitán Rápido have done a lot to return our city back to normal, but a lot has yet to be done."

Victoria couldn't watch this. She patted Vance on the shoulder and retreated to her bedroom for the night.

EMMA
in Shadow Town

It was late when Estevan plopped down on the springy, hotel mattress. Emma would have loved to stay at her sister's place in Shadow Town, but then she'd have to explain Estevan's odd behavior. In the years they'd been married, she'd decided that avoiding situations was a lot easier than trying to lie your way out of them.

"Tough day?" Emma asked, pulling the covers tightly against herself.

Estevan's face was smashed into the pillow, his words slurred and his Spanish accent thicker than usual. "Yeah, you could say that. I tried to keep up with my email from work, but managing this with the earthquake cleanup, looters, thieves, and supervillains, I didn't have time."

Emma rubbed her husband's back. "But you can handle it. I know you can. Not only are you amazing, but you've got superpowers too."

"I can handle it, can't I?" Estevan turned over, renewed with energy.

"You bet. I have complete faith in you." Emma rubbed his shoulder. "You already know what's going on here in Shadow Town, right?"

Estevan's forehead turned up in wrinkles, then they smoothed themselves again. "Yes, of course. What specific thing are you referring to?"

Emma bit her tongue. She kept The Kite's amazing capture of the one supervillain silent for now. She'd tell Estevan that when he wasn't so tired and his ego could handle it. "You know how Mayor Payne was the underdog? How someone was out to get him? Well, his ratings are shooting up. Everyone is rallying support, pulling together in the time of crisis. It helps that he saved his twelve-year-old nephew from the earthquake. He pulled him out of the way before the roof of the building collapsed. They're saying he's a hero."

"A hero?" Estevan arched an eyebrow.

Emma smiled. "I thought that'd perk you up a little. Of course, he's not as big of a hero as you, but it was still a pretty impressive rescue." She wrapped her arms around her husband and gave him a tender kiss before snuggling into his arms.

"So, what did you do today, *mi gatita*?"

The day's stream of activities played in her mind. She spent all day rescheduling her City Council engagements, coordinating meetings in Shadow Town with the government officials, and investigating what could cause this earthquake, if it wasn't a natural disaster. Emma feared that if it was deliberate, it could happen again. And if it happened again, Shadow Town may never recover. "Oh, nothing much. A little of this, a little of that. Nothing important."

There was silence.

"Estevan?"

Nothing.

His eyes were closed and a small snore escaped his mouth. *Oh, well.* Emma slipped down into the covers and joined him in dreamland.

ARIANA
in Windy City

Ariana spent the rest of the evening "slaving" over the stove. Chicken scampi with a butter pasta. The smells of the rich butter and herb mixture had her mouth salivating for hours already. She didn't know why she bothered, who knew where Adam was anyway…other than out gallivanting with his protégé. He had to be home soon. She hadn't seen him all day and felt the need to make something fancy.

It's not to cover up your inadequacies, Ari…even if you couldn't even get a cat out of a tree. Some superhero wife.

Adam's voice startled her. *'Ari?'*

She spun around, hoping he was at the front door, but realized it was his telepathic ability, she sent a reply. *'Adam?'*

'I will be late.'

Of course. *'I missed you today when I needed you.'*

'I'm sorry. Have you checked out the news? I caught one of the escaped supervillains in Shadow Town.'

Ariana knew she should stroke his ego some, but she couldn't get herself to do it. Instead, she thought back to her conversation with her parents. She needed to come clean. *'When will you be home? I want to talk to you.'*

'About what?'

She took a deep breath. *'About being married.'*

'I was hoping it'd be about the weather?'

'Why? Is something going on?'

*'No, it's just that it'd **blow** over.'*

With his chuckle, her hands tightened into balls. Couldn't he be serious for a moment? She snapped the connection closed and waited for him.

An hour passed that she had the scampi set to "warm." It was after eight, he had to come home sometime.

Eating this late gave her heartburn,, but she wanted to show her husband she loved him and was trying. Her stomach growled, and she didn't know how much longer she could hold off. She washed all the dishes, except the salad bowl, and busied herself with housework while she waited.

Still no signs of Adam. She focused and reached out with her mental connection. '*Adam?*' She took a deep breath.

'*Hi, Ari! Sorry for my delay. I'll make it up to you, I promise. My day was so busy.*' His voice was smooth in her head.

'*Anything good?*'

'*No, just superhero stuff.*'

Ariana waited. Would he ask about her day? Only silence came. Was it because she was boring? No special powers. Not fighting crime. She filled the awkwardness. '*You're still not home. I was hoping you could give me an estimate what time you'd be here.*'

'*Do you need me for something?*'

'*I'm just gonna go…to bed if you'll be out a bit yet.*'

'*Yeah. I'm behind. I thought I'd be there earlier, but things didn't go as planned today.*'

'*Okay. I'm gonna hit the sheets then.*'

'*Enjoy. And Ari? I love you.*'

'*You too.*' The words were automatic. She didn't think about them, or she'd have held them back. Their telepathic connection halted and an emptiness replaced it. He hadn't told her a joke. No terrible pun. Was he sick of her? Did he wish he never married her?

She stared at the two plates she had set. Her stomach rumbled again. She went to the kitchen to serve herself a plate, then thought of Lenny.

Why'd he have to have a cat named Sir Fluffypants? Like Peter Pan? And had a girlfriend that passed away? Perhaps she felt guilty for almost killing his cat today.

Her legs carried her down the hall and before she allowed her brain to think about it, she knocked on Lenny's door.

"Hi, I made dinner tonight for my husband, but he's working late. Did you want to try something with more substance than chocolate cake?"

"You can't get enough of me, can you?"

Ariana bit her lip. "No. I'm just being nice. Never mind."

"No, no, no. I'd love to have dinner with you." He stepped outside his apartment.

Her cheeks tingled and heated.

He arched an eyebrow. "Strictly as friends and all."

"I'm married," Ariana blurted out.

"You keep telling me that, but I haven't seen him yet."

Ariana wouldn't let him get to her. Despite everything, she didn't want to eat alone. She'd eaten alone for more meals than she cared to number.

"Wow," Lenny said, entering her apartment. "You really got this place all decked out for dinner." He stopped and sniffed the air. "It smells heavenly." A soft smile appeared on his face.

Any frustration Ariana held dissipated. "Thank you." She poured two glasses of red wine.

They both sat down to a plate of chicken scampi.

"This is nice," Lenny said. "I feel…at home."

"Yeah, me too…probably because I am at home."

They both broke out in laughter.

Hours passed as Lenny and Ariana sat at the kitchen table, drinking wine and discussing cats, *Peter Pan*, and clogged sink drains. Boring stuff Adam wouldn't have liked, but for Ariana, it was nice to connect with someone and have things in common.

It was well after midnight before Lenny went home and Ariana retreated to bed.

The room spun slightly as she lay flat against her cool sheets. *I'm gonna pay for this at work tomorrow.*

She laughed.

If only Adam could see me now! Where are you, dear husband of mine?

She rolled over and smooshed her face into her pillow.

Her thoughts changed to the discussion she had with Lenny about the timeline in *Peter Pan and Wendy,* and fell asleep determined to re-read the entire story.

Wednesday, April 14th

ARIANA

in Windy City

Ariana's alarm had been beeping for way too long before she turned it off. Her head throbbed, and she squinted at the digital display—quarter after seven.

Urgh!

"Do I have to get up?" she whined as she rolled toward Adam's side of the bed.

It was empty.

Had he been home?

She sprang out of bed and gripped her head as a wave of dizziness settled on her.

Note to self: Drinking that much wine is not worth it.

"Adam?" she called. When silenced returned, she reached out with her mind. *'Adam?'*

Nothing.

Was he okay? She rushed into the bathroom where she found a damp towel laying on the center of the floor.

"Adam?" She scooped up the towel and headed toward the laundry room.

Folded in a neat tent on her dining room table was a note.

> *I left early to pick up Scarlet Macaw before heading to Shadow Town. Lots going on over there.*
> *Love ya!*
> *Adam*

Ariana threw the towel in the washing machine, took three ibuprofen, and headed for the shower, sure she had another busy day at work ahead.

While showering, innocent thoughts of Adam flying around saving people changed to Lenny's words. *It sounds like he has another woman.*

Yeah, named Scarlet.
Enough, Ari. You need to get to work.

EMMA
in Shadow Town

Emma arrived at Shadow Town's government building Wednesday afternoon. She spent all morning coordinating a monetary donation from Actionville to aid Shadow Town in their time of crisis.

Soon, she sat in a leather chair in front of a dark cherry desk, waiting for Mayor Payne to return to his office. His secretary, Jack, sat in a separate room off to one side.

"He's very busy," Jack said, adjusting his dark glasses. Emma thought he looked like that reporter guy with the weird glasses from that giant city near Kansas... Clark something or another.

The leather chair squeaked as Emma adjusted herself. "This will be quick. I imagine it's been chaotic this week for you both."

"You have no idea!" Jack said.

The intercom buzzed, then came the mayor's crackly voice, "I'm on my way."

"He'll be right here." Jack smiled, then turned his attention to his computer.

Out of the corner of her eye, Emma caught movement. An aquarium with a light yellow-colored snake with whiter spots along its spine. Perhaps an albino? The hair rose on her arms, and she felt frozen in place.

"I see you've found Fred," came a voice from behind her.

She sprung to her feet. "Fred? The snake?"

The mayor made his way to the aquarium and gave it a little tap. "I'm actually afraid of snakes. I keep Fred here as a reminder to conquer my fears."

Behind the glass, the snake's tongue outstretched while it raised its head, then sprang at one of a dozen crickets crawling in the cage. When the reptile recoiled, its mouth was a display of insect legs.

Emma shivered. "I don't like them much either." She pulled her focus away from the aquarium and shook the mayor's hand. They both sat down. "I brought a donation from Actionville. We had a budget item approved for disaster relief and voted to send it over here, with one stipulation."

"What's that?" The mayor rubbed his mustache.

"It has to be used specifically for medical aid."

"No problem. We're definitely in need of that."

"I had Jack coordinate the money transfer already."

The mayor folded his hands on top of his belly and leaned back in his chair. "Fantastic. Thank you."

"Your last few weeks have been quite exciting. With what happened when you visited Actionville, and then I hear you were injured in the earthquake." Emma's eyes examined his arm, which was no longer in a sling.

The mayor lifted his arm. "It was nothing more than a few pulled muscles. It's all better now. It's not me I'm worried about, though. I was spending time with my nephew when it happened. We were going down to the old campaign headquarters to pick up some flyers. Luckily, a few red lights delayed our trip. We were minutes away from being inside the headquarters." His words grew quiet. "My nephew could have died."

"The headquarters crumbled, right?"

"Yeah, nothing's left but a pile of rubble."

Emma was careful with her words, "Do you think this could be related to whoever is coordinating the attacks on your life? I understand the smoke bomb we experienced over in Actionville was not the first problem you encountered."

The mayor shook his head. His words were firm. "This was nothing more than a natural disaster. I don't see how it could at all be connected."

Emma nodded and bit her bottom lip. "Well, we're

lucky you're here today. I imagine a situation like that makes you reexamine life."

The mayor nodded.

"Even if it was connected, I don't think that activist group thought about what this would do for your approval ratings if it didn't succeed. The entire city's behind you. With support like that, you could run for president."

The mayor looked away, and his lips tightened.

"Is that next for you? President?"

"I'm not saying anything at this time, but the election's coming up next year and candidates will have to be announced soon."

Emma nodded, understanding his intentions. "Well, that's all I have. I don't want to hold you up from saving the city and all." Emma stood and shook the mayor's hand again.

"Make sure Actionville knows how much we appreciate their donation." Mayor Payne motioned toward his secretary. "Jack can lead you out."

"That won't be necessary. I've been here a few times in the past."

With that, Emma turned toward the door. Before leaving, she called back in, "If Actionville can be of further assistance, please let us know."

The mayor laughed. "You've given us money. You've lent us your superhero when ours is nowhere to be found. I think you've done enough."

With a nod, Emma was out the door.

ARIANA
in Windy City

After work, Ariana spent an hour cleaning up until there was no sign of Adam's presence. She had cleaned up his towel this morning, but there were dishes in the sink, dirty clothes in the hamper, and he had dumped out the pens and paper writing her that note. How was this mess possible when it felt like she never saw him? Maybe she expected too much.

Exhausted, she plopped down on the sofa and clicked on Netflix. She wanted to enjoy herself, but her mind only filled with images of Adam…and Scarlet flying around, hand in hand. Of Adam telling his cheesy puns to that flying bird…puns he should have been telling Ariana instead. She stared at Adam's empty chair and bit her lip.

Unable to focus on watching anything, she clicked off the TV.

She needed her mom.

Dialing her parents number, her stomach tingled. Why was she excited to call them?

"Hello?"

"Hi, Mom, it's Ari. I wanted to see how you're doing."

"Hi, honey. We're good. How's married life treating you?"

"Great." It sucked. She rubbed her hand on the sofa's armrest.

"I'm glad. Usually, it takes some adjustment. The important part is to always be there for each other."

Ari bit her lip so hard it drew blood. She needed to tell her mom her troubles. "Um, can I come over?"

"When?"

"Actually, right now?"

"That won't work, honey. Your dad's taking me to the casino."

"The casino? You never go there."

"Well, we've been wanting to go since you moved out. Now that you're officially married and have your own life, we thought we'd start being a little adventurous." She laughed. "Never mind. You don't want to hear that."

"Urgh. Mom. I didn't think that at all until you added the 'never mind' part."

"I have a few minutes now though, is there something you want to tell me?" She heard giggling and then a quieter whisper. "Trevor, stop it. Ariana's on the phone."

Double urgh. "Thanks Mom...um, we'll talk later. I have to go."

Ari hung up. It appeared everyone had their own life except for her. Maybe she shouldn't have been so hard on Adam a few days ago.

She stared at Adam's chair, the worn green fabric with a few strings hanging off the seat.

You're his wife, Ari. You need to be with him and show your support.

'Adam?'

Nothing.

'Come on. This is getting ridiculous! I know you're alive, you leave signs all over...but...'

Was he too busy with Scarlet to answer her? How would Ariana ever compete with that? Scarlet was a lean, mean, crime-fighting machine.

Ariana laughed at that as images of herself dressed up in a red cape and blue eye mask floated through her mind. How would that be possible? She couldn't even turn a wrench to open the kitchen sink drain.

You have to do something. You're losing your husband. To make him like you again, maybe you need to be more like Scarlet. Then he'll want to spend more time with you.

Ariana opened her laptop and began searching for

martial arts classes. She needed to toughen up. Be able to handle herself. Maybe then, she could help Adam in the crime-fighting world.

VICTORIA
in Shadow Town

After work, Victoria and Vance found themselves inside Vance's home once again. They waited until nightfall and turned the lights off. Victoria secured all the curtains, hoping the darkness would keep his freeze power under control. They both clutched a flashlight in their hands, taking the chance that an artificial light bulb wouldn't recharge his special power.

"This feels weird," Vance said. "It's like I'm intruding on someone's life, even if it's my own."

"What feels weird is that if you had your memory, you'd hate me looking through your things. Are you ready?" Victoria stood in front of Vance.

When he nodded, she slipped the mask off and moved out of his line of sight.

"Where do we start?" he said.

Victoria stayed a step behind him while they walked around the living room. He picked up a magazine, sat in the most worn chair, staring at the TV screen, then opened the cabinets below the TV, shining his flashlight inside.

"Does anything seem familiar?" Victoria asked.

"No. Not even déjà vu. In fact, I'm more comfortable in your apartment than here." His head tilted toward the windowsill, and he made his way toward it.

Shit. He'd seen the tipped down photo. She didn't want to explain it all to him and relive the memories.

Victoria grabbed his hand. "Maybe we should check your bedroom or the kitchen."

Vance kept moving toward the photo that Victoria really didn't want to explain.

"What's this?" He picked it up and turned it toward him, shining the light upon it.

"Just a photo from a long time ago."

"It's us. We look so happy."

"Looks can be deceiving."

"We weren't happy?"

"Well…we were then, I guess. Things change."

"Victoria." Vance set the photo down and turned her toward him.

The emotion in his eyes made her heart melt. She reached for the mask wrapped around his wrist. "Maybe you should put your mask on again."

Vance shook his head. "I'm fine. Tell me. What was our story?"

Victoria tightened her lips.

"It may help me find my memories."

Victoria blew out the breath she hadn't realized she was holding. She looked away from Vance, settling her eyes on the photo. "We were married."

"*Were* married?"

"Yeah. It didn't work out. We were young. Neither of us were ready to let each other in. You had spent your whole life hiding your identity…and I…well, I'm flawed." Victoria examined the lines of the photo frame, unable to look at Vance.

He reached over and took her hand. His voice was soft. "I don't think you're flawed, and I doubt I'd feel that way if I get my memory back. Why else would I keep a photo of you right in plain view?"

Victoria blinked away tears and pulled her hand away.

Vance's eyes pleaded. "Victoria. What's wrong?"

"It's nothing." She laughed, uncomfortable. "I like you better with the mask on. When you can't see me."

Vance sank down into the chair and rubbed his beard. "How could I have let you get away?"

Victoria reminded herself of all the reasons and composed herself. "You didn't let me get away. I left you. Now let's keep searching for things to jog your memories. Let's check your bedroom."

"You left me?"

"Yeah. We weren't good for each other."

"You mean, I wasn't good for you?"

Victoria stayed silent, and Vance turned away, retreating to his bedroom. Victoria followed, and they resumed their search through his belongings.

They spent the evening digging through things, but nothing triggered any memories. The good thing was Vance kept control of his power the entire night. He didn't have many personal items other than a few photos of his parents and of Victoria. Spreading all these photos out on the bed, Vance picked up one of him and Victoria.

"I must live a sad life," he commented.

"I don't know." Victoria rubbed her head. "You've always been strong and confident. Maybe you keep so little in case someone discovers your secret identity."

"To give my life up, to protect others, it's heroic, yet sad. Is that why you left me?"

Victoria shook her head. "No. It was because I gave up my life to support yours. We were too young. I was only nineteen years old when we got married and didn't know what it meant to be committed to someone for a lifetime. You were perfect, or so I thought. More than I could ever hope for, but we weren't ready."

"I held you back?"

"It doesn't matter anymore."

"Sure it does. It seems like we're not over what happened yet."

Victoria looked away. They should be over it, since six years had passed. She took a breath and let it all out. "We held each other back. I had always seen myself going to college, and that was impossible. Your early twenties are the best time of your life, right? While all my friends were out having fun and meeting new people, I was at home, playing wife. You wanted to create your superhero identity and figure out your method of helping this city, but were torn between your duty to the city…and to me."

Vance tipped her chin up and she didn't look away when his eyes bored into her soul. "Thank you, for everything. This can't be easy."

Victoria nodded and relaxed into his hand.

Vance's fingers glided across her cheek, before entangling in her hair. He whispered, "Something in the back of my mind keeps telling me that this is right. That we're right."

He leaned in closer, and she closed her eyes. Butterflies danced in her stomach. *Pull away, Victoria. This isn't right. It's not even really him.* But just as she felt a slight tingle on her lips, Vance yelled, "Oh no!"

Her back cooled, and when she twisted around, the nightstand right behind her was covered in ice.

"I'm so sorry! I almost got you. That can't happen again!"

Victoria sprang from the bed, memories of their almost-kiss quickly forgotten. "No. It can't."

Vance rushed to the living room, found his frilly purple mask, and replaced it over his eyes. "You can leave me here. I'll be fine."

"I can't leave you." Victoria never thought she'd hear herself say those words.

"Yes, you can. I want to be alone for a little while."

Victoria let the tears come. He couldn't see them, anyway. He was right. She needed some time apart. Time to think. They weren't getting anywhere, anyway. "Okay. I'll stop by and check on you tomorrow." She turned to leave, but hesitated. "For what it's worth, I did love you." …And maybe still did. *Stop it, Victoria. That thought's absurd.*

She turned and left without another word.

Thursday, April 15th

VICTORIA
in Shadow Town

An unidentifiable knot twisted Victoria's stomach all day at work. With Vance's memory loss, the escaped supervillains, and an earthquake where it shouldn't have been, Victoria suspected Vance had been deliberately targeted. What other explanation could there be for all the coincidences?

She spent way too much time at work researching the cause of the earthquake, not buying the "old fault line" explanation.

It turned out that there were a few articles on the online newspaper that had been overshadowed by the mayor, the city cleanup, and the arrival of The Kite, Scarlet Macaw, and Capitán Rápido to Shadow Town.

One article stated that communication outages were worse than expected for an earthquake. Upon further investigations, scientists found a large surge of sonic energy at about the same time as the natural disaster. They were unsure which came first, whether the earthquake released the sonic energy or the sonic energy caused the earthquake.

Now, Victoria sat outside SynPharmaTek's sonic division laboratory, waiting to talk with the head scientist, Dr. Felicia Burg. Victoria hadn't met her before, despite working in the same company. People working in accounting and the lab didn't cross paths, as they were in separate towers.

Victoria had set up an appointment to meet with her, saying it was because she wanted a better understanding of the new pharmaceutical technique of eradicating tumors and cancer combining radioactive isotopes and soundwaves. Victoria was impressed she even knew those words. The technology her company worked with was a little more advanced than she could grasp. Yes, she had always loved math, but science wasn't her strong suit.

While waiting, she flipped through the Superhero News Network, mindlessly scanning through photos. The main headline contained a photo of Capitán Rápido dressed in his black leather suit and a black mask over his eyes. Then she flipped to another photo of Scarlet Macaw in her red and yellow costume and The Kite in his gray and black. Who were those heroes behind their masks? They obviously hadn't lost their powers too.

The door opened and out walked a graying woman wearing a white lab-coat. She smiled warmly and shook Victoria's hand. "I'm happy you stopped over. It's about time someone from accounting came down and saw where all the money was going."

Victoria returned her greeting. "You know, things are just so busy and we're perpetually behind. Making time for a tour isn't top priority."

Dr. Burg motioned Victoria to follow her back into the lab. "I'm glad you found time. We're concluding phase three clinical trials this week. If everything looks good, we'll be releasing the technology to the world. It'll be a breakthrough. So far, preliminary data shows the cure rates are unheard of. Nearly eighty percent success in cancers that had twenty percent or less success with conventional treatment."

"It is exciting times to be working at SynPharmaTek, isn't it?" Though Victoria was proud and really wanted to know more, she had more specific things to discover.

"It is. This new discovery will put us in the history books and make us a pile of money."

Victoria nodded as she figured out how to ask the question that had her twisted in knots. "Could you tell me more about the technology? I understand you were recruited here specifically for your expertise."

Dr. Burg laughed. "More like I sought out SynPharmaTek for funding. I had been playing with isotopes and these sonic waves at my previous job, but it didn't align with their overall goal of crop technology. I saw more and wanted to get into human medicine. SynPharmaTek is the biggest player, so it seemed like a natural fit. I had played with it in my garage, so to speak, before coming here a few years ago."

"No matter how you came, it's great to have an actual supergenius on our payroll."

Dr. Burg laughed. "I wouldn't call myself that. I think the term only came out after the superheroes emerged. People needed to place wits on a pedestal along with superpowers. I'm not that different from everyone else."

But she was different, and they both knew it. Dr. Marchant had made a special position at the company just for Dr. Burg, because they both had special abilities. Victoria had just started working for SynPharmaTek and needed to do some accounting magic to allocate funds for Dr. Burg's research. "From what I understand of your research, tumor cells are marked with an isotope, then soundwaves are blasted to destroy the cells."

"That's the way the company is explaining it, but it's not really soundwaves. More like a vibration of the energy contained in the space between air molecules. Sort of a combination of cell phone frequencies, radio frequencies, and sound."

"We don't hold a patent on that device, do we?"

"We do for medical treatment, small scale."

"What about large scale?"

Dr. Burg tilted her chin.

Victoria laughed to cover up her nervousness. "Large scale like--" *Okay, Victoria, just say it.* "--like causing an earthquake. Has anyone suspected the connection?"

Dr. Burg turned to some white equipment laying on a long counter. Each tubular device was the size of a telescope. "These devices are way too small. Plus they only target isotopes. You would have needed to drench the city in radiation for it to work, and if that was the case, the radiation levels would have been the top news story."

Victoria scratched her head.

The sound of vibration drowned out the gentle humming from the other equipment, and Dr. Burg pulled a phone from her pocket. "Excuse me a moment."

Victoria nodded.

"Kyle did what?" the woman exclaimed, her pacing stopped. "What does that mean?"

Victoria bit her nails. She had the information she needed and tried to get the woman's attention, to tell her she was leaving, but she was too focused on the phone call.

A thought fluttered through Victoria's mind. Had Vance been right to suspect Dr. Marchant in this fiasco? Her boss had always been kind, and she trusted him.

Stop it, Victoria. He saved you from a purse napping. Trust your instincts.

There was no way, despite him having access to enough energy to create the earthquake.

Dr. Burg slipped her phone back into her pocket and grabbed a purse off a hook by the door. "I have to run. It appears my son got himself in a little trouble at school. After all the publicity with his uncle saving him in the earthquake, he seems to be acting up a little…again."

Victoria put two and two together—his uncle was the mayor. "Yeah, go. Family always comes first." She thought of Vance and felt her heart squeeze. He used to be her family. Too bad she couldn't teach an earlier version of herself that life lesson.

EMMA

in Shadow Town

After spending most of the next day reading whatever speculation she could find about superpowers and what happened to Icy Tundra, Emma needed a break. She headed to the middle school her sister taught at to surprise her.

When she made her way into the school office for a visitor's pass, she immediately found Becky. She was crouched in front of a boy wearing a black t-shirt displaying the periodic table of the elements. Hmmm. He looked familiar. He had sandy blond hair, thick glasses, and a face littered with freckles. Why was he in the office? Was he sick? Hurt himself?

The sharp tone in her sister's voice told her differently. "It doesn't matter if your uncle's the mayor, that just makes this situation worse."

The boy's voice hadn't grown deeper yet. Emma guessed he was about twelve. He folded his arms over his chest and leaned back in the chair. "I'd like to see your proof."

"You know there's no proof. The video footage has been erased."

"Then, why are you keeping me here?"

When Becky noticed Emma, she motioned toward the hallway. "You can go. I'll let your mother know our concerns when she arrives. I just see your potential and want so much for you."

With wide eyes, the boy took off, and Becky led her sister back to her classroom.

"Rough day?" Emma asked.

Becky blew out a breath. "That boy. He's too smart, yet refuses to apply himself."

"Trouble with his grades?"

Becky laughed. "Oh no, his grades are perfect. He

makes sure of that."

"So what's the problem?"

"He's a computer hacker. He gives himself grades and never does the work. We have him on a manual system, but those papers and files always end up missing too."

"You said he was the mayor's nephew? Is that the boy that almost died in the earthquake? Um… Kyle Burg?"

"Yeah, that's him. Not only is he gifted, but his mother's a supergenius that works at SynPharmaTek. I'm sure the boy will be a supergenius too. It's an interesting family. I wonder if he doesn't get enough attention at home. Anyway, what brings you to Shadow Town?"

"I had some business with Mayor Payne, but wanted to visit with you too."

"Where's the hubby?"

"Busy with work." And saving the city.

"If I didn't know better, I'd say he didn't like me. He's never with you."

Emma sighed. She'd long gotten over the loneliness of being a superhero's wife. It took a strong woman. "Luckily, you know better." Emma smiled and gave her sister a friendly shoulder nudge. "I was hoping I could pick up Samantha and take her to your house."

"Oh, that'd be great. I have some extra paperwork to fill out before I go home, anyway."

Emma's stomach filled with excitement while Becky called the after-school daycare and made arrangements. With a nod, Emma headed toward the door. "I'll have her back at your place before midnight."

"Seven's her bedtime. You know that."

"Okay. Eleven." She winked at her sister and disappeared through the door.

ARIANA
in Windy City

Lucky to get into self-defense training so soon, Ariana stood on a blue spongy surface in the middle of a gym. *This is good for you, Ari. It'll give Adam a reason to hang out with you, plus you can blow off some steam...and keep in shape, too.*

She wiped her sweaty palms against her yoga pants. How was it possible she was sweating and class hadn't even started yet? She never saw herself taking a self-defense class. *It's good for you to try something new—all by yourself.*

A dark-haired man with a full beard wearing a black karate-type uniform stepped to the front of the room, right in front of the mirrors. "Good afternoon, everyone. I hope you've had a nice day so far."

"Afternoon," the handful of people in the class said in unison.

"I'd like to introduce our new classmate, Miss Ariana Turano." The man motioned toward Ariana.

"*Miz* Ariana Turano," she corrected, feeling her naked ring finger and giving a little nod in response to everyone's welcomes.

"We always start our class with physical practice. We can teach you all the principles of self-defense, but if you never use them, the skills won't be there for when you need them. Everyone, partner up. I'll take *Miz* Turano." The teacher smiled at Ariana.

After a warmup, the students practiced various moves with their partners that made them look like they were wrestling. Ariana had to look away, especially since she didn't want to see anyone get hurt. She focused on her instructor, admiring the fullness of his beard.

"My name's Jake, by the way," he said, giving her a little nod. "There are two components we use here during our initial practice session. Strikes and ground defense."

"Ground defense?"

"Yeah, what to do if you're brought down to the ground. Kinda the last resort. Let's start with the strikes first."

Ariana nodded.

"This is the hardest part for a woman. Females struggle with unleashing the aggression needed to throw an effective punch. They're just not wired that way—too passive. So, women have less power, by physiology, and less aggression. Combining these two things makes them an easy target."

Unless your name's Scarlet. "Are you trying to scare me off?"

"No, not at all. On the contrary. I want to show you that despite your size and your physical strength, you can still stand up for yourself if faced with trouble." He brushed his hand down his beard. "The thing you have going for you is women can be fast and smart about an attack. We'll teach you how to use these strengths to your advantage."

Ariana nodded again, and butterflies fluttered in her stomach. She hadn't been this excited since…well, her wedding day.

After discussing proper balance and positioning, the instructor retrieved a black-cushioned pad and gloves from a shelf in the back of the room. "Put these on." He tossed Ari the gloves before pulling the pad onto his hand. "Okay. Hit this pad."

Ariana raised an eyebrow at him. "Now? Don't you want to show me how or something first?"

"No. It's okay. Go ahead. Keep your wrist straight, elbow relaxed, and show me what you've got." He slugged the pad with his free hand. "This is a self-defense class. Oftentimes, you'll be taken off-guard."

Ariana looked around the room at the other classmates throwing punches. She took a deep breath, focused on the black pad, and extended her arm out, hitting the soft foam-covered pad with her covered knuckles. "Ouch," she said, shaking her hand out.

"Okay. I didn't even feel that. You're kinda wimpy."

"Kinda wimpy?"

"Yeah. All the other women can hit much harder than that." Beneath the beard, she saw her instructor's taunting smile.

She bet Scarlet hit harder than that. Anger simmered.

"There." Jake hit the pad with his fist again. "That anger I just saw in your eyes. Pull it. Use it to hit right here." He slugged the pad again, then held it toward her.

Ariana took another swing.

His arm recoiled from the force of her fist.

"Okay. Better. Now try again, swing with your hips, think of punching *through* the pad. Don't stop at the surface."

This time, Jake took a step back when her fist crashed into the foam.

He laughed. "You're a quick study."

Ariana smiled.

"One more time. Do everything the same, use that anger again. Channel it and take it out on the pad."

What angered her?

Dishes.

She took a swing.

"Good. Keep going." Jake widened his leg stance and braced his arm with the other.

Clothes stained with blood. Laundry.

"Another," her instructor said.

That Adam's not there when I need him. And Lenny. Why can't I keep thinking of him as a jerk? Why does he have a cat, like the same books as me, and had a girlfriend that died?

Another blow.

That she married Adam and hasn't felt married at all. That she left her parents for him...and she never sees him.

Another strike.

The redhead he spends his time with. Ariana pictured her face. Her seducing smile, her well-glossed lips, and her laughing at Adam's cheesy puns.

Another strike and another. Ariana's mind filled with images of Adam's hands on his partner. Showing her how to use her powers. Flying with her. Spending all his time with her while Ariana was in Windy City. Trying to make enough money to support them both.

"Whoa there, Ariana. Hold it. No need to show off now." Jake took a few steps away from her. "Okay, here's the first real lesson. All that anger you felt? You need to push it away and stay calm. If you ever need self-defense, you need to keep a clear head. Check out your arm."

Ariana looked down to where Jake pointed. There was a bright orange sticker.

"You didn't even realize I did that, did you?"

Her cheeks heated from more than the exertion.

"Always be aware. When you're angry, you lose that awareness." Jake clapped his hands, raising his voice. "Okay. Now it's time to move to throws and ground defense."

Half an hour flew by where Ariana worked one on one with Jake, doing various throws, twists, and shields. When her instructor switched to the classroom instruction part about being aware of your surroundings, Ariana caught her breath.

The lesson went by in a blur. Ariana struggled to control the anger she hadn't known was inside her. She wanted to run out the door and hide. Instead, she blankly stared ahead, wondering who she had become.

EMMA

in Shadow Town

It was official. Emma was a pushover. All Samantha had to do was look at her with those big, beautiful brown eyes, and she had Emma wrapped around her finger.

"Can we go to the park, Auntie Ems?"

Emma sent her sister a text and soon finagled a parking spot on the busy main street. Maybe if they got here earlier and didn't stop for ice cream, they would have gotten a better spot. But, of course she'd do anything for that girl. When…um…*if* she had a child of her own, would she give in so easily? Yeah, probably. She smiled thinking of that possibility.

"Ready?" Emma asked, clutching the swing's chains in her hand.

Samantha squealed and nodded.

"Okay, hang on!" Emma pulled the swing back and pushed her all the way forward, doing an underdog. She turned around and watched the expressions change on Samantha's face. Gritting her teeth and eyes wide as the swing sucked her backward to a huge smile and laughter when she returned toward Emma.

They spent over an hour at the park, swings, slide, jungle-gym, and all sorts of new plastic gadgets Emma didn't know the names of. Playgrounds had really changed since she was a child.

It wasn't until the sun dipped behind the multi-story buildings that they headed back to Emma's car.

On the way out of the park, Samantha skipped beside her. "Auntie Ems, could you move in with us?"

"Oh, why is that?"

"You're so fun!"

"You don't have enough room in your house."

"I could get bunkbeds. I get the top, though!"

Samantha's movements were exaggerated and jerky and filled a hole inside Emma she kept trying to hide.

As they approached the road, Emma took Samantha's little hand in hers. Her warm, fuzzy moment was shattered from screeching car tires coming down the street. She stopped and pulled Samantha into her arms.

There was a traffic jam, and Emma scanned the cars for the squealing tires. Next, the sirens caught her attention. She snapped her head in their direction, and a dark car, being chased by two police cars, nearly flew through the air as it traversed the curb, darting around the backed-up vehicles and using the park as a passing lane.

It'll stop.

The car picked up speed and headed right toward them. Emma grabbed Samantha and dove to one side...then the other, but there was no escape. The car was still coming right toward them, through the grass.

Samantha's scream rang in her ear, and Emma couldn't breathe. The car was only thirty...no, twenty...ten feet away.

Emma screamed herself, realizing that there was no way she could dart out of the car's path fast enough.

Then, her body jolted as an arm wrapped around her. She relaxed a moment, wondering how Estevan knew where she was. Her world moved fast—but not quite as fast as she was used to. The park came into view and the car passed below her feet. She and Samantha were up in the air.

"What's going on?" She tried to twist around, but couldn't see who held them.

Flying... She listed what superheroes she knew of with this power. There was the guy who wore red and blue...she always forgot his name, he was kinda old news. That new woman hero, The Crimson Macaw...no, Scarlet Macaw.

Before she sorted through the long list of

superheroes she knew, her feet touched the ground and the grip around her disappeared. She spun around to a black cape with silver feathers sewn into it. A white hood over a man's head. The Kite.

His voice was breezy, almost sounding young. "I have to go. They stole that car." In a whoosh, The Kite was flying toward the car once again. All she saw was the flapping cape.

Emma looked around for the police, but they were still stopped in the traffic jam. Off in the distance, The Kite landed on the car's roof and punched out the passenger side window. He shook his hand out as he crawled inside.

It was then she realized Samantha's cries had completely stopped. When she looked down at the curly-haired kid, she saw a huge smile.

"That was awesome!" the girl lisped. "Which one was that?"

Emma smoothed Samantha's hair down. "The Kite. He's from Windy City."

"Auntie Ems, do you think you could buy me a cape like that?"

Emma shook her head and spoke as calmly as she could despite her racing heart. "What about Capitán Rápido?"

"He can't fly."

"No, I guess that's true." Emma grabbed Samantha's hand. "I think we need to take you home first. You have quite an adventure to tell your parents about."

~ ~ ~

Estevan met Emma at Becky's house later that night. He had been in the middle of capturing the last escaped supervillain and couldn't stop. It turned out one of the escaped villains had lost their powers and the other gained a new power that he couldn't control. It seemed that she was right—whatever had happened during the earthquake had affected the superhuman powers. Was that what happened to Icy Tundra?

Emma had just finished telling her husband about her save by The Kite when a voice sounded from upstairs. "Ready? Here I come!" Samantha exclaimed.

Emma snapped her head around to see her niece dart down the stairs and jump off the last few.

"I can fly! I'll save you!" The little girl spun around, showcasing her new black cape with silver feathers sewn in. Yup. Emma hadn't been able to help herself and had pulled off at the nearest department store to please the child. Samantha had no idea they almost died, and Emma wanted to keep her attitude positive.

Estevan leaned in toward Emma. "What's she wearing?"

"Oh, we bought that for her. It's The Kite's cape."

Estevan almost choked. "The Kite? What happened to her obsession with that other handsome superhero? Capitán Rápido?"

"He didn't save us!" Samantha yelled before Emma could soften the blow.

"Well, maybe he was busy. Protecting the city. Capturing the bad guys."

"But he can't fly!"

"But he can see the future."

"The Kite can read your mind."

"He can't read your mind," Emma corrected. "He can only talk through telepathy. Now Capitán Rápido can read your mind...kinda."

Emma reached out and gave her husband's hand a squeeze. "It's okay. She's six."

Becky interjected, "I keep trying to get her to like Icy Tundra to support our town, but I guess he's flown the coop."

"Or something happened to him," Emma added, thinking about how her own husband had lost his powers momentarily...plus the supervillains issues. If Icy Tundra had the same phenomenon, perhaps one of the villains got to him…or he met his demise, crushed in the earthquake debris. What a shame.

Emma rubbed her hands against her jeans. What if the earthquake was just a side effect of something else? Some superweapon designed to take away powers. A master plan to eliminate the superheroes. She looked over at her husband. Could they leave the city? Escape before something big happened? How many innocent people would perish in another attack? No, that wasn't their way. They needed to figure out who was behind this.

"Emma?" Becky waved her hand in front of Emma's face.

"Oh, sorry. I was just deep in thought. I had a tiring day." She smiled.

Becky glanced at her watch. "Oh my, it's eight-thirty. I need to put Samantha to bed."

"Can I have a cookie first, Auntie Ems?"

"Of course," Emma said with a smile.

Becky interjected, "Samantha, you know you can't have sugar so close to bedtime."

Emma couldn't help the words that flowed from her lips. "Come on, Becky. We had a stressful day. One cookie can't hurt."

Becky's words were stern as she scooped the little girl up into her arms. "She'll never get to sleep with the sugar. When you have your own kids, you can do whatever you want with them."

Emma bit her lip to stop it from quivering. She let Becky carry a whining Samantha upstairs. *When she has her own kids.* If only it was possible. She looked over to Estevan, and he sensed the tears swell in her eye.

He reached over and rubbed her shoulder. "I'm sorry. Maybe you'd be better off with someone else."

Now the tears flowed, and Estevan pulled Emma into his arms. He rubbed her back, and she inhaled his woodsy scent. She steadied her voice the best she could. "But I don't want anyone else." She wiped her eyes, and they slowly dried. "Sorry, it's just been an emotional day."

"I understand, *mi gatita*. If it helps at all, I wish we could have a child, too, but I gave up on the idea long ago. I guess I was tired of the emotional rollercoaster."

Maybe Estevan had the right idea. "What if we…"

"Considered adoption?"

"Dang you." She gave his shoulder a jab. "Your darn power again. Yes. Adoption."

"Now that's an idea I hadn't considered."

"Well, we should at least think about it." Emma took a deep breath and refocused on Shadow Town's current situation, no longer wanting to dwell on her child issue. "I think this whole earthquake fiasco was planned. Intentional for some reason, but I'm not sure why. The escaped prisoners didn't do anything but hide, and they're now both back in custody."

Estevan whispered, "And what if it is? That means something big is going to happen soon. Another earthquake would wipe out this city…but if nothing happens? How can we be sure it wasn't just a coincidence?"

Emma rubbed her cheek. "Well, we know you lost your powers. It'd be nice to know if the same happened to Icy Tundra, but we can't find him. Who else could we ask about losing superpowers?"

Estevan stared blankly ahead.

Emma continued. "If only there was another superhero running around this town, saving people." Her mood picked up some.

Estevan perked up. "I have an idea!" He raised one finger and pointed at the ceiling, his lips curling up into a bright smile.

Emma put her hand on his upper arm and gave it a squeeze, waiting patiently. "And what's that?"

"What if I…um…Capitán Rápido goes out and

finds this Kite fellow? We could see if we both had issues after the earthquake."

"I think that's a brilliant idea. How'd you ever come up with that?" Emma kissed her husband on the cheek, then headed upstairs to tuck Samantha in bed. She wouldn't let her anger with her sister be taken out on her sweet little niece.

While Estevan was busy finding The Kite, she wanted to pinpoint who could create such an earthquake.

ARIANA
in Windy City

For the rest of Ariana's evening, she couldn't stop thinking about her self-defense class. Specifically fantasizing about the look Adam would give if she was able to sneak a move in on Scarlet. She was invincible, right? But did she have any formal self-defense training? She'd never attack Scarlet, but the thought made her excited for the next class. At some point, Adam would realize what he was missing.

She felt like she could take on the world, and on her drive home, she stopped off at the mall and picked up some lacy black underwear—she wouldn't put the red stuff on from her honeymoon. Red reminded her of Scarlet, and she wanted no reason for Adam to think of her too.

She shook that thought out of her head and focused on her husband.

'Adam?'

'I'm here.'

'When will you be home tonight?'

'I'm finishing up and heading that way.'

'Great.'

Once she arrived home, she showered, shaved everything she could, and got ready for Adam. She waited…and waited. Images of him opening the door and how she would seduce him played in her mind. Her mind was filled with one hundred and one ideas and she laid on her bed waiting.

When a few hours passed, she reached out to her husband.

'Adam?'

'Yes, dear.'

'I'm waiting for you.' She sent an image of her black lace underwear.

His words were eager. *'I'll be right there.'*

Ariana sorted through her ideas and knew how she'd greet him. She positioned herself against the wall, leaning into one leg and bending her other knee. She grasped her hand on her side, then in front. What should she do with her arms? She brushed her fingers through her hair. There. That was it. She positioned herself ready to pounce. When the door opened, instead of raw, carnal, adrenaline, she felt...raw carnal exhaustion.

Instead of pouncing, she snapped. "It took you long enough." What evil creature had she become? Who kidnapped Ariana and how much ransom would it take to get her back?

"If I would have known, I would have been here sooner. It takes time to get here from Shadow Town."

"How could you not know?" Ariana now stood with her legs hip width apart and her arms folded across her chest. She felt kinda ridiculous having this discussion in her underwear, but she wasn't gonna retreat now.

"Ari, I can't read minds."

She unfolded her arms and pointed at him. "Actually, Adam, yes, you can!" She realized what she was doing and forced her hand to her side.

"You know it doesn't work that way."

She glared at him. Holding her ground.

"Oh, come on. Give me a break. I've got a lot going on."

Like Scarlet? She threw her hands up in the air. "Never mind. Just go back to *her*."

"Her?" He cocked his head.

"You know, the big red bird."

"You mean Scarlet?" He raised an eyebrow. "It's not that way. I love you."

"You're never home."

"Things are complicated right now. I'm a little..." His shoulders sagged. "...overwhelmed."

She blew out a breath. "I'm gonna go to bed."

"Ariana…" Adam followed her across the room. "I'll give it all up for you, if that's what you want."

"I shouldn't have to ask for your time and attention. Please leave. I want to be alone."

"Ari—"

Ariana crawled under the covers and turned her back to Adam. She held in a sob.

Adam's voice was soft. "Okay. I'm going."

Ariana heard him shuffle around, then the front door opened and clicked shut. That was when she let it all out, sobbing into the pillow.

How could he leave?

He should know better. To prove a point, she sent him a feeling of her sadness. Her hopelessness. Her…anger.

He was getting good at leaving.

What if, someday, he didn't come back?

Friday, April 16th

EMMA

in Shadow Town

From their hotel room in Shadow Town, Emma spent the next morning making phone calls and searching the internet. Everything she read had pinpointed the earthquake's strongest force to be in the block where East 104th Street intersected with Sparrow Avenue.

Emma pulled up a map on her laptop and assessed what was there. She then called in a few favors down at the government building and determined that nearly the entire block was owned by the wealthiest man in town, Montgomery Marchant. The man involved in the high-speed train proposal to connect Shadow Town to Actionville.

An earthquake was an awfully convenient way to demolish some old buildings, but Emma shook the thought away. That would be a lot of work for a project that wasn't even approved yet.

Now, Emma walked down the sidewalk of 104th Street, trying to find anything of interest. The buildings were still in shambles; glass, lumber, and concrete blocks littered the sidewalk. There were a ton of volunteers cluttering the streets, working on cleaning it up.

Emma easily slipped right in to investigate without anyone noticing how out of place she was. She made her way to the corner of Sparrow and 104th and stopped when her feet crunched on broken glass.

Volunteers passed in front of her while she examined the building across the street. All the glass windows were blown out…more than blown out. They were completely shattered to the point where the glass littered the opposite sidewalk.

It appeared the building had been a bakery of some type and had taken the biggest blow from the earthquake. Surrounding the building was yellow caution tape interlaced with red danger tape. Despite this, she needed to get inside.

A worker stopped in front of her with a wheelbarrow of crumbled bricks.

She stood straight and smiled, trying to appear like she belonged there. "Great job."

The man nodded, his hardhat slipping some. "This part was definitely hit the hardest." He kept pushing the wheelbarrow around the littered street.

It had been nearly a week. Emma wondered what this place looked like right after the event.

She returned her focus to the bakery. Above the missing windows was the shadow of letters. The sign had been removed well before the earthquake. She squinted and made out the words, "Cupcake Corner."

Emma dashed across the street, lifted the caution tape, and crawled through a spot where a window had been. Her heart hammered. She always left the dirty work for her husband. Tucking herself away in a corner, she scanned the inside of the building.

What if some debris falls on you?

What if someone catches you inside?

She was sure nobody had seen her. She made her way through the building. The main room was empty, the display cases just shells with the glass shattered like the windows. The plaster from the ceiling had fallen down in multiple spots and lay across the floor, creating a thick blanket of white dust.

She followed two sets of footprints to the back room, then saw the dust stir at her feet. *Crap.* She turned around to a trail of her own steps. There was nothing she could do about it now, and did it really matter? It depended if there was a criminal mastermind behind this or not. She continued to follow the footprints. One set of steps was a smooth shuffle of large feet and the other were smaller tennis shoes. A woman's, perhaps?

Emma scanned the room from the doorway. Dusty ovens lined the far wall, and the stainless tables were tipped over, also covered by a heavy layer of dust. The footsteps lead around the equipment to the corner where a lot of shuffling went on…and a dust-free spot, as if something that had sat there was moved.

Emma scratched her head. There may have been dust before the earthquake, but this heavy layer had settled after the quake. These two people had been there after the disaster…taking something out of the vacant shop. Could it have been looters, stealing whatever was inside?

Or was it something else? If Emma's hunch was right, and the earthquake was not a natural disaster but caused by a person on a mission, maybe there was a device here. Where could a device, capable of causing this devastation, be tucked away?

She scanned the room and her set of footprints. Just being here would make her look suspicious, especially if this whole thing was caused by criminal activity. She needed no reason for anyone to investigate her…she'd hate for that investigation to lead to her husband.

Emma snuck outside and walked around the block. Across the street was a bank. Beside the shop was the mayor's campaign headquarters. That explained why he had been so shook up. They had been right in the heart of the disaster. Careful where she stepped, Emma walked past the headquarters trying to look like all the other volunteers.

The place was destroyed and full of debris. If she thought the glass from the cupcake shop was bad, this place was worse. Soggy papers were scattered across the floor, destroyed by the water from the sprinkler system that must have gone off. The desks were crushed by the fallen ceiling. Was that a smashed computer? What a loss.

"Excuse me?"

Emma spun around. "Yes?"

It was a policewoman. "Are you helping clean up?"

"Yes, of course."

"What team are you on?"

Team? Crap. "Um, no team. I just came down to see if I could help."

The policewoman pointed down the street. "There's a tent set up on 103rd Street. You'll need to register there."

Emma nodded, hearing her heart pound in her ears. "Yes, of course, I'll get on that right away." Were her hands shaking?

Not waiting for the officer's approval, she turned and headed toward 103rd. She needed her City Council computer access so she could figure out why someone would destroy this specific area of the city.

Since she knew that Dr. Marchant owned the block that was hit the hardest, she had three scenarios running through her head.

Did someone have it in for Dr. Marchant?

Or did Dr. Marchant want this area destroyed?

Or was something else going on?

Emma needed to clean herself up and look presentable. She was going to pay Dr. Marchant a visit. After all, as the Chair of the City Council, Actionville would want information about the high-speed train and whether the earthquake interfered with that project here in Shadow Town.

And perhaps while obtaining this information, she'd answer some of the questions she kept turning over.

VICTORIA
in Shadow Town

Victoria was going to pay for the day, um, week she'd had at work. She had literally spent no time actually doing accounting work. She'd have to catch up next week and maybe put some time in on multiple weekends, but it didn't matter. It was her duty to help Vance…and Icy Tundra…and the entire city of Shadow Town get their superhero back.

The first part of her day, she couldn't get her mind off how she left Vance alone at his house… No, it wasn't that she left him alone. It was that she left him hanging.

It was what she did. It was how she'd left their marriage. She didn't even say good-bye. One day, while he was out saving the city, she was busy packing her stuff and driving halfway across the country. If she stayed and explained to Vance what she was doing, she would have never left. She'd had the opportunity to go to the college she'd dreamed of her whole childhood, and saw only three choices back then: stay in Shadow Town with Vance and miss her chance, take Vance along and make him give up everything he worked hard for, or go without her husband, allowing them both to live out their dreams.

Now, she realized that it didn't matter what college she had gone to, staying with Vance would have been worth it…without a doubt. But deep down, she knew what would have actually happened if she had told him: he would have given it all up for her, and she didn't want that guilt. The guilt of him giving up his dream for her…and the guilt of leaving Shadow Town without a superhero.

Honestly, she understood why he hated her now and treated her the way he did. He had a broken heart. She liked to think that she would be more adult-like than him if the situation was reversed, but she wasn't so sure. Strong emotions could make you do strange things.

And now, she couldn't face him again. She couldn't express her feelings. Couldn't do what she truly wanted. She should have learned from her mistakes.

Her phone buzzed, and she opened the text message.

Dinner tonight? We need to talk.

It was from Mike. Yet another man she couldn't tell how she truly felt.

Victoria: *Not tonight. Sorry. I have book club.*
Mike: *You've been avoiding me.*
Victoria: *No. I've been busy.*
Mike: *We really need to talk.*
Victoria: *We will. Later. I have to get back to work.*

Which wasn't the truth either. She already proved to herself she wasn't getting anything done today. In between her long periods of self-reflection, she filled her time searching through accounting records for unexplained purchases in the Sonic Division Lab of SynPharmaTek…or that Dr. Marchant made directly. Anything that may indicate the building of a weapon that could cause an earthquake and wipe out a superhero's memory.

And that was how she'd start thinking of Vance again. Her day was a vicious circle.

By early afternoon, she decided to head home. She still had the book to read for book club, and she wanted to attend that meeting. Something to get her mind off this past week. Besides, Mike might come looking for her.

On her way out the door, Victoria had a peculiar thought. It was no secret that Dr. Marchant opposed Mayor Payne. In fact, he had been an opposing candidate in the mayoral election last fall.

How was it that Mayor Payne's sister-in-law, Dr.

Burg, worked for Dr. Marchant? What were the dynamics there?

She found herself calling Dr. Marchant's office. His secretary answered.

"Hi, Fanny. This is Victoria Chesney down in accounting. I'm working on fund allocation and was wondering if you had information on the sonic lab's big announcement next week."

"Yeah. Actually, I have some flyers made up. Did you want to take a look at them?"

"That'd be great. I'm heading home now, I'll swing by on my way out the door. Oh, were you involved in Doctor Marchant's campaign for mayor? I know we made a big donation and was wondering how the funds were allocated." Victoria laughed. "You know us accountants love closing loopholes."

"Yeah, actually, I did the books for that. I could include the fund summary with the sonic lab promotional materials."

"That'd be great. See you in a few minutes."

EMMA
in Shadow Town

"I'm coming along," Estevan had insisted over lunch.

Emma took his hand and gave it a caring pat. "I don't know how I'll explain why I brought my husband along to a business meeting."

"Just say we were in town together."

"Don't you think your time would be better spent trying to find The Kite?"

"What if this Doctor Marchant *hombre* is the bad guy? Then what? I want to be near. This may not be the right thing to say, but your safety will always come first."

Emma sighed. Why couldn't she refuse that man? "Fine, but you'll need to stay quiet."

Now, Emma sat in the waiting room inside SynPharmaTek tower beside her husband. She took his callused hand in hers and gave it a little squeeze. It was so easy to overlook all those small things that make your spouse happy as you fly through life, but stopping to appreciate things was crucial, even in between saving the world...or at least the current city.

A curvy woman with long chestnut hair entered the room and approached the reception desk. "Hi, Victoria." The receptionist held out a manila envelope. "Here's the info on the sonic lab you requested."

Sonic lab?

"Thanks, Fanny. You've been more of a help than you can imagine."

As the woman left, she gave Emma and Estevan a nod. It was amazing how some people radiated charisma and you couldn't help but watch them.

The receptionist looked up. "Okay, Missus Rodríguez, Doctor Marchant is ready for you now."

Emma and Estevan stood up. "No, just you, ma'am.

I'm assuming it's official business?"

"Yes, of course." Emma swallowed and turned to her husband, who was eager to force his way inside. "It's okay. I'll be right back."

She turned away from Estevan, not waiting for his answer. She didn't want to draw suspicion about the visit.

Fanny led her back to Dr. Marchant's office. The hair rose on Emma's arms, but she straightened her blouse and tried to focus on something else. It was just this guy had superpowers...and could be behind this town's missing superhero. Interacting with potential supervillains had always been Estevan's job.

She thought through what she knew about Dr. Marchant. His power was the ability to manipulate time somehow...or at least a human's perception of time. Emma was sure there was more to it, but it wasn't something Dr. Marchant flaunted.

Stepping into the office, the first thing she noticed was the big grandfather clock in the back corner. The pendulum swung, back and forth. She heard the ticking of a clock...no, multiple clocks. On his desk was another clock, an old-fashioned tambour type. Then on a shelf sat an anniversary clock. Two more hung on opposite walls as well. She pulled her eyes away and focused on the man behind the desk.

Dr. Marchant twirled a pen with his fingers. "You've noticed my collection?"

"Yes, they're very nice." She wanted to raise her voice to be heard over the ticking, but it wasn't necessary. "Doesn't the ticking get distracting?"

"You'll tune it out, everyone does...except me. I like to focus on the steady noise. It ensures I'm not playing with time."

Emma sat down. "I've read you never use your power."

"I try not to." He rubbed his fingers through the

graying hair at his temples. "You see, I may be able to stop time, but it stops for everyone else except me. I keep aging. How old do you think I am, Missus Rodríguez?"

"I couldn't say."

"Please, take a guess."

Emma's eyes focused on the gray hair, then to the gentle wrinkles around his eyes. "Maybe forty-eight?" Emma was being generous. She really thought he looked over fifty.

Dr. Marchant laughed. "Not quite. I'm thirty-nine."

"I don't understand where you're going with this."

"Deep down, you're nervous being here. You wonder if I actually use my powers to manipulate time. Stop time, specifically. Well, no, Missus Rodríguez, I don't. Because when I stop time, everyone stops aging, except me. I learned that the hard way in medical school. For every exam, I stopped time to study, and what took me eight years on paper actually took me twelve. My hair was graying, skin wrinkling, and I had high blood pressure. I haven't played with time since graduating."

She sat back in the chair with her business smile plastered on her face. If he only knew how closely she understood superpowers. Instead of commenting on that, she sat back in the chair with her business smile plastered on her face. "I've come to see how the earthquake is affecting the high-speed train project."

Dr. Marchant leaned forward. "Is Actionville in support of the project?"

Emma shook her head. "The town hall meeting hasn't been rescheduled since the incident with the mayor and the smoke bomb. I don't know how they feel, so I thought I'd gather more information for the council."

"I hate to find fortune in other's misfortune, but this will speed up the plan if it's approved. The train depot needed to be put on the East Side. Now with the damage, the demise of the buildings has become a priority."

"You needed to tear buildings down?"

"Yeah, I own a block out there that was going to become the main train station. One of my buildings was recently condemned and the rents are low. I thought the train stop would be a better use of space."

Emma rubbed her sweaty palms on her thighs, thinking back to her trip down to the rubble. "The condemned building. Had it been a cupcake shop?"

Dr. Marchant nodded. "You know the place? Cupcake Corner?"

"I stopped down there to check out the devastation for myself and saw the shadow of the sign against the concrete."

"It had been shut down this past month for bugs. We had even hired an exterminator, but there was still bugs on the repeat inspection. It's okay though, it's for the better."

"The mayor's campaign headquarters is also on that block."

Dr. Marchant laughed. "Headquarters can easily be moved. I understand that building took the worst of the earthquake."

Emma found herself holding her breath. She couldn't outright ask Dr. Marchant if he caused the earthquake. And if he did cause it, she didn't want to lead him to believe she was on to him. "Let's get back to the business at hand. Tell me more about this new technology you're rolling out. Using sonar to modify the molecular compounds used in medications—vaccines specifically?"

He gave Emma the elevator pitch on how the vibrations in soundwaves caused the molecules and atoms to shift around, creating new compounds. "I don't know everything, though. Doctor Burg is the expert."

Dr. Burg? That name was familiar…that boy her sister had been reprimanding in the office. The supergenius… "Is Doctor Burg any relation to the mayor?"

"Yes, that's his sister-in-law. The whole family has supergenius powers…well, except the mayor."

"And she's your main scientist on the project? She's using sonic waves that destroy and rearrange things?"

Dr. Marchant cocked his head. "What are you saying, Missus Rodríguez?"

Nothing. She was saying nothing. She needed her husband. "Oh, it's just fascinating that soundwaves can manipulate the physical world, but I guess there are stories of opera singers that can break glass with their voices."

Dr. Marchant nodded.

"Oh, I have one more question. You led the group opposing the mayor. Asking for an impeachment. There had been multiple attempts on the mayor's life…" She held her breath and waited. She hadn't asked a question but hoped he would fill in the blanks.

"I pulled out of that group. Gave a speech that we all needed to support the mayor in this time of devastation. And those attempts on the mayor's life were not my doing, if that's what you're insinuating. Every group has a few zealots that are known to take their beliefs to an extreme."

Emma released the breath she had been holding and reached out to shake his hand. "Thank you for your time…um…no pun intended, but it's after three and I need to get going. It's been a pleasure, Doctor Marchant."

Emma rushed from the room, searching for her husband. Something inside her said that SynPharmaTek was connected to the earthquake; she just needed to figure out how.

ARIANA

in Windy City

Ariana sat on the couch, ignoring the dishes in the sink. She had given in and washed the salad bowl, but now, it was full of a whole new set. The dishes were proof Adam had been here, but it was like they were ships passing in the night. During the day, Ariana was at work and Adam was home. At night, he was out with his too-beautiful partner, fighting crime. Being a hero.

Ariana should have been happy, but she was...lonely. Where did she fit into his world? How did she deserve to be married to a superhero? She was nothing more than an average woman.

She mindlessly flipped through Netflix, but her usual genre, romantic comedy, didn't excite her today. She had just finished a kung fu movie, but had to turn it off. All she could think about was doing a flying roundhouse kick at that Scarlet Macaw.

When there was a gentle knock on the door, she was more than happy to answer it. Seeing Lenny's soft blue eyes through the peephole made her stomach do a somersault. She eagerly flung the door open. "Hey, I haven't seen you in a while."

Lenny dug his hands deep into his pockets. "Yeah. I've been busy."

"What brings you here?"

"I'm just going to be honest with you. I have two tickets to the Rec's showing of *Peter Pan*, and I was hoping you'd come with me."

Ariana shook her head. "I'm married." Boy, she wished the jeweler would finish up fusing her wedding band to her engagement ring.

"You keep saying that, but I'm not listening. It'd be just as friends, anyway."

"Friends?"

"Yes, of course. I mean, unless you want more, you did cook me a fancy dinner the other night." Lenny gave her sly smile.

"Urgh. When is it?" She used to love live theater, but she had never seen *Peter Pan*. Of course he'd have tickets to the one show that would make her cave.

Lenny pulled two tickets from his back pocket. "Seven tonight."

Ariana took the tickets from his hand and examined them. Third row. "Um, I need to check with my husband first, but I'll let you know."

"Check with your husband?" Lenny laughed. "Hey, whatever you need to do. You know where I live." With a nod down the hall, Lenny took off toward his apartment.

After closing the door, Ariana mentally reached out for her husband.

'Adam?'

Nothing.

'Adam? Are you there?'

Still nothing. What use was it having a telepathic husband if he never answered you? He had to be busy with Scarlet. Ariana groaned. She pulled out her phone and sent a text.

I'm gonna go see Peter Pan with a friend tonight.
No rush on coming home.

Like he'd rush home, anyway. Should she have told him her "friend" was male? Did it matter?

After waiting a few minutes for a reply that didn't come, Ariana rushed down the hall, let Lenny know she'd be joining him, then returned to her apartment with only an hour to get ready. Would that be enough time? It'd had been so long since she'd seen live theater, so this event called for her fancy black dress.

Maybe her new lingerie too.

VICTORIA
in Shadow Town

Arriving home, Victoria spent the next few hours attempting to connect the dots between campaign funds, the sonic lab at work, and Dr. Marchant's relationship with the mayor.

She had nothing, but still felt there was something not right about the whole situation.

When her head began to hurt, she skimmed through the novel for book club, pulled a bottle of wine from her wine rack, then headed out the door, looking forward to a distraction.

~ ~ ~

"Did everyone get a chance to *read* the book now?" Megan was less giggly tonight, but she was hosting the meeting this time, and they hadn't cracked the wine yet.

"I did…mostly… Okay, I skimmed it," Victoria said. "Hey, that's better than last time."

"I did too," Dora chimed in.

Faye stood up. "Not me. I just come for the wine." She held the bottle up. "Anyone ready for a glass?"

"Aye, aye, captain!" And the giggling started. Victoria had to chuckle as well.

They began discussing the book and one glass of wine led to another…and another.

"So…" Megan had the giggles again. "Have you seen The Kite?"

"He's ten years younger than you." Dora slapped Megan's hand.

"I don't mind," Megan said.

Victoria fisted her hands. She felt…betrayed.

"Now, I prefer Capitán Rápido. He monopolizes my fantasies. I like the dark hair…the start of a little gray. And that accent? Mmmm mmm."

"I'll take either," Faye said. "Or both." A little

giggle. "Seriously though, I'm happy they came. The city's a mess and they've already captured both escaped supervillains. I hope they stay."

Victoria stood up. "Ladies, it's been fun, but I have to go."

"You did that to us last time too. Do you have something against superheroes?"

"No," Victoria snapped. "Icy Tundra disappears for a few weeks, and you've already given up on him?"

"Hey, weren't you the one against him at our last meeting?"

"No…yes…maybe. I just think we should be more loyal."

"But Capitán Rápido and The Kite have come to help us. Icy Tundra is nowhere around. He's abandoned us. Those two have been busy cleaning up Icy's mess."

"Maybe he can't help. Maybe he's hurt or something." Victoria forced her hands to unclench. "I just think we should have some faith in him. I do really need to get going, though." Victoria flew out the door.

~ ~ ~

Victoria knew she should have gone home after book club, but she couldn't get herself to do it. Instead, she swallowed her pride and went to check on Vance. She knocked on his door once…twice…no answer. Leaning over the railing, she peeked in the windows—complete darkness. Her stomach sank while she retreated to the bus stop.

When she shuffled into her apartment complex, a familiar figure leaned against her door.

"Vance, how'd you get here?"

"Come on, Victoria. I may not be able to see, but I'm not disabled. I called a taxi."

"How long have you been waiting?"

"Long enough." He stepped closer to her.

"Is everything okay? Do you need something from

me?"

Vance shook his head. "I...miss you."

Victoria rubbed her eyes. The wine was making her emotional. "Let's go inside."

While sitting at the kitchen table, the ache inside her grew, and Victoria was so tired of keeping her feelings to herself. She dug deep to pull the words from the back of her mind. "I have a confession. Um... I missed you, too." Not only did she miss him over the past twenty-four hours, but over the past six years as well. "I went to your house after book club tonight, but you weren't there."

Vance stood up and gave a half-grin. "You came looking for me?"

Victoria nodded, then realized he couldn't see her. "I guess I did."

Vance felt his way around the table and took Victoria's hand. "So you don't hate me?"

"Not anymore. Not when you're like this."

Vance pulled Victoria to her feet. "Whoever that man was that you hated, I never want to be him again. He was a fool to let you get away, whether you wanted to leave or not."

Victoria laughed. "He was a fool, but maybe he let me go because it was what I wanted. Maybe he knew I'd never go after my dreams if he'd begged me to stay."

Vance brushed Victoria's cheek with his warm hands. "Is there any hope for us?"

She nuzzled her face deep into his touch and shook her head. "It's over, Vance. Sometimes, you've hurt so bad, there's nothing that can fix it. Maybe a Band-Aid could help for a little while, but there will always be that scar. And what happens when you get your memories back?" She pulled away and wiped her silent tears.

Vance wrapped his arms around her. "I'm so sorry. I think it's time for me to figure out what I'm doing next. I can't allow The Kite and Capitán Rápido to continue to save this city—they have their own cities that need them. It's my duty, whether I remember things or not."

"What do you propose?"

Vance sat down. "I've been doing research and want to talk with Doctor Marchant."

"I'm way ahead of you. I spent all morning today, scrutinizing his files and records, and don't think it's him."

"How can you be so sure?"

"I don't know if you remember, but he's my boss."

"There are so many connections, though. His superpowers, his company's technological abilities, his opposition to the mayor—"

"But I know him." Victoria sighed. "You're right, though. He is our best lead right now, and we should investigate all his connections."

Victoria walked around the table and took Vance's hand, giving him a gentle tug toward her. His body radiated heat inches from her, then he pushed up his frilly mask, giving her a glimpse into his eyes.

Victoria pulled his mask down again. "When I said that I missed you, I really did. We may not be able to start over, but I don't want you to go. Please, stay here tonight. Stay here until this is all over."

Vance wrapped his arms around her as she leaned into his chest. "Of course. And if you believe Doctor Marchant is innocent, I believe you."

Tears welled in Victoria's eyes. Since when did Vance take her word for things? If only he had done that years ago. She blinked away the wetness and focused on their job instead. "I'll help you with your powers again in the morning. The blankets and pillows are still on my sofa."

Vance kissed the top of her head. "I feel at home here…and with you in my arms."

ARIANA
in Windy City

The next five hours flew by, and in what seemed like only a blink of her eye, everything was over. Ariana and Lenny had left the theater and walked back to their apartment complex.

"That was fantastic!" Ariana gushed. From the music, to the costumes, to the playfulness in the room. Nothing like the energy of a real crowd.

Lenny shrugged. "I've seen better renditions of that play."

Ariana grabbed his arm and turned him toward her, stopping them in the middle of the sidewalk. "You didn't like it?"

"I liked it. I always like it, but I just thought it could be better."

"What didn't you like?"

"The music."

"I thought that was great."

"Well…it was *good,* but the sound system in the theater left something to be desired."

"I thought it was just fine."

They continued their walk home, bantering back and forth about the play. Eventually, they were at Ariana's door.

"Well, I had a nice time," Lenny said.

"Actually, so did I."

Lenny looked away a moment, and all traces of sarcasm left his voice. He took a single step toward her. "Hopefully, we can do this again."

Ariana nodded, her eyes meeting his. They paused, and when Lenny's lips curled up in a smile, Ariana looked away.

Gently placing his hand on her shoulder, Lenny gave it a little rub. "Okay. Sleep well." And he headed toward his apartment.

Within fifteen minutes, Ariana had changed out of her black dress, washed up, and was enveloped by the soft cotton sheets of her bed. While humming the theme song to the play, she drifted to sleep not feeling lonely at all for the first time in a while.

Saturday, April 17th

EMMA
in Shadow Town

Emma rolled over on the worn-out hotel mattress. A spring dug into her side as she reached over Estevan for the phone buzzing on the nightstand. She squinted at the display: *Becky.*

"Hey, sis. What's up?" Emma croaked.

"Did I wake you? I'm so sorry. It's like Samantha never sleeps, and I forget how early it is."

Emma squinted at the alarm clock. 7:30. "Nah, it's okay. I should be up already anyway. I've just been so tired lately."

"Well, Samantha had a brilliant idea this morning, and I was hoping you were up for it. She wanted to have a girls' weekend. Just us three."

"Um…this weekend?"

"That was the thought. Do you have anything going on?"

In the background, Emma heard Samantha. "What did she say, Mommy? Is she coming?"

Emma couldn't say no. Family had to come before her wild goose chase into Dr. Marchant, Cupcake Corner, and whatever sonic energy could have caused an earthquake. Besides, that was superhero stuff. Shadow Town had The Kite, Scarlet Macaw, and Capitán Rápido to finish cleaning up. "So, what were you thinking?"

"Samantha wanted to go to that new water park resort over in Actionville. You're always coming here to see us, and we thought we'd head over to your town to see you. Samantha wanted to spend the night. We could go around in the lazy river until our fingers shrivel." Becky laughed.

Images of joy displayed on Samantha's face made Emma smile. "That actually sounds fantastic. I could use a distraction, anyway. I'll meet you at the resort's front desk…like at three p.m.?"

Samantha's voice perked up again. "Come on, Mommy. What'd she say?"

Becky whispered, "She's coming."

Samantha squealed, and Emma laughed. "Okay. See you then."

"Oh, and, sis, I wanted to apologize. The other night I was harsh. I know you struggle with having a family and I shouldn't have made the comment I did about when you have kids of your own…"

Emma took a deep breath. "It's okay. Really. I shouldn't have tried to mother your child."

"I give you permission to mother her all you want this weekend. See you soon."

When Emma ended the call, Estevan was awake and smiling. She reached over him, returning the phone to the nightstand. "I'm heading back home to meet up with Becky and Samantha."

"I know." Dang that superpower again. "No problem. I have enough work here to keep me busy."

"Great. I have a few more things I want to follow up on too, but you know what we say: family first."

She leaned over and kissed her husband. "Unfortunately, you know what day tomorrow is?"

He laughed. "Sunday."

"And I may not see you all day."

Estevan grabbed her hips and pulled her close. "Then, we'll have to pretend today's Sunday."

Emma laughed and rubbed her hand down her husband's bare back, causing him to shiver.

ARIANA
in Windy City

Adam came home after the sun had already risen.

"You made it home," Ariana said, the song from *Peter Pan* still playing in her head.

Adam's eyes were heavy. "Yeah, I made a *home run.*" His lip curled up like it wanted to let out a laugh, but nothing came.

"That one wasn't even close to funny. Tough night?"

"Shadow Town's overrun with crime. It's taking longer than expected. I'm having a hard time splitting my time between the two places and am going to need to stay in Shadow Town a little while to help with their out-of-control citizens. They need a superhero to give them faith."

The song in the back of Ari's mind fizzled. Alone again? For longer? "When are you leaving?"

"We're leaving today."

"We?" She took a step away from Adam.

"Yeah, Scarlet and me."

"You're taking *her* with you?" It was like they were an inseparable crime-fighting duo. The Kite and Scarlet Macaw. Maybe if she had to wash his dishes and do his laundry, she wouldn't want to be around him all the time.

"Why wouldn't I? I'm mentoring her, and she needs to learn."

"Can't you just send her there without you?"

Adam shook his head. "She's not ready."

Of course not.

Ariana's eyes focused on the pile of Adam's clothes in the corner of the bedroom. "Go then. Get out of here."

"Ari, don't do that."

"What can I do to stop you anyway? Saving an entire city is more important than a single person."

"Well, I can't leave you now."

"Go. I don't want the guilt of holding you up." Ariana forced a smile and kissed Adam's cheek. "It'll be okay. I'm adjusting to this married life anyway. I have a friend down the hall to keep me company, and it'll be nice to only have to clean up after myself for once." Did he get the hint?

When Adam leaned in and hugged her, she realized that she missed it.

"Thank you. You're the best," he said.

Ari hoped he meant that and remembered it when flying around with Scarlet Macaw. "I have to get going, it's my Saturday to work."

"I got work to do too. Love ya."

She should have said she loved him too, but the words wouldn't come out. "I know," was all she managed.

~ ~ ~

When ready for work, she slipped into the hall and did a double-take when a beautiful redhead left Lenny's apartment. Not red like Scarlet Macaw's hair, but a more subdued orange. Ariana looked again. Yeah, it was definitely Lenny's door the woman just shut.

What was going on? Her stomach tightened in a way she only could describe as jealousy.

"Hey, do you know Lenny?" Ariana asked, unable to hold it in.

"Are you his neighbor?"

Ariana looked back at her door. Wasn't it obvious? "Yes, his neighbor. Actually, his friend too."

"Oh. I'm surprised we haven't run into each other before. Lenny and I have been hanging out quite a bit the last few weeks."

But that didn't stop him from taking Ariana to the play. "Did you come in last night?" Ariana squinted some, thinking this woman looked a little familiar.

"I came after work. It was quite late."

Ariana tried to place the woman's familiar face. She

was Wendy from the play last night. Is that why Lenny had invited her? To see his girlfriend on stage? She fisted her hands. "Well, I'll see you around. I have to get to work now."

"'Kay. See ya."

It took Ariana the whole twenty-minute walk to work to reason with herself that her feelings were ridiculous. She was married. She was just jealous about having to share her new friend's time. Adam was her one true love, right?

Yes. Without a doubt.

Then why was she confused?

Adam was her husband, and they were bound together through marriage. So why'd he leave her again?

The feelings she was developing for Lenny were wrong. She needed to forget about him and focus on her relationship...if only Adam was around.

VICTORIA
in Shadow Town

"Hi, Mike. What brings you here?"

Mike stared at Victoria, like she should already know.

She sifted through her thoughts. "Oh, yeah, that's right. It's Saturday." They had a bowling league every Saturday morning. She hated bowling.

Mike's eye caught something behind her. Victoria spun around to see Vance standing with his shirt off. Frilly mask still on. She swallowed. How did this look?

"Um, Mike." Victoria spun around to see his jaw drop. "Vance hasn't been well. He had surgery and can't see."

Mike cocked his head. "And you're the only one who can take care of him?"

"Yes."

"Victoria, I know you have an ego, but—"

"An ego? Really?"

Mike raised his voice. "Yes. An ego. Nobody can ever do it as good as you can."

"Okay. This is over. Please go."

"That's not what I meant. It's obvious you're hung up on him. He's always around. What's really going on?"

Victoria was done avoiding her feelings. "It's not going to work, Mike. It doesn't matter if I have feelings for him or not. This is about us, and I just don't feel the spark."

"We should discuss this in private."

When Chewy began to sniff Mike's leg, he pushed the dog away. That was it. Nobody pushed Chewy.

Victoria raised her hand and turned her palm toward Mike. "Nothing to discuss. I've made my decision, and if you knew anything about my past, you'd realize you're lucky I even told you. Have a nice day."

His face turned red and his lips puckered, but then

he spun around and flew down the hallway, disappearing down the stairwell.

Vance's body radiated warmth behind hers. He spun her around in his arms, pulling her in for a hug. "He's a fool if he doesn't come back."

"Don't worry about it. I hope he doesn't return. He was always a little creepy. Nice to me, but it just didn't feel right. Maybe it's because he never liked Chewy." She relaxed and laid her cheek against Vance's bare chest. "It really is okay. And he's right. I do have an ego when it comes to you." She laughed.

Vance pulled away and tipped her chin up to meet his eyes. He had pulled the mask back some. "I think you're perfect."

Victoria didn't back away from his advance. She edged up on her tippy toes and met him halfway. Their lips touched and a flood of memories filled her mind. Memories of leaving him. Of her nights alone, hugging a pillow and crying afterwards.

Of seeing him with that other woman. Of the look on his face when she returned to Shadow Town. A tear rolled down her face, and she pulled away.

Her voice cracked. "I need to shower, then we can get going."

"Victoria."

She held her hand out. "We can't do this. When you get your memory back, you'll understand. It's not fair to you…or me."

ARIANA

in Windy City

Despite only having a four-hour shift at the bank, it felt longer than eight. With everything happening in Shadow Town, people in Windy City were panicking and pulling their money out. Ariana had to float over to the teller window for her whole shift and boy, did her feet hurt.

Outside her apartment door, she fumbled with her keys.

"Ariana?"

She jumped and grabbed her chest. "Hi, Lenny." She quickened her search for her apartment key. She needed inside. Needed to get away from him and focus on her own life.

"What are you up to?"

"I'm tired. Gonna rest. It was a long day at work." All day, she'd formulated ways to avoid him. Was this really the best idea she had?

"I was wondering if you wanted to listen to the *Peter Pan* soundtrack. I downloaded it this morning."

"After Wendy left?" *Oh, Ari, why'd you have to say that?*

"Wendy?"

"Your girlfriend."

"Oh, from *Peter Pan*. Her name's Meredith, and no. We broke up." Lenny's eyes darted to the floor.

"Oh. When?"

"After the show last night. It didn't feel right."

"I saw her leaving this morning."

Lenny's eyes darted back up, squinting at Ariana. "I let her crash on my couch since it was two in the morning when we finished our argument. What's going on? Maybe we need to talk."

"About what? We don't have anything to talk about."

"You seem upset. Did I do something? I thought we left on good terms last night."

You're being ridiculous, Ari. He didn't do anything.

"Can I come in? It'll be good to get things out in the open."

The softness in his blue eyes had Ariana pushing the door open and waving him inside. *Note to self: Be stronger next time.*

Stalling, she made her way to the kitchen and opened the refrigerator. "Want anything?"

"Yeah, actually, I'd like a drink. Do you have anything alcoholic?"

Ariana shook her head. "It's only two in the afternoon."

"It's five o'clock somewhere."

She crawled up on her countertop to see in the cabinet over the refrigerator. "I've got some brandy here. I save it for when my dad comes over because he enjoys a Wisconsin Old-Fashioned."

"That'd be great." Lenny helped her down and opened the bottle, giving it a whiff and wrinkling his face. "That'll do it."

He opened her fridge and pulled out a gallon of orange juice. "Interesting. This may taste good. Want one?"

He had already found the glasses and was pouring her one.

"Yeah. Sure." Maybe it would make the ache in her feet go away and give her the courage to shove Lenny out the door.

He poured a few fingers' worth of brandy in a glass, sucked it down, then refilled it, adding the orange juice this time.

"That bad?" Ariana asked.

"Nah. Let's watch some TV, then we can listen to the soundtrack."

After a show or two and an equivalent number of

cocktails, Lenny took the seat beside Ariana on the sofa. "Why can't more women be like you?"

Ariana smiled. "Why?"

"I don't know. You're funny, and we share interests. In fact, it's what made me call it off with Meredith. Every time I was with her, I thought of you."

Ariana laughed, but words flowed from her mouth. "I'm married."

"Married, shmarried. You keep saying that. Even if you are, he's foolish. Where is he? He's never around. If I was married to you, I'd spend every moment I could at your side." Lenny's words began to slur.

"Well, Mister Smooth, I *am* married." Ariana focused on her words, attempting to prevent them from slurring too. "I can prove it. Then will you believe me?" She stood up and stumbled to the closet, pulling out a man's winter coat. "See, this is his."

"Uh huh. Is that all you have?" Lenny came up behind her. She smelled the alcohol on his breath as he leaned over her shoulder.

"No, I have this." She pulled out an umbrella.

"That's just an umbrella."

"Yeah, but it's his."

"It could also be yours."

She pulled the basket off the shelf and pulled out a pair of men's gloves. "And these?"

"Still could be a coincidence."

She dumped the basket out. Lenny reached down and scattered the various hats and mittens. Ariana eyed something white and her chest did somersaults. She snatched her hand out to grab it away, but Lenny beat her to it.

"What's this?" He held up the white hooded mask.

"It's nothing."

Lenny smiled. He put it on. "It looks like you have a little obsession with someone who wears a costume."

"No, I don't."

"Really? Then why is it here?"

He can't know the truth. Focus, Ariana. "Okay, you're right. I have a fetish." No more references to her husband. She couldn't let him put the pieces together. "Okay. You need to go. My world is spinning, and I'm gonna hurl." She pushed Lenny out the door, not allowing him to protest.

Ari, you're making it worse. Drawing attention to the situation.

Maybe he'd just think she was embarrassed. She picked the things up and cursed herself. How did she get here?

Sunday, April 18th

EMMA
Back in Actionville

Emma lay across the top of a clear inner tube floating down the lazy river at the indoor waterpark. Her sister slowly spun in a circle beside her while Samantha led the way, walking her tube more than floating it.

Rubbing her stinging eyes, Emma reached over to turn Becky's tube to face her. "Thanks for this weekend. We haven't even been at this resort a full twenty-four hours yet, but it feels like I've had a mini-vacation."

"What else would you do on a Sunday, anyway?"

Emma held in a childish giggle, thinking about Estevan.

Becky continued, "I imagine with that job of yours, life can be stressful."

"I don't know. I think raising a child would be stressful too…and being a teacher—that's like raising thirty children!"

"Samantha's pretty easy, but everyone says that one child's great, the second's a handful."

Emma lost her words, and her smile dissolved, thinking about her younger sister having two children. She'd be ecstatic with just one.

"Hey, sis," Becky said. "Don't worry. It'll happen for you, too."

Would it?

Before Emma could ponder that thought, a little face with a huge grin and wide eyes popped up in front of her. "I'm ready," Samantha giggled.

"Ready for what?" Emma asked.

"For the big one." Samantha pointed to a huge waterslide that wrapped itself over the lazy river.

"I don't think so," Becky said. "You're not catching me on that thing."

"Come on, sis. Where's your sense of adventure?"

Emma pried herself out of the tube. "I got this one."

Emma led Samantha out of the lazy river and up the eight flights of stairs to the top of Demon's Flight, a double-person inner tube ride.

"Wave to your mom," Emma said, giving Becky a huge grin and a giant wave from way up top.

Samantha squealed and did a little happy dance as she waved at her mother.

Settling into the tube, Emma wrapped her legs around her niece. "Hang on!" Emma coached as a lifeguard gave them a push into the long dark tunnel.

As they took the first major drop, Samantha screamed...a happy scream, but when the top of the ride opened up and they whipped up one side of the slide to the other, Samantha's scream turned terrified.

One more corner and a huge wave of water crashed over the side of the tube. It was like time slowed down as Samantha lifted her hands from the handle to shield her face from the water.

"No!" Emma screamed, trying to wrap her legs tighter around her niece, but it was too late. Samantha tumbled out of the tube and Emma whizzed past her. Behind her, Samantha rushed down the slide as roaring water splashed over her head.

Emma threw herself out of the innertube, spreading her legs against the slide's surface to slow her down. Her skin burned as it scraped against the fiberglass slide. Her knees and elbows bruised as she created friction, waiting for the water to carry Samantha to her.

Stretching herself forward, Emma's fingertips grazed Samantha's ankle. Not quite in reach. She flexed her toes to create more friction and reached for Samantha again. With one finger, then another, she gripped the girl's ankle and pulled her into her arms.

Emma rolled over, cradling the girl to her chest as they slid the rest of the way down and flew out the bottom of the slide.

Water sprayed over their heads as they plunged into the pool, and Emma pushed Samantha to the surface, only to be knocked over by more rushing water. She lifted the child up again, hoping Samantha's head was above the surface, but then fell over from the current. A pain radiated in her arm as a lifeguard pulled her to her feet, still clutching Samantha in her arms.

Emma's heart raced as she coughed water from her lungs and watched Samantha's look of pure terror.

"Are you okay?" Emma croaked out.

Samantha's expression melted and a slow smile painted her face. "That was awesome! Do you think there are any superheroes that can breathe underwater?"

Emma found a beach lounge chair right beside the pool and lay back, still hacking water out of her lungs. "Probably. I don't know all the superheroes."

"But you know some?" Samantha asked.

They were interrupted by a concerned Becky hovering over Emma. "What happened there?"

Emma coughed again. "Just a little superhero adventure." She sat up. "Come on. Let's get out of here. I've had enough water for a while."

"I wanna go again!" Samantha said.

"I don't think so."

"Please, Auntie Ems?"

Becky folded her arms over her chest. "What did you say before? I quote, '*Come on, sis. Where's your sense of adventure?*'"

Emma laughed. "Gone. It's all gone. How about some ice cream instead? I'll buy both of you a double scoop."

When Samantha's eyes lit up, Emma leaned back into the chair. Boy, was she ready to return to her life of behind-the-scenes superhero assistant.

Did Estevan enjoy the adrenaline rush?

Well, he could keep it. First the car that almost hit them, then her encounters with the policewoman in Shadow Town and Dr. Marchant, then this adventure on the Demon's Flight.

What else could possibly happen?

VICTORIA
in Shadow Town

After another unsuccessful morning of Vance trying to regain control of his powers, they ended up at a small café for a late lunch. The outdoor, pet-friendly seating kept Chewy happy.

"Doesn't it bother you wearing that purple eye mask? We can get you something a little more… manly."

Vance smiled and adjusted the lace. "Why would it bother me? I can't see it."

"It just…looks ridiculous."

"Does it bother you?"

The waitress interrupted them. "Well… Hello…" Her eyes raked up and down Vance's body, then when she turned to Victoria, her flirty smile disappeared. "What can I get you to drink?"

Victoria dropped the menu. "A Diet Coke for me."

"Just water," Vance said.

The waitress stepped away, and Vance leaned in. "It seems that even with the mask, women still find me irresistible."

"It appears women like men in masks. I prefer to know what's behind them."

"That sounds like there's more to that story."

"There is."

The waitress returned with their drinks. "Are you ready to order?"

Vance picked up his menu and tipped the eye mask up some, then dropped it. "Not yet. I had surgery, and my wife here--" He smiled at Victoria. "--still needs to read me the menu."

"I don't need to read it. He'll take the liver and onions."

"Somehow, I don't think I like liver and onions."

Before Victoria could laugh, a commotion caught

her attention.

"Give that back!" a man with a booming voice exclaimed. He chased after a younger man wearing a hoodie and clutching a backpack.

Victoria tensed. Another thief like the one who'd tried to steal her purse? What would happen if Vance never regained control of his powers?

The older man flung himself at the kid, tackling him toward where Victoria and Vance sat. Victoria stopped breathing as one table crashed after another—the men still headed in their direction.

They'll stop, right?

Before Victoria could contemplate what to do, Vance leaped up and threw her out of the way.

Chewy whined, hiding beneath the table, and Victoria struggled to get out from under Vance. "Chewy!"

Both men gripped the backpack. The older man gave a tug, but the younger man yanked it away, making the older man tumble forward, right on top of the table Vance and Victoria had been sitting at—breaking the table legs and smashing it down on top of Chewy.

Victoria's heart pounded as she pulled herself from Vance's chest, focused solely on Chewy's yelps from beneath the crushed table. Throwing his mask off, Vance effortlessly flung the men away and dug Chewy out from beneath the wreckage.

The dog whimpered.

"Shit, no!" Victoria brushed the fur on Chewy's neck. Tears streamed down her face. "It'll be okay." Her hands came away coated in blood.

Security had the two men pulled aside and were questioning them. Victoria didn't care what happened or what they were saying. She had only one thought. "Chew-Barka's injured. We need a veterinarian."

Vance looked at Chewy and a stream of cold came out of his eyes. "Crap!"

Chewy yelped at the same time. Vance had frozen the dog's leg.

"I'm so sorry!" He squeezed his eyes shut.

"Get away!" Victoria screamed, struggling to pull Chewy into her arms. Sitting on the ground, she cradled his frozen leg to her body to warm it. "He'll lose his leg!"

"I'm sorry," Vance repeated, stepping away from them.

"I need to get him to a vet. I can't lose him! He's all I have." She adjusted the heavy, whimpering dog in her arms, leaving a trail of blood on her yellow shirt.

Vance easily lifted the dog and put him in the back of Victoria's car. Once the door was closed, Victoria crawled behind the wheel, leaving Vance standing alone on the sidewalk.

It wasn't until she was a few blocks away that she realized what she'd done.

ARIANA

in Windy City

Ariana hadn't heard from Adam all day, and she finally admitted to herself that she was lonely. Being an only child, her parents had taken her everywhere with them. Gave her all the time she needed. Now, she felt she couldn't go to them. She telepathically reached out to her husband multiple times, but received no reply. Perhaps her throbbing headache from the brandy last night was impairing her ability to talk with Adam.

After her third failed attempt, she called his phone, but that went straight to voicemail. This wasn't unusual, as when he was The Kite, he didn't carry his phone. What was unusual was that Ariana was approaching twenty-four hours since she last heard from her husband.

She put the Superhero News Network on TV, listening for anything that might have gone wrong. Other than the crisis in Shadow Town, there wasn't anything specific that made her worry. If she could only get a glimpse of The Kite, to know he was okay. Anything at all. The Kite rescuing someone, someone thanking The Kite, or even just a scene of him flying in the sky. Hell, she'd even take a photo of him with Scarlet Macaw right now.

She bit her lip as she booted up her laptop, searching for anything current about her husband, but came up emptyhanded again.

Enough!

She slammed the cover shut, needing to do something to take her mind off this. Attempting to busy herself with laundry, dishes, cooking, eating, or whatever else she could find, her brain still couldn't relax. She needed a friend.

Ariana called her parents.

No answer. She hung up the phone and sighed.

After feeling sorry for herself for way too long, she

found herself knocking on a neighbor's door.

Lenny greeted her shirtless again. Ariana snapped her eyes away from the ripples in his abdomen. "Um… Can you put a shirt on?"

Lenny smiled. "Don't you like what you see?"

"Now's not the time for a joke."

"Okay. What's wrong?"

Lenny led her into his apartment and fetched a shirt from the back of a kitchen barstool, draping it over his head.

"Okay. Don't judge me, but my husband hasn't been home in twenty-four hours."

"I told you he was having an affair."

Images of Scarlet Macaw filled her head. "I can't deal with those comments right now either. Could you…help me pass the time? Take my mind off him for a bit?"

Lenny rubbed his chin. "Sure, I can do that." He went to his living room. "Have a seat." He pulled a blanket from his sofa. "I have the perfect thing. I just rented a movie, and it's always more fun to watch it with someone."

Lenny started the movie and took a seat beside Ariana.

The opening credits weren't even over before Lenny handed her a tissue. "Please don't cry. I'm sorry for the comment about the affair."

Ariana shook her head, but couldn't say anything. Her thoughts were still on her missing husband.

"Come here." Lenny motioned for her to come into his arms.

Ariana stared a moment, but Lenny reached forward and pulled her to him.

"We're friends. Friends comfort each other. Now, turn around and enjoy the movie."

Well into the film, a voice in Ariana's head startled her.

'Ari?'

She stiffened and pulled out from Lenny's arm. How long had she been sitting there?

'Adam, are you okay?'

'Yes, just busy. I wanted to let you know I made it to Shadow Town safely.'

'Don't do that to me.'

'Do what?'

'Make me worry.'

'You worried? Oh, Ari. I'm so sorry. I thought... Well...I guess I didn't think. I gotta run, but wanted you to know that I love you. I wanted to make sure I check in every day.'

Ariana looked at Lenny, but let the words come out automatically. *'Love ya too.'* Then severed their connection.

She scooted away. "I have to go. This is wrong."

"So, that husband of yours really does exist, huh?"

"Of course. I've been trying to tell you that. What makes you believe me now?" There was no way he had heard her and Adam's conversation.

"Guilt is written all over your face."

"I should be with him."

"But you're here with me." Lenny moved closer.

Ariana looked into Lenny's eyes as he leaned down. His lips softened.

No. No. No. This wasn't where she was meant to be. She needed to be with her husband, no matter where he was. How could their marriage get off on the right foot if she didn't put the effort in?

"I have to go."

"What? Where?"

Her dad's voice echoed in her mind. *Men sometimes have a hard time expressing their feelings...their wants and desires...sometimes you need to whack them upside their head.*

"I need to go find my husband. He needs me whether he'll admit it or not."

On her way out the door, the apartment floor rumbled beneath her feet. "Do you feel that?" She glanced over her shoulder to see Lenny rushing to the window.

"It feels like major road construction." He scanned the street below the apartment. "Nothing's going on out there."

Ariana stumbled against the door when a large jolt shook the apartment. Adam's image filled her mind.

'Adam!' She didn't wait for a response and called again. *'Adam? You okay?'*

'Of course. Why?'

'Didn't you feel that?'

'Feel what?'

'I think there was another earthquake. Somewhere near me.'

'Are you okay?'

'I'm fine.' Ariana looked up at Lenny. "Lenny, put on the news. I wonder if that was another earthquake."

Adam's voice pulled her back. *'Lenny? Who's he?'*

Ariana sighed. *'Our neighbor. He's been keeping me company while you've been gone.'*

Across the TV scrolled a red banner.

Earthquake hits New Shore. Two cities along our coast in a week. What's next?

Ariana sent Adam the image of the TV. *'What if it's more than a coincidence?'*

There was a pause, then his words were conveyed with sincerity. *'I'll investigate. Thanks for letting me know and checking in on me. I'm truly a lucky man to have you.'*

Pride filled Ariana's chest, and she straightened herself against the door. Was there more she could do to help her husband even if she didn't have superpowers?

Well, she couldn't find out if she was sitting here watching movies with the neighbor.

EMMA
in Actionville

At home, Emma sat at the kitchen table and scrolled through the Superhero News Network on her phone. The headline caused her heart to pound.

Another Earthquake Hits the East Coast. This Time, New Shore Struck.

Emma couldn't scroll through the article fast enough. It appeared the earthquake caused some minor damage, but nothing like Shadow Town had experienced.

Perhaps she had been wrong and the earthquake was simply a natural disaster.

She pulled out her phone and texted Estevan again.

Another earthquake? Are you OK??? Call back ASAP!

No sooner had she hit send then her phone rang. "*Mi gatita, ¿Estás bien?*"

"Yes, I'm fine. I didn't feel a thing. You?"

"Nothing here either. Where did it happen? Do they need my help?"

Emma switched her phone to speaker and pulled the article up again. "It happened up the coast in New Shore. Per this article, they seem in much better shape than Shadow Town." Emma fell silent.

"*Mi gatita*, are you there?"

"All this time I kept thinking that the earthquakes were intentional, created by some supervillain. What if they weren't?"

Estevan softened his words. "What are your instincts telling you?"

"That there's something fishy going on."

"Then you need to keep pushing forward. What's the worst that can happen? You discover it was just an earthquake, and you can't do anything about it. But what if there is some mastermind with a grand plan behind it? And you give up? Think of all the damage that can happen not just to the city, but also its people."

Emma sighed as images of nearly drowning while saving Samantha haunted her thoughts. "Sometimes, I feel we're missing out. We're spending all this time saving people we don't even know when there are other people we should focus on."

It was as if Estevan could read her mind. "How was the waterpark?"

"It was…" Awful... Terrifying… "an adventure, for sure. I was thinking, life's short. How about you come home for the night?"

"You okay, my kitten?"

Oh, he switched to English. He must be worried.

Estevan continued, "It's not the baby thing again, is it?"

"No… Well, maybe a little, but more than anything, I wonder why we do it all. All this running around and saving people, when we should be enjoying each other. Living our lives and enjoying our family. At any moment, we could lose someone we care about."

"Emma, I do think about that…all the time. When I first discovered my powers, I thought I was gifted, but then I realized the responsibility I had, and it ate at me. It drove me crazy. I couldn't possibly be everywhere, all the time. But I tried. And it wore me out…to the point that when someone really needed me, I couldn't help."

"You've always balanced it well. Saving the world, yet still making me feel special."

"You *are* special, *mi gatita*. I realized that having someone like you made everything else I do worth it. I can't be selfless all the time. I need something to look forward to. Someone wonderful like you."

"So why do you do it?"

"Because I have a gift. Because I'm willing to share it. Because I'm needed…just like you're needed."

"What about a normal life?"

Estevan laughed. "Neither of us would be happy with a normal life."

Emma was silent. What was normal? Becky's life? But how many people actually had a life like hers? She pictured herself with a child on her hip, cooking dinner, running off to a Monday through Friday day-shift job. But it wasn't her face she pictured, it was her sister's. No, her life did not fit that picture.

Estevan's voice was soft. "So, this *is* about having a child."

"Our life will pass us by. It'll be over before we know it."

"Whatever you want to do, *mi gatita*. I'll be there for you. Whatever you feel is 'normal,' I'll support."

Emma took a big breath. "I suppose I don't want 'normal.' I'm just at this point in my life where I'm looking for something."

"It's okay not to know what that 'something' is. Sometimes, that 'something' actually finds you. Like how you found me."

"Hey, there's nothing wrong with online dating," Emma laughed. "And someone had to make the first move."

"I'm not complaining! I'll use my superspeed and be home in thirty minutes. I'd love to take my wife out to dinner tonight."

Emma gripped the phone tighter and smiled. "I'd love that. It feels pretty normal to me." Then she thought of what else would feel normal. "Maybe we can figure out our next step. How are Shadow Town and New Shore connected, besides both being along the coast?"

Estevan laughed. "That definitely sounds like a normal evening for us."

VICTORIA
in Shadow Town

Victoria left the veterinarian emptyhanded. Chewy had to stay the night after they amputated his leg and stitched up his side. Victoria didn't know how to explain the frostbite, but the doctor said Chewy's leg had been smashed by the falling table and couldn't be saved. Victoria cried the whole way home.

Vance sat against her apartment door still wearing the frilly purple mask, rubbing his hands against his jeans. He fumbled to his feet when Victoria cleared her throat.

"I'm so sorry," he said.

Victoria couldn't say anything as sobs escaped. More than sobs for Chewy. Vance had come to check on her, despite how she left him stranded on the sidewalk. It was just that Chewy had been with her for so long, and he was her responsibility. She wasn't used to having Vance around. She composed herself. "I'm sorry I left you. Chewy will be fine...just had his leg amputated."

"Oh my god. I'm so sorry." Vance reached out, then shoved his hands in his pockets and stiffened. Did he want to hug her? Had she hurt him by leaving him...again?

Victoria didn't hesitate. Despite everything, she needed him. She dove into his arms and squeezed. "I'm happy you're here." She relaxed against his solid body. "My poor puppy. He's always been there for me. Stayed by my side...loved me no matter what."

Vance brushed her hair off her forehead and planted a kiss. "I'm so sorry. I should have never removed the mask. Let's go inside."

Vance pried the keys from her hand and felt for the doorknob. Once it was unlocked, he pulled her in. "Okay, I'm going to go. I've done enough damage today."

Victoria shook her head. "His femur and knee were shattered. Your freeze vision wasn't the reason for the amputation. Maybe it even helped with the pain."

"It could have been so much worse. I'm a danger to everyone around me and don't know what to do. I don't know if I'll ever get my memory or control of my powers back."

"Hey, stop it," Victoria said, taking Vance's face between her hands. She rubbed her hands through the brown hair that fell over the elastic of the mask, twirling some of it in her fingers. "You'll get them back. We'll just have to work harder at it."

Vance nodded, but the way his jaw softened told her something different.

"You don't agree with me?"

Vance pulled her in closer and rested his chin on top of her head. "I don't know. I'm tired and think I just need a good night's rest. You can come by in the morning if you still want to see me."

Victoria's heart stopped. She took his hand and gave him a small tug toward her bedroom. "I could really use your support tonight. With Chewy injured, I need someone to…" She wiped the tears away. "Hold me. Can you do that?"

"I'll do anything you want."

She led him into her room and shut the door. With Vance's arm wrapped firmly around her, she realized she needed to figure out where her life was going—completely independent of Vance regaining control of his superpowers.

Monday, April 19th

ARIANA
in Windy City (and Shadow Town)

Ariana's request to transfer to her bank's branch in Shadow Town was approved almost instantly. People were fleeing that city like crazy, including the employees. Patrons were frantically withdrawing their money, and the bank needed all the help they could get.

Ariana didn't hesitate. Immediately after work, she threw a week's worth of clothes into her suitcase and headed off to find her husband.

The moment the bus dropped her off in Shadow Town, she opened her mental connection to Adam. The connection was much stronger when they were near each other.

'Adam?'

'Ari, is that you?'

'Yes. Where are you?' She struggled to drag her broken-wheeled suitcase and sat down on a clean bench at the bus stop. She touched random buttons on her phone to make it look like she was doing something other than staring off into space. Of course, no one would suspect she was actually talking to her husband telepathically.

'Why do you ask? You sound close. Are you in Shadow Town?'

'Yeah. I thought we should be together. Maybe I can help?'

His mental voice was sharp. *'It's not safe here. You should go home.'*

She bit her lip. Why did he want her to go? Was it Scarlet? *'I'm not going.'*

'Crime's out of control, and what if there's another earthquake?'

'Obviously, an earthquake could happen anywhere.'

Adam sighed. *'Where are you? I'm coming.'*

'The bus station.' She looked up from her phone and sent him a visual image of her surroundings.

'Hang on. I'll be right there.'

Ariana returned her attention to her phone, connecting to the Superhero News Network while she waited. She searched for any news articles about what was going on in this city. She read of the hopelessness, the destruction, the unknown evil, and stopped at the headline: "The Kite is our Savior!"

A smile spread across her face as she paged through other articles with similar themes. She stopped cold when she found the article entitled: "Shadow Town has Gone to the Birds." Next to it was a picture of Adam with his arm around Scarlet.

Glancing away, she tucked her phone into her purse and clutched the handle of her suitcase until her knuckles turned white.

With a gust of wind, she was pulled from the park bench and lifted off the ground. She'd recognize the strong arm wrapped around her anywhere.

"Hey, sweetie," came Adam's…The Kite's voice from behind her.

"You found me." Despite everything, she felt butterflies in her stomach. They had been apart too long.

"Always."

He flew her to the top of a nearby building and set her down. "My room's number four-one-three. I'm kinda in the middle of something and have to go." He slipped a keycard in her hand.

Ariana noticed the gun in his other hand. "What are you doing?"

"Stopping a hostage situation. One suspect down, two to go." He winked.

"What are you doing here then? You have to get going!"

He kissed her. "I know, but you come first."

Before she processed the fuzzy warmth in her belly, he was off.

His words were sincere. *'I'll be back soon.'*

Ariana dragged her suitcase to the roof stairs. *Please be unlocked.*

She turned the handle and the heavy door opened. When she found Adam's hotel room on the fourth floor, her chest constricted. Here she was, alone again at a hotel—just like their honeymoon.

How would she get over this feeling?

EMMA
in Actionville

Emma pulled a few strings down at City Hall this morning. Now, the reports from the health and building inspectors condemning the cupcake shop for bugs sprawled across her kitchen table.

She took Estevan's advice. Her instincts told her that there was someone behind the earthquakes, and she needed to keep moving forward. Her current lead was the cupcake shop. Her husband sat across from her, the cutest worry lines across his forehead as he tried to make heads or tails of the documents.

"Do you know what's interesting?" Emma flipped back and forth between the two different inspection reports.

He calmly waited for the answer.

"The mayor signed off on them both."

"Isn't that his job?"

"Yeah, but if his campaign headquarters was situated right next to that building, you'd think he'd worry about bugs too."

"Maybe he did. Maybe he used an exterminator."

When Emma snuck into the destroyed cupcake shop, there had been dust all over the floor, but no signs of bugs. She clicked to an internet browser on her computer and searched for any news on the cupcake shop.

"Local favorite sweet spot, Corner Cupcake, shut down for bugs," she read out loud.

Below the headline was a photo of an older woman frosting a cupcake. Emma read the caption, "Owner Suzie Quintano can't believe her shop was condemned. In her ten years of being in business, she'd never seen a bug before."

Estevan scratched his head. "What kind of bugs?"

Emma scanned further down the article. "Quintano states: 'The health department tells me that the building was shut down due to a cockroach infestation. Growing up in the South, I know what cockroaches look like, and those bugs I saw were not cockroaches.' It's undetermined if Cupcake Corner will reopen."

"When was it shut down?" Estevan asked.

"It looks like only two weeks before the earthquake." Emma looked at Estevan. "Isn't it odd that cockroaches suddenly appeared in a large enough quantity to condemn a shop? And she says they weren't cockroaches."

Estevan cocked his chin. "What are you saying?"

"And isn't it odd that the owner admitted there was bugs, and she happened to close up shop just two weeks before the earthquake?"

Estevan sat beside Emma and scrolled through the news article, his face focused on the screen.

"And it's interesting that something large was removed from the shop after the earthquake."

Estevan cocked his chin. "How do you know that?"

"Oh, I went down to check things out."

"You did what?"

"Never mind that right now." Emma leaned forward and began to lead Estevan to his idea. "Let's see... Cockroaches suddenly appeared. Footprints in the dust and object that was removed. It seems like there's more to this story."

Estevan snapped his hand up and pointed toward the ceiling. "I have an idea!" His eyes nearly sparkled.

Emma held in her smile, loving the excitement on her husband's face. "And what's that?"

"Let's find the cupcake shop owner and see if she has some clues."

"I think that's a brilliant idea. How'd you ever come up with that?" Emma kissed her husband on the cheek then closed her computer. She tapped her pen against the device. "I spent all morning trying to draw connections between both earthquakes. All I've come up with is that

SynPharmaTek has a small research facility in New Shore, but they have small facilities all over the country. Other than both being on the same fault line that runs along the coast, there's nothing else."

"What about the high-speed train?"

"There's no discussion about it extending that direction."

"New Shore doesn't even have a superhero, if the underlying reason was to wipe out Icy Tundra…or other superheroes for that matter." The worry lines reappeared on Estevan's forehead.

"Even without a superhero, the town is nearly recovered."

"That doesn't make us superheroes look good, does it?"

"I don't know how you can even compare the two earthquakes." Emma tucked her laptop into her bag. "New Shore's much smaller and didn't have as much damage. Speaking of superheroes, how's your search for The Kite going?"

"It's hard to cross paths. I've been splitting my time between here, Shadow Town…and you. It appears that he's splitting his time between Windy City and Shadow Town, plus he's not as fast as me. Travel probably takes quite a bit of his time."

Emma nodded. They needed a better way to track him down, but first, it was time to find Suzie Quintano and get to the bottom of her cupcake shop's bug infestation.

VICTORIA
in Shadow Town

Victoria sat beside her ex-husband on his bed, photos sprawled across the comforter, trying to trigger some memories. Earlier, they had drawn the blackout curtains closed and used a small flashlight to go through the photos one by one.

Victoria told him stories of their life together. Of the time they decided to go camping, and it rained. They had put the rainfly on, but the tent was on a slight angle, so a river of water ran across the floor, right between them.

She told him about their wedding. Their honeymoon on the sailboat. Of the day they adopted Chewy.

Nothing jogged Vance's memory.

Victoria picked up one photo after another and began making a nice stack. Vance leaned close, and his arm rubbed against hers. She stopped gathering the photos and wrapped her fingers around his forearm, giving it a little squeeze. "Thank you."

A deep chuckle rolled from his lips. "What are you thanking me for? You're the one doing so much for me."

"For the support last night. For...not trying anything while I was vulnerable. You could have taken advantage of me, and I appreciate that you didn't."

Vance leaned in enough to nudge her shoulder with his own. "That goes both ways. I was vulnerable too and you could have taken advantage of me."

She laughed. "And you're glad I didn't try something?"

"Not exactly." A familiar mischievous look grew on his face, that one lip curled up Elvis impersonation, but now, Victoria found it charming. She darted her eyes back to the photos.

Vance picked up a photo of his parents, arm-in-arm, standing below a giant tree. "They're both dead?"

Victoria nodded.

"How'd they die?"

"I'm not going to tell you."

"Please. It may be the key to unlock all of this."

Victoria bit her lip. She took the photo from Vance's hand and intertwined her fingers with his, noting the small sparkle his eyes seemed to reflect. "May I do something first? I want to remember this moment."

Vance nodded.

Victoria leaned in and kissed him with as much passion as she had locked away from their six years apart. This past week, remembering what it was like during the good times of their marriage, made her completely forget all the terrible things they'd done to each other. Eventually, her hands tangled in his hair and she straddled his body while he gripped her hips. Her barrier had disappeared and all that was left was her and the man she fell in love with.

Eventually, he broke their kiss with a taunting laugh. "I think you're avoiding telling me."

Victoria playfully nibbled his bottom lip, then pulled away. "I am."

Vance turned serious, scooting to the edge of the bed. "I'm ready. Tell me now."

She looked away. "It's awful."

"I need to know."

Victoria balled the fabric of his comforter up in her hand. "You know what happened with Chewy?"

Vance raised an eyebrow, followed by the other, then they both came crashing down with the realization. "I froze my parents?"

A single tear fell down Victoria's cheek. "You were a teenager. Your father wasn't a good man. He verbally abused you and your mother. One day, you came home from school and your father was calling your mom all sorts of names. You were angry and your emotions got out of control. His heart stopped instantaneously."

Vance was silent.

"And my mother?"

"She died a few years later of liver cancer. After that, you changed schools and moved in with your grandfather. That's how we met. You were already an orphan."

"I froze my father? Killed him...and you allowed me to sleep in your bed last night?" Vance jumped off the bed, scattering some of the remaining photos on the ground. "You married me? A murderer?"

"Vance, he wasn't a good man—"

"It doesn't make it right, Victoria!" Vance paced at the foot of the bed. "You shouldn't be here. You need to leave." He jabbed a finger toward the entrance.

"You really think I'll go anywhere?"

Vance brushed his hair back, and he looked like he wanted to say something, but he tightened his lips.

Victoria scooped up a pile of photos and set them on his nightstand. "It was an accident. Everyone wants powers. If they only knew the consequences. Your powers had just formed, and you know how hard they are to control. He was in the wrong spot at the wrong time. Nothing more."

Vance dropped his hands from his hair. "No wonder you left me."

Victoria took a deep breath as everything clicked into place. "We married right out of high school. Part of me knew we were passionately in love, but the other part wondered if I couldn't say no...you had already been through so much tragedy."

Vance stopped, and his jaw fell open.

Victoria continued, "Since our divorce, I realized that wasn't true. Your tragedy may have brought us together, but it wasn't what made me love you." She stood up and took his hands, but he pulled away and continued pacing. "I left you because I was selfish. I felt I was missing out on life. Maybe we married too young. I didn't realize what a treasure I had. I wondered if we rushed into things without knowing what else was out there. I've thought about it, over and over, tortured myself over the decision for six years."

Vance looked up at Victoria, tears filling his eyes that matched hers. "Come here," he whispered.

Carefully, she took a few steps and wrapped her arms around his body.

He rubbed his hands up and down her back. "I may not remember things, but my heart seems to remember that I still love you. I'm certain I never stopped."

Victoria squeezed him tightly. "I don't think that's true. You morphed into a bitter man—"

"I'm sure I was hurt...bad. Forgive me, please. I'm so sorry. Right now, though, I realize that I'm a menace if I don't regain control of my powers."

Victoria wanted to argue, but she knew it was true. She silently stayed in her ex-husband's arms as long as he continued to hold her.

ARIANA
in Shadow Town

Hours later, Adam finally showed up at the hotel. Ariana had showered, unpacked a few of her things, and ordered Chinese. She felt better being in Shadow Town, focusing on supporting her husband and knowing he was near. This was a new start, and she was determined to make it work.

"How'd it go?" she asked Adam, already knowing. His heroic save had been all over the Superhero News Network. A mother who had been in the bank had spoken to a reporter about how he saved the lives of her twin five-year-old boys. Ariana had been proud, but was also filled with a sense of inferiority. How could she compare to a superhero? Maybe that was why she was attracted to Lenny. They seemed to be equals. And her issue with Scarlet? Ariana feared her because she seemed to be Adam's equal.

Adam beamed. "I'm so happy Scarlet was there. It makes my job so much easier. She's really learning fast."

Ariana bit her lip. Just like that, reality returned and all her suppressed feelings resurfaced like they had never left. Memories of when she'd lashed out at her self-defense teacher filled her mind. What was wrong with her?

Adam continued, "I think she'll be amazing. Not only can she fly and is invincible, but she also has a little extra speed and strength. No wonder she struggles with control sometimes. That's a lot of power to manage at once."

Ariana nodded, clenching her hands behind her back.

"And she's funny." Adam shook his head and laughed. "She has the same sense of humor I do."

Ariana couldn't hold it in anymore, and the words burst from her lips. "It sounds like you're falling for her."

Adam wrinkled his eyebrows and tilted his chin. "Seriously?"

"Yes! You spend all your time with her. You talk about her nonstop. She does sound pretty amazing!"

"Is that why you came here? To keep tabs on me?" He laughed.

Laughed? Really? "Of course not!" She took a few steps back. Was he trying to push her buttons?

Adam cocked his head and lifted an eyebrow, waiting for her to continue.

"I came here to be with you. My husband. But, maybe you don't want me anymore?"

"That's ridiculous. Of course I want you. It's just not safe here."

"And you're not trying to get rid of me because of *her*?"

"Ari, stop it. All I'm doing is helping Scarlet, like I help everyone. Once upon a time, you told me that was what you loved about me. Remember, you're the one I'm married to. The one I love."

She inhaled deeply, crossing her arms over her chest. "How do I know that? You haven't been around." She sat on the bed.

Adam paced in front of her. His words were humble. "You're right. I'm so focused on proving myself…" He turned toward Ariana, grabbed her arms, and looked in her eyes. "A week ago, I lost my job and felt like I was worthless. Now, I feel like I'm doing something. Having me just sitting around at home didn't work for either of us. I guess I'm trying extra hard to show you…me…and everyone else, that I deserve the title of superhero. That I'm useful. With all my heart, I love you, Ari. Be patient with me, please."

She bit her bottom lip, then sighed. Pulling out of his arms, she crawled toward the headboard. With the blanket wrapped tightly around her, she spoke, "I need a little bit to think about all this. I didn't mean to drive you away."

"You didn't, Ari." He sat down and dropped his head in his hands. "It was something I needed to do for me. I get fulfillment from helping people—whether it's Scarlet or the citizens of Shadow Town. I now see that I took on too much."

Ariana had so many emotions swirling inside, she couldn't grasp hold of any of them. Married life. Did anyone actually enjoy it? She turned over in bed.

The bed bounced when Adam got in behind her. "I know this isn't what you expected, but I'm doing all this so we can have a better life. Once this crisis is over, I swear I'll find some type of balance and give you the attention you deserve. We'll figure this out, together."

Those words were what Ariana had been waiting to hear, only now, guilt filled her. Had she gone too far with Lenny? And was she even good enough for a man with superpowers? How did she fit into that world? Maybe Lenny intrigued her because he represented a *normal* life... Was that what she wanted? And what was *normal*, anyway?

Don't think about it now, Ari. He's here and you're together. That's what counts. You knew what you were getting yourself into, didn't you?

At that moment, Ariana's chest tightened with another thought. What about the next crisis? And the next? There would always be something monopolizing Adam's time.

He was a superhero.

Tuesday, April 20th

ARIANA

in Shadow Town

Ariana's morning at work went great…well, great for having to adjust to a new facility, but not so great since the city was still in chaos. There were long lines, tense customers, and they nearly ran out of money.

She came "home" for lunch to the hotel, hoping to run into Adam.

On her way into their room, she checked her phone. Her dad had left a message.

Hi, honey. I need you to call me back as soon as you get this. It's urgent.

Ariana's hands shook as she swiped through screens to return his call.

His voice sounded wrong—hesitant and gentle. It made her palms sweat. "Hey, Ari. I have news. What are you doing?"

"I'm on my lunch break."

"Okay. Um… There's no easy way to say this, so I'm just going to blurt it out. Your mother had a heart attack a few hours ago. She's in the ICU at Windy City Medical Center."

Ari's world dropped from under her feet, the tacky room disappearing. *A heart attack?* Her mom wasn't old enough for that, was she?

"Ari, are you there?"

Her voice was as shaky as her hands. "Was it bad?" She felt for the hotel's lumpy mattress and plopped down, asking louder, "Dad? Was it bad?"

"She's stable. The doctors say the next twenty-four hours are critical."

"Critical? I'll be there as quickly as I can."

"That would be best. I thought you'd want to know

as soon as possible. I'm sorry I didn't call you earlier, but we were in the ambulance and then in the emergency department. It was so chaotic, and I wasn't thinking."

"Take care of yourself, Dad. I'll be there as fast as possible." She wiped away tears, and her voice cracked. "Tell her I love her, okay?"

"I will."

Ariana ended the call and opened her connection. *'Adam?'*

Nothing.

She yelled with her mind, using all the force she could gather, *'Adam! Where are you? I need you, now!'*

'Yes, Ari, what's up? I'm a little busy right now.'

'My mom had a heart attack.'

'Is she okay?'

Ariana's mind fogged. She couldn't concentrate enough to talk to Adam this way. She let out a few audible sobs, and instead of answering Adam, she sent him her emotions.

'Wow, Ari.' A moment of silence. *'What can I do?'*

She focused her thoughts enough to send a message. *'I need to go back to Windy City ASAP to be with my mom.'*

'Um... I'll figure something out.' He sent the image of a movie theater with a hostage at gunpoint and a man with a bomb strapped to his chest. *'I'll send Scarlet. She's not here, and I've already told her all about you.'*

At this point, Ariana didn't care who got her there, she just needed to be with her mother. Scarlet was faster anyway. *'Fine. Tell her I'll be on the roof, waiting.'*

'Take care. I love you. Give your mom my love.'

Ariana didn't pack. Instead, she ran straight to the roof. Scarlet arrived in her standard red dress and yellow tights moments later.

"I'm sorry," Scarlet said.

Ariana nodded as she let the strange woman wrap her arms around her.

Scarlet looked at her and whispered, "Ready?"

Ariana nodded again, wrapping her arms around the woman she despised. The woman she blamed all her problems on. Now, though, she didn't care about any of that. In fact, deep down, she realized that the only person making her problems worse was herself.

In a flash, they were up in the air, and Ariana shivered as they made their windy journey.

EMMA

in Shadow Town

After her bakery closed, Suzie Quintano found a job at the local grocery store, making cupcakes in the bakery department along with a variety of other baked goods. She looked like a sweet, old grandma. Suzie had agreed to meet with Emma and Estevan during one of her breaks.

They sat on a small table tucked away in the deli section. The scent of rotisserie chicken made Emma's stomach growl.

"I don't know how I can help," Suzie said, futzing with her apron. "I haven't been in that shop since it was condemned."

"We realize that, Miz Quintano. It's just that the earthquake destroyed a lot of it, and they want to change that whole block into a train depot." Emma leaned her elbows on the table. "I read there were bugs."

"The report said *cockroaches*, but that's not true."

Under the table, Estevan placed his hand on Emma's knee before asking, "Who mentioned cockroaches?"

"I don't know where it started, but it's in the final inspection report. The mayor even signed off on it despite my protests. Apparently, he's too busy and didn't have time to discuss it with me. I told him they weren't cockroaches, they were crickets."

Crickets? How could crickets condemn a building? Things weren't adding up. Either she was lying or someone obviously wanted Ms. Quintano out of her cupcake shop for some reason…and fast.

Emma rejoined her husband and Ms. Quintano's conversation in time for Ms. Quintano to say she needed to return to work.

Emma stood up and shook her hand. "One more

question. Is there any reason someone would want you out of the shop?"

Ms. Quintano's eyes widened. "No, I had been there for so many years and had so many loyal customers. I loved it and never planned on going anywhere…unless they kicked me out for the train depot."

Emma's feet couldn't carry her out of the grocery store fast enough. She had to discuss all this with Estevan and come up with a plan.

ARIANA
in Windy City

Scarlet set Ariana down in a corner of Windy City Medical Center's parking lot.

"Thank you," Ariana said. "I owe you one...maybe two. You did save my neighbor's cat, too."

Scarlet smiled. "No need. I already owe Adam so much. He's been such a huge help in training me. You're lucky to have him."

"I don't know about that. I've been..." She couldn't believe she was admitting this to the enemy. "...struggling a little."

"Well, you need to know that Adam's crazy about you. Being married to a superhero can't be easy." She laughed. "I mean, I can't even hold down a boyfriend. To be the spouse of one of us has to be a job all on its own— and a thankless one at that. You may not think I know you well, but from what Adam tells me, you're pretty special. I mean, he talks about you all the time."

"Even recently?"

Scarlet nodded. "Yes. All the time. All he wants is for this be over, so he can get home and let you teach him how to be a *fantastic husband*. His words, not mine."

"But what about the next time? There will always be something taking his time away from me." Ariana bit her lip. At that moment, she realized how selfish that sounded.

Scarlet shrugged. "Yeah, even if he wasn't a superhero, he'd have a job, friends, and hobbies that took time away. At least you know he's out making a difference and not sitting at a bar somewhere. I know he doesn't like being away either."

Ariana took a deep breath.

Leaning in, Scarlet whispered. "And one more thing—for someone like me, you know, someone with a secret identity they've struggled to hide their whole life, to find someone worthy of telling my secret to is incomprehensible. And Adam, he found that special person in you."

Ariana looked at the pavement. "I'm not that special."

Scarlet patted Ariana on the shoulder and took off into the sky. Ariana felt a new presence in her mind. It was Scarlet's voice. *'Don't underestimate yourself. You are special.'*

Ariana ran into the hospital, contemplating Scarlet's words.

When she pushed the curtain aside in her mother's hospital room, the first thing she saw was her father's long face. Everything drooped like it was made of wax and melted from the midday sun. She firmed up her chin and tightened her lips; she was sure her face must have been as long as her father's.

"Hi, sweetie," her dad said solemnly.

Ariana didn't reply. Instead, her eyes glided over to her mother. She had a tube coming out of her mouth. Her skin was pale, her cheeks hollow, and her normally well-groomed hair pointed in multiple directions. Even though she didn't look like the spunky woman who picked her up from the airport or the woman who played cards with her every Tuesday, Ariana knew that woman was still in there. She had to be.

Her vision clouded, and she wiped her eyes while grasping her mom's unmoving hand—the one her father wasn't holding. It was limp and heavier than it should be.

"She doesn't look good." Ariana sniffled.

"She's actually doing well. The doctor said her heart rhythm has stabilized, and they'll try to take her breathing tube out later this afternoon. She only needs it because they have her sedated while she heals."

Ariana focused on her mother's chest, rising and

falling. "I'm so sorry I wasn't here."

"Ariana, you couldn't help it."

"Sure I could have. I could have not gone to see Adam. I should have stayed here with my family." Ariana sat back with a realization. She loved her parents, whether she was with them or not. Nothing would change that. When Adam was away from her, was that how he felt, too?

Ariana's father reached across the hospital bed and grabbed Ariana's arm. "Honey, Adam's your family too now. It's time you accept that. We know you love us, and we'll always be here for you, but you need to support your husband. It's him that will be there for you long after we're gone."

Gone? Ariana looked up to see a tear drip from her father's eye.

"It's not that easy," she whispered.

"Letting go is never easy."

"Being married isn't easy either."

Her dad let go of her arm. "Nobody ever said it was. Being married takes communication, dedication, and accepting each other's faults. There's no such thing as Prince Charming and no white horse, but what I see between you and Adam…is pretty close. So close, that someday you'll realize he may not be THE Prince Charming, but he's YOUR Prince Charming. Like your mother here. She's my Cinderella, Snow White, and now…Sleeping Beauty. Actually, she's more than all of them."

Ariana clutched her mom's hand tighter. She thought of her dad's words, of Scarlet's words, and her own thoughts.

'Adam? Can you hear me? I love you, and I'm ready to start over. Can you come now? I need you.'

VICTORIA
Outside of Shadow Town

Victoria drove Vance to another spot in the mountains. This one was special. Surrounded by the fragrance of pine, she led him down a path to another cool mountain lake. This one was deep and crystal clear.

Victoria stood behind Vance and began to slip off his mask, but Vance stopped her. "Maybe we should start with hide and seek or testing my strength. Those are less dangerous."

"That's exactly why we should work on your freeze vision. You need to master the one that could do the most harm."

Vance dropped his hands, allowing Victoria to remove his mask. At first, he shielded his eyes from the light, but after some blinking, he scanned the scenery. "This place is beautiful."

"It is. It also holds some special memories."

Vance shook his head. "I'm sorry. I don't remember."

"Well, it didn't look like this when the memories were made. Freeze the lake."

"What?"

"You've done it before. Stare at the water until it's frozen." Victoria stepped behind him and weaved her fingers through his, leaning against his back and whispering in his ear, "You can do it. I know you can."

And a few moments later, a sheet of ice covered the lake's surface.

"Perfect." Victoria replaced the blindfold and pulled Vance out onto the frozen lake. "Whoa, there." When he almost fell, she helped steady him.

Vance wrapped his arm tightly around her waist. "What are we doing?"

"We're ice skating...only without skates." She

pulled Vance across the surface, elaborately twirling him in and out of her arms—both of them laughing.

After making a few trips around the lake, Victoria stopped. "Close your eyes." She removed Vance's mask. "Open them quickly and take in the view."

He shook his head. "Not with you in front of me."

"One moment's all I ask."

With that, Vance opened his eyes.

"Isn't it beautiful?"

Vance's eyes never left Victoria. "Yes, it is."

Victoria knew what had to happen next. "Close your eyes," she whispered.

He obeyed.

"Picture what you just saw in your mind. Feel the cold ice beneath your feet. Feel my warm hands in yours."

Vance nodded.

"This is how you told me about your powers. You took me on a hike out here. Asked me if I trusted you. If I loved you for who you were. If I'd still love you if you were someone else." Victoria wiped away a tear.

"And what did you say?"

"I thought you were joking, but your face told me different. I said, 'Of course. How could I not love you?' Hell, we were already married." Victoria paused while she regained her composure. "Then you froze the lake. I swore a few times, but you pulled me out here and skated me around. When we stopped in the middle of the lake, like we are now, you kissed me. You told me you were sorry for not telling me sooner."

"I think we should replay that kiss." Vance smiled. "It might help trigger my memory."

"So, do you want me to do to you what I did that day?"

Vance nodded.

Victoria slapped him across the cheek. Vance easily shook it off. "I blew up at you. I couldn't believe you had married me without telling me everything. That you took that choice away from me."

"I'm sorry."

"Do you remember any of this?"

"No. I might be a lost cause."

Victoria's shoulders sagged. "I had hoped this would work."

"I'm sure I regretted not telling you about my superpowers sooner."

Victoria shuffled her feet, sliding back and forth in front of Vance. "We all have regrets."

"What do you regret?"

Victoria took his hand again and wrapped it around her waist, then reached up, placing her fingers on the back of his neck and pulling him down to her. "I regret that I slapped you that day. Keeping a secret that big, for so long, had to be hard. And then telling me…so late into our relationship couldn't have been easy either. I should have seen the other side…and did this instead." She kissed him with as much fire as she had on their wedding night. Perhaps more.

Vance's fingers dug into her hips, then he hesitated a moment before lifting her up. She wrapped her legs around his torso while his hands raked over her back, deepening their kiss.

"I love you, Victoria," he breathed, voice full of sincerity.

"I love you, too. I never stopped."

"Neither did I." Vance flipped off the mask and he carried Victoria to the grass. Running his hands through her hair, he stared into her eyes.

"Vance… you're going to freeze…"

He shook his head. "No, I won't. I remember. I remember everything. I think the passion in your kiss brought it all back. Do you want to know why I didn't tell you about my powers until after we were married?"

Victoria nodded.

"I wanted to make sure you loved me for me...not because I was a superhero. I needed to make sure what we had was real, and that you'd marry me, thinking I was an average man. Women flocked to Icy Tundra. Nobody flocked to an orphan who was socially awkward...except you. Besides, telling you I was Icy Tundra was the first step to me telling you my deepest secret, what happened to my father."

"And that's not why I left you."

"At first, I didn't know, but after harassing you for so many years, I realized it was more than that. You left for you, and I'm sorry I held you back." He wiped a tear from her eyes. "Stop crying! That was a long time ago already. But I still have one question unanswered."

"What?"

Vance smiled. "How could you take my dog away? It's one thing to lose you, but to kidnap Chewy? That was low."

"I—"

He laughed, then stopped her argument with his lips. Surrendering, she wrapped her arms around him. She'd had dreams about this, dreams she tried to forget, yet they haunted her. Here was her chance to redo a memory. Her chance to redo a mistake. If he'd have her.

~ ~ ~

Victoria dropped Vance off at his home, and he kissed her good-bye, saying he had a city to save. Victoria went to the animal hospital to check on Chewy and then home, to her empty house. Vance had his memory back, Chewy could come home tomorrow, and her life was back to normal. Everything was great, but why did she feel like her world was falling apart?

Victoria began to fold the blanket Vance had been using, but stopped, instead laying her head on top of his pillow and inhaling his scent as she drifted to sleep.

Wednesday, April 21st

EMMA

in Shadow Town

Emma sat beside her husband on the motel room bed, holding a cup of terrible tea. The TV was on for background noise. "We need another superhero or two. How have you been looking for The Kite?"

Estevan looked down at his paper cup. "Um…I've been running around the city, looking for a man with a black cape with silver feathers sewn in."

"And Icy Tundra?"

"Um…the same way? Only looking for a blue cape. I'm glad he's back and nothing happened to him."

Emma prodded him further. "How would someone find you?"

"They'd contact you." He smiled and patted her thigh.

"Oh, come on. How do you get a hold of the mayor? Or how did we coordinate our meeting with Doctor Marchant or Miz Quintano?"

"We called them."

"How would you call a superhero?" Emma's eyes darted to the TV.

Estevan turned his head, then looked back, his eyes slowly lighting up. "I have an idea!" He raised one finger and pointed at the ceiling.

Emma let her huge smile out. "And what's that?"

Estevan dropped his finger and looked her intently in the eyes. "You realize that I let you spoon-feed me these ideas, right?"

Emma bit her lip hiding her smile. She nudged him with her elbow. "Oh, come on. Let me feel important. You can see the future, and even if you didn't have the idea, you'd blurt it out much sooner than you do."

"It's that obvious?"

"Yup," Emma said. "So, what's your idea?"

"First off, you are important, super important, and I know that you know that already. Secondly, here's my idea. What if Capitán Rápido goes on TV and asks for a meeting with all the superheroes in town? This Kite hombre can speak telepathically. Maybe he could help us secretly create a meeting spot."

"Once again, I think you have a brilliant idea." Emma kissed her husband on the cheek and clicked off the TV. "Let's get you ready for a news broadcast."

VICTORIA

in Shadow Town

A pounding on the apartment door woke Victoria. She dropped the pillow she had been hugging and wiped the drool from her lips. Was it morning already? The light outside told her it was approaching noon.

"I'm coming," she called, pulling her hair into a ponytail in a fruitless attempt to fix it. She peeked through the peephole at Icy Tundra, wearing a white suit and blue cape. She flung the door open and pulled him inside. "You can't stand out there in your costume."

He shook his head. "Remember, I can sense people. Nobody's around."

"Oh yeah, I'm not used to you having your powers back. Why are you here?"

Vance pulled his dark blue hood off and removed his white mask. Victoria found herself, once again, lost in his eyes. "Because I can't stop thinking about you."

Butterfly wings beat in her stomach and a tingle shot up her legs. "It's okay. Things can get back to normal. The way they were before the earthquake."

"But I don't want them to. We've wasted all this time apart. These six years have been torture. There were things I wanted to tell you. Things I wanted to share with you, but couldn't. It made me regret all the opportunities I had during our marriage that I missed. All the times I left you out."

"You did exclude me from that side of your life." She motioned to his superhero costume.

"I thought I was keeping you safe, but was actually pushing you away."

Victoria bit her lip.

"Then after our divorce, I was so angry and grudgeful that you left me. Mad you took Chewy with you."

"That, I feel bad about. I didn't know any better. I've been trying to make it up to you by giving you visitation rights…I've been putting up with you being a jerk because I feel awful. Deep down, I know you're a good guy. I've been wanting to break through your façade and find that Vance again."

"Yeah, that's another thing. I've been trying to punish you, but you never crack. You're the strongest woman I know…the only woman for me."

Victoria wiped a stray tear. The softness in Vance's eyes got to her. "So, what you're saying is you'd like to try again?"

He laughed. "Of course that's what I'm saying!"

"Things will need to be different. We're older and wiser now."

"That's true," Vance said. "Like you, I didn't know what being married meant. All my life I have had to keep secrets from everyone, and I assumed that included my wife. Without a doubt, I now know that was wrong. Can we forget about the past?" Vance pulled Victoria into his arms and held her tight.

When he loosened his embrace, Victoria reached up. She cupped his cheek, feeling the prickles of his beard against her hand. "No, we can't. And I wouldn't want to." Victoria pulled away and wiped her eyes. "But we can start again. Move forward from here."

Vance smiled. "Is that a yes?"

Victoria nodded.

"Well, I'm not letting you get away again. I gotta run now, though. I stopped by to give you a quick kiss."

"What are you up to? Did you find something out? You used to always come for a good-bye kiss before facing someone unstoppable."

Vance gave a sly smile. "Oh, I'll stop whatever it is. I have something to come home to…plus I have help.

Capitán Rápido made an announcement on TV. Did you see it?"

"No, I've been catching up on sleep."

"Well, The Kite telepathically reached out to me to set up a meeting between all the superheroes in town. They have a theory about the origin of the earthquake and the crime spree. We're gonna work together."

"We? That's great." Victoria felt her heart drop. "Oh, you didn't mean me." She crossed her arms when old feelings surfaced. He had kept his crime-fighting adventures a secret for the first part of their marriage, and when she finally found out his alternative identity, she had to pry out information. "We're not doing that again this time. I want to be beside you. An equal partner in everything. I won't be easily pushed aside—superpowers or not."

"You know that's dumb. You could be hurt. I can't have that worry."

"And I'm not one to sit at home and wait. That's not who I am."

Vance squinted at her, but the smile on his face said she was getting somewhere.

She threw his words back at him. "You're leaving me out again."

Vance shook his head. "No, I'm not." He leaned down and kissed her. "Let's go...but maybe I should change into my civilian clothes first. Imagine the Superhero News Network showing Icy Tundra running around with a beautiful, curvy brunette."

ARIANA
in Windy City

The doctor removed the tube from Ariana's mother's mouth yesterday, but her mom slept until late this morning. Everything was looking better. She had been weaned off all medications and was now alert. Tired, but awake.

Once the situation was explained to her mom, she turned toward Ariana and gave her daughter a beautiful smile. She croaked out in a hoarse voice, "I'm sorry I scared you. So sorry you had to rush here for me, but I'm so happy to see you."

"Shh," Ariana hushed. "It's okay. Of course I'd rush here." She took her mother's hand. The dead weight of it was gone, and instead, it was infused with life. Ariana leaned down and planted a kiss on her mom's knuckles.

Her dad rubbed his hand along his wife's cheek, brushing the hair from her face. His words were gentle. "The doctors say you can move to a step-down floor tomorrow, and if that goes well, home in a few days. They put three stents in your heart, and you're as good as new...for now."

"Honey..." She looked at Ariana. "You don't need to stay. You can go back to Adam. I'll be fine."

"He's okay, Mom. You need me more."

"Let me tell you a secret. Men need their women. They become dependent on them. The women keep the men going, connected, and grounded. Adam may not tell you this, but he needs you. No matter how much strength he shows, he needs you more than you need him. Isn't that right, dear?"

"Yes. That's true." Ariana's dad wiped a solitary tear that had made its way down his cheek. "I don't know what I'd do without you."

"And I know that. That's why I'm certain I'm

gonna get out of here. I'm not done yet because I'm still needed." She turned toward Ariana. "But, Ariana, remember life's short. You never know how long you have, so don't waste any time. There's no sense holding a grudge, or being stubborn, or not showing or telling someone you love them."

Turning those words over in her mind, Ariana filled with guilt. She had avoided telling Adam she loved him because she was mad. What if something happened to him?

The TV in the corner of the room caught her attention. It was a photo of Capitán Rápido with a headline, "Are the Superheroes Working Together?" Ariana reached over and turned up the volume.

The news reporter's voice was deep. "Earlier today, Capitán Rápido made a special announcement. He agrees with the suspicion that the earthquakes experienced in Shadow Town and New Shore were not natural disasters, but rather orchestrated by someone. At this time, he's not stating whether or not we have a new supervillain in town. He asked for The Kite to reach out to him, using his telepathic ability, and coordinate a meeting between him and the other superheroes helping Shadow Town. This recent development looks promising for the future of our city."

Ariana felt like she was being pulled apart, ripped right down the center. Duties as a daughter versus duties as a wife. She realized she kept forgetting about one set of duties…duties to herself. What did she want?

Ariana squeezed her mother's hand. "I love you, but I have something to take care of. I'll be back as soon as I can." She then extended her mental connection to Adam. *'Adam?'*

No response.

She wasn't going to wait around. Scarlet's powers were stronger, so she reached out to that crimson-haired woman through the connection opened when she dropped

Ariana off at this hospital. This time, there was no jealousy.

'Scarlet?'

'Yes?'

'Could you send Adam or come and get me? I'm ready to go back home.'

'Which home?'

'Home is wherever my husband is.' Ariana would do everything possible to make her marriage work. She loved Adam with all her heart and wouldn't keep her troubles to herself anymore, no matter how hard it was to admit what was wrong.

'I'll send Adam. I'm going to my home, too. I know Shadow Town still needs help, but so does Enormopolis.'

Ariana leaned back. She was almost sad for Scarlet to return home.

VICTORIA
in Shadow Town

Vance took Victoria to an empty building. Inside were two men. One was younger…perhaps in his early twenties. The other man was five or more years older with dark hair. He appeared to be of Spanish descent.

The older man stood up. "What's going on here?"

"Who's our guest?" the younger man asked.

Victoria tucked a hand in her pocket, but Vance snatched it, holding it tight. "This is my wife, Victoria. She's part of my team."

Wife. Victoria realized the urge to argue was gone. The dark-haired man did it for her.

"Wife?" the man asked. "You're married?"

The younger man stepped forward. "I have one at home, too."

"You do?" Vance asked. "And how do you make it work?"

He laughed. "We're newlyweds, and right now, I don't think I'm doing a good job of making it work."

The older man added, "I've got one too, and admittedly, most times, I don't know what I'm doing either. I'm sure our wives would have a lot to talk about."

Victoria laughed. "I know what happens when women get together…especially if you throw a little wine in the mix."

The older man took a deep breath and rubbed his hands down his face. "*Mi gatita.* Come on out." He waved someone from the back room.

The young man stood up, rubbing a hand through his hair. "I should have sensed her here, but I've been preoccupied."

From the other room, a woman stepped out wearing dark jeans and a black top. Her hair was slicked back into a bun. Victoria had seen her before on the news.

The woman stuck out her hand, shaking Victoria's first. "Hi. I'm Emma Rodríguez. I'm happy to know I'm not the only better half." She winked at Victoria as she shook Vance's hand as well. "This is my husband Estevan, but you may be more familiar with him wearing his black leather costume."

"Capitán Rápido?" When the man nodded, Victoria turned toward the younger man. "Then you must be The Kite."

The Kite stepped forward and shook her hand. "Adam."

Emma turned to face the young guy. "Thank you for saving me and my niece the other day when that car you were chasing almost hit us."

He winked. "It's what I do."

Soon, they all sat around an old table. Vance started the conversation. "I want to thank you both for taking care of this city while I was…not myself."

Estevan nodded. "My wife tells me we need to put all our heads together. She's uncovered some things that led her to believe the earthquake was deliberate. Both earthquakes, in fact."

Emma continued. "I'm hoping we all know a little piece of the puzzle, and together, we can put this mess behind us. Vance, since it's your city, I was hoping you'd go first."

"I don't know much since I lost my memory in the earthquake." He looked to Victoria.

"I have a theory," Victoria said. "There have been some scientists reporting the earthquake was manmade. At SynPharmaTek, we're working on a device that disrupts and rearranges drug molecules using sonar energy. I wonder if this was made on a larger scale, and tuned into the right frequency, if it could disrupt superhero DNA. The device isn't big enough to create an earthquake, but perhaps something with the same technology could."

"That makes sense," Emma said. "Estevan had a temporary loss of powers. He wasn't as close to here as you were, but Actionville still felt the effects. The supervillains that were caught had issues too. Not everyone lost their powers, though. Some had a power surge. Others discovered new abilities."

"I kept my powers, but I didn't remember how to use them. Maybe they were a little haywire too, making them harder to get a grip on." Vance motioned toward Adam. "How about you? Any power changes?"

Adam shook his head. "No, but I'm much farther away. What about the other earthquake? I understand there were no superheroes and no power disruptions in New Shore."

"I haven't been looking into that," Victoria admitted.

"I have," Emma said. "A distraction perhaps? I'm not really sure. I do know New Shore had a surge of sonic energy during the earthquake just like Shadow Town did."

"Do you think SynPharmaTek's behind this?" Adam asked.

"I checked them out the other day when I was following some leads." Emma motioned toward Victoria. "Didn't I see you in Doctor Marchant's office last week? Do you think he's involved in this? They do have a small facility in New Shore."

Victoria shook her head. "My gut tells me he's not. Perhaps someone accessing the knowledge of one of his scientists might be involved. I talked with Doctor Burg, the lead scientist on the sonar drug project and a supergenius. She says the device could be made in someone's garage."

"Doctor Burg?" Emma rubbed her chin. "I know that name... That's the mayor's sister-in-law. I ran into her son, Kyle, at my sister's school. He was in the office, in trouble for computer hacking."

Victoria's eyes widened. "I saw the mayor's brave

rescue on the news. Isn't the nephew a supergenius like his mom? It's weird the mayor has multiple superhumans in his family. I mean, to us, it's an everyday occurrence, but there's really not that many out there. Then they seem to be connected to this event."

Vance leaned forward. "I've watched quite a bit of TV lately, and Mayor Payne's approval rating has been phenomenal ever since he saved the boy."

Victoria asked, "Do you think that was staged? I mean, look at how much the public loves a good hero? Plus, nothing was on camera."

Emma rubbed her temple. "I don't think so. He lost his campaign headquarters in the quake. Everything was ruined. All his files… Wait. He did hint that he may be running for president next year. With all the support he'll get for cleaning up the city, I'm sure that will really help his campaign." Emma's tapped the table with her finger. "The cupcake shop next door to him had recently been condemned for bugs. The owner says they were crickets."

"Crickets?" Vance asked.

"Yeah, that's what I thought. The report actually said cockroaches. It's also interesting that I had the pleasure of watching the mayor's pet snake eat a cricket when I visited him. If he has to keep the snake fed, I'm sure he has a supply of crickets."

"I'm sure there are thousands of people in this town with pet snakes," Victoria added.

"Yeah, but the mayor also signed off on the inspection reports, despite Miz Quintano's objections. The heroic rescue the mayor had of his nephew? The leveled campaign headquarters? He had to be hiding something."

Estevan flashed a smile and his finger pointed up toward the ceiling. "I have an idea."

Emma's jaw fell open, which she quickly righted. "You do?"

"Yes, I do. What if the Mayor had files that needed

to be destroyed…say he rigged the election…or a supergenius computer hacker nephew of his did?"

A bright smile flashed on Emma's face. She turned toward the young man beside her who'd been silent this whole time. "What do you think, Adam?"

Adam was staring off into space. He stood up. "I have to go. I know we have important things to do, but I need to get my wife. Family first. When I'm done, I'll come find you." In a swoosh, he flew from the room.

Victoria turned back to the others. "So, where do we go from here?"

They spent the rest of the afternoon piecing together everything they had discovered and figuring out what their next step would be.

ARIANA

in Windy City

The moment Ariana saw Adam, she wanted to wrap her arms around him. She didn't, though. Something still held her back. Adam didn't hesitate and pulled her into his arms. It was what she needed.

"How's your mom?" he asked.

"She's okay. They're moving her out of the ICU today."

He cocked his head and wrinkled an eyebrow. "She's still in the ICU? Why'd you want to come with me to Shadow Town?"

Confusion swirled inside Ariana, then the weeks of pent-up anger resurfaced. Didn't he want her with him? Why hadn't he checked in with her at the hospital? That anger she tapped into at her self-defense class grew once again, and her hand tightened into a firm ball. Energy gathered in her arm and Adam's face began to resemble the pad she had punched in class. She wound up.

"Ari, what are you doing?" Adam raised his hands and took a step back.

She tried to find the words, but they escaped her. She tightened her fists.

"Breathe, Ari. Breathe. What's bothering you? Tell me. Get it all out."

The words finally exploded from her mouth. "You've ignored me for weeks! You didn't come to see my mother. You're spending your nights with another woman...and I had to move to another city to be with you while my mom had a heart attack! You have no idea what's been going on in my life!"

"Ari, I had no idea. I'm sorry."

A flood of tears washed down her face.

Adam pulled her into his chest. He brushed the hair from her forehead and replaced it with his lips. His breath was warm and comforting. "I...never thought of the other perspective. I'm so sorry. You're right. You're right. I'm done with that. You're number one in my book. You've always been number one."

He squeezed her, and she tensed. His hands rubbed up and down her back until she eventually relaxed into her husband's body. He had been a stranger for these past few weeks, and now, suddenly, she felt some familiarity again.

Adam's voice was calm and laced with sadness. "We'll go home together tonight...our real home here in Windy City. I'll call Scarlet back to take over for me in Shadow Town."

Ariana nodded into his embrace. Home. That word had never sounded so good.

Adam continued, "We just need to be patient with each other and communicate. I didn't understand what was going through your mind and didn't know what I was supposed to do. I thought giving you space was the correct thing. Maybe I'm a coward. Obviously, I was wrong."

A delirious chuckle that couldn't be from anything besides tension and stress rolled from Ariana's mouth. "I'm glad I'm not the only foolish one in this marriage. I've always been an only child. Never having to share attention. I just feel I should be cherished. Put up on a pedestal. But that's unrealistic. I realize that."

"No, you should be cherished. I'm so stupid for not seeing it." Adam wiped her eyes and smiled. "I love you, and I mean it."

Ariana let those words sink in. She also thought of what her mom told her about never missing an opportunity to say it back. Despite her frustration, she returned his term of endearment with sincerity. "I love you too."

As right as this was, a part of it was wrong. Ariana leaned back. "You still have your duty in Shadow Town, and we need to see it to the end."

"We?"

"We're a team. Even if you're in the spotlight as The Kite, I'm still part of you. What was the statement at our wedding? Two become one."

Adam nodded. "Then I think it's time to go to Shadow Town and finish this. I've met with the other superheroes and their wives, and it'll be really nice to have you along."

Ariana smiled. How could she go from an outsider to feeling like she belonged with the flip of a switch? It didn't matter. She gave Adam a nod, and he lifted her up into the sky.

Thursday, April 22nd

ARIANA

in Shadow Town

Ariana followed her husband into an apartment complex in Shadow Town. Adam had told her that he had someone for her to meet. On her way inside, she couldn't stop glancing at her husband's hand. She wanted to reach out and grab it, hold it, and tell him she was there for him, but didn't feel now was the time. It wasn't until she saw the shimmer of his gold wedding ring that she finally reached out, thinking of her mom's words. *There's no sense not showing someone you love them.*

He stopped immediately when her fingers intertwined with his, squeezing her hand. "What's this for?"

"You're wearing your wedding ring."

Adam smiled. "I've been wearing it for a while now. Ever since I came to Shadow Town, I've kept it on. It's a reminder of you. I may not have been with you, but you were right here with me the whole time." He wiggled his finger.

"But, you always said you couldn't wear it when..." Ariana looked around to ensure the coast was clear. "...you were out in costume."

"It's just a simple gold band, and I'm going to wear it because I want to. It's a symbol of our life together."

Dropping Adam's hand, she rubbed her ring finger and wished it wasn't bare. This time, it wasn't to prove to Lenny that she was married, but to connect with her husband.

"I was going to wait, but I have a surprise for you." Adam dug a hand into his pocket and pulled out a little black bag. A golden ring tumbled out and onto his palm.

"It's my ring! How long has it been ready?"

"Way too long, but with everything going on, the timing wasn't right. I was waiting to do something romantic. Since I can't wait forever for the perfect moment, I'm making one now."

Ariana picked the ring up and turned it over in her hand. Before she slipped it on her finger, she noticed words etched along the inside. "You had it engraved?"

"I did. I had mine done, too."

Ariana twirled the ring around, reading the saying out loud. "To the woman who knows all my secrets. I love you." Tears welled in her eyes. "I love you, too." She wiped away the wetness and smiled. "What does yours say?"

Adam handed over his ring.

Ariana rotated it between her fingers. "Above all else…" She looked up at Adam, waiting for an explanation.

"You are the most important thing in my life. Nothing else compares to that. Not even saving the world."

Ariana slipped Adam's ring back on his finger. "I don't think that's realistic. We need to find a good balance."

"Maybe, but I forget sometimes. I push things off, thinking you'll always be there. It's foolish, and this is my reminder to stop." Adam pulled her close and placed a perfect kiss on her lips—one that made Ariana sigh with longing. "Maybe things would have gone better if I got you a necklace instead."

"A necklace? Of course not."

"Well, if I did, it might start a *chain* reaction." He chuckled.

"What?"

"*Chain* reaction. Get it?"

Ariana shook her head. It'd been too long since she heard one of his cheesy jokes, and she didn't realize how much she missed them. "Okay. Enough of this. You have a city to save. Then, we can get back to Windy City and really start our married life together."

"That sounds wonderful, so let's get this over with."

Adam turned around and knocked on the purple apartment door behind him.

A curvy woman with dark brown hair opened the door.

Adam smiled. "Nice seeing you again, Victoria. I'd like you to meet my wife, Ariana."

Victoria gave Ariana's had a firm shake while exchanging pleasantries.

Adam continued, "Thanks for agreeing to entertain my wife. I gotta meet up with Estevan and your husband for some important business." He winked.

"Ex-husband." She winked back, then opened the door wider. "You bet. I've been looking forward to this. Come in."

"Uh oh," Adam continued. "I have a feeling I'm in trouble." He flashed a smile.

Victoria grabbed Ariana's hand, pulling her inside. "We're gonna have so much fun! Don't worry. I'll make sure to tell her everything NOT to do in a special kinda marriage, so she doesn't end up divorced like me."

Ariana swallowed.

"Don't worry, sweetie," Victoria said. "I know how to make it right too." She turned to Adam. "Okay. Now go. It's girl talk time."

Adam nodded. "Thank you. I'll go round up the men and be back soon." He hesitated. His eyes latched onto Ariana and made her want to kiss him. Did he feel the same? Hell, there was no reason to hold back. She wrapped her arms around his neck and planted her lips on his. When his firm grip left her, she opened her eyes just in time to see him disappear down the stairs, and she couldn't help but smile.

After some small talk, Ariana asked the question that had been eating at her. "So, ex-wife, huh? I know we just met, but could you tell me what happened? See, I'm afraid I almost headed down that path…maybe I still am."

She twirled her wedding ring.

Victoria cocked her head. "Why?"

Ariana sighed as she followed Victoria into the kitchen. They sat at the kitchen table. "Um… I've been lonely and almost kissed another man."

"You did what?"

"*Almost* kissed him. It was more like he tried to kiss me. The details don't matter—it was still wrong."

Victoria tilted her chin. "But nothing happened?"

"No. Of course not."

"Get over it then. Stop blaming yourself. Tell Adam; he'll probably laugh about it."

"It seems so easy when you say it." Ariana rubbed her hands along the edge of the table.

"It is easy. It's only complicated in your own head. My advice is not to let him get away. If you both love each other, that's really all you need. Being married to a superhero can be lonely if you let it be. It can also be quite fulfilling if you take that path instead." She left the table and made a cup of coffee in the kitchen's single-serve.

"Fulfilling?" Ariana leaned back in her chair.

"Yes, in many ways. You may not be the center of attention, but you are still the support system for your superhero. Actually, not a support system. You are equals. Partners. You're all he has. The only one he can tell his secrets to. Sometimes, the men's egos cause them to forget those details, but that's okay. We just need to be there, bringing them back to reality." She laughed. "We ground them." She pulled the cup of coffee out of the machine. "Want one?"

"No, thanks."

Victoria made her way to the table and sat down again beside Ariana, smelling her coffee. "Being a superhero wife is more fulfilling than that. It's not about being his wife. It's about being confident in who you are and what you bring to the table. You're not him. You're not a superhero, but you still can do amazing things. So, what brought you to Shadow Town?"

"I guess... I'm here so Adam doesn't get away."

"As long as you both care and talk about things, you can get past this. You can overcome anything. I saw the way he looked at you. He loves you deeply."

"That's what Scarlet said too."

Victoria shrugged. "Well, if everyone's saying it, it has to be true."

"You think so?" Ariana straightened in the chair.

"I do."

EMMA

in Shadow Town

Behind the purple painted apartment door, two beautiful women greeted Emma. She'd met Victoria yesterday, but today there was a new woman, younger than both of them. She held out her hand. "You must be Adam's wife."

"Ariana." The woman brushed her golden hair off her face and shook her hand.

"Newlyweds, I understand. I feel bad for you. You have a lot of adjustments to make. It takes a special woman to do what we do. Strength to recognize you belong in this world."

"I'm realizing that," Ariana said.

"Don't worry. You have the strength. These men only pick women they feel can handle them." Emma took a seat beside Estevan at the kitchen table, pulling her chair close to him. The room felt oddly comfortable with some of their secrets out in the open. "What have we figured out?"

"We think Estevan's idea is the best," Vance said.

"That the mayor is behind this all?" Emma looked over to her husband and pride filled her chest. "So...let's say the mayor's nephew rigged the election results and the earthquake was a coverup. What about the earthquake in New Shore? Or the superhero power loss?"

Victoria rubbed her forehead. "New Shore doesn't have a superhero, right?"

The group nodded.

"If the mayor was involved, why would he attack that city?" Victoria asked. When no response came, she continued, "I still say we move forward. Any ideas on what we do next?"

"We could approach the mayor and ask him directly what he knows," Ariana suggested.

Emma shook her head. "That never goes well. If the mayor is our villain, he'll deny it. They always deny it."

"Obviously, we need proof." Adam put his arm around his wife, rubbing his hand down her upper arm.

"We need to find the weapon. The thing that caused the earthquake." Estevan reached over and took Emma's hand. "It's big, right?"

"The empty space I saw at Cupcake Corner was about six by six," Emma said.

"Where do you think the mayor keeps it?" Estevan asked. "I doubt he'd have incriminating evidence like that in his own home."

Ariana tapped her finger against her lip. "Does the mayor own any other property?"

"I don't know," Emma said.

"That's an easy online search. I do it all the time at work. Can I use that?" Ariana motioned toward a laptop on a small writing desk in the corner of the living room.

"Yes, of course." Victoria left the table and retrieved the computer.

Ariana flipped up the laptop and clicked a few keys. "Nothing came up in the tax documents. Maybe there are loan documents under his name…connecting him to…" Her fingers flew across the keyboard. "There it is. He owns a boathouse down at the docks here in Shadow Town. It's under the name 'Three Dogs LLC'."

All three men leaped out of their chairs, ready for action.

Estevan lifted his backpack with lightning speed, pulling out his leather suit. "We should go check it out."

"Wait." Ariana motioned for them all to sit back down. "He owns other property, too. It looks like a vacation home in New Shore. We have a connection." Ariana closed the laptop and a smile filled her face. She sat up straight. "Dang! It's nice to feel useful."

The men were out of their chairs again.

"Now can we check out the boathouse?" Estevan asked.

"You don't know what you're looking for. I'll come along. I may be useful for identifying the object," Emma said.

Victoria stood up, planting her feet firmly on the linoleum floor. "Well, if you're going, so am I."

"Hey, hey, hey. I'm not being left behind," Ariana chimed in.

Emma leaned back in her chair. "Well, it looks like we have quite the team right now."

"Maybe we are onto something new." Estevan smiled and wrapped his arm around his wife. "The difference between success and failure is a great team. Emma's always been on my team."

Emma's cheeks heated as Estevan leaned down and kissed her. Her heart may have even missed a beat.

Seven years of marriage, and it only got better.

VICTORIA

in Shadow Town

Down at the docks, the entire superhero and wife crew waited to enact their plan. On top of a nearby abandoned shipping warehouse sat Adam with Ariana in his arms. Next to Victoria's car, Emma and Estevan sat in theirs. Everyone waited for Vance to locate the sonic device.

"Anything yet?" Victoria rubbed her sweaty palms against her jeans. Anticipation danced in her chest. Sure, she'd had other run-ins with criminals in the past, but nothing this big. Nothing capable of causing harm to her husband…um…ex-husband. The plan was for the wives to stay back. Let the husbands do their jobs…they were the invincible ones.

"Just wait," Vance said with his sly smile. He closed his eyes and focused.

Their plan was simple. Vance would find the device, then neutralize it with his freeze vision. It appeared the whole plan hinged on him. The other superheroes were there for support. Estevan's ten-second foresight would keep them safe, and Adam could easily keep watch from the sky.

Once they had the device, they'd confront the mayor about it. Take it to the police. Typical superhero stuff.

Outside the car, a blur of black streaked past the window and a man with a white cape dropped from the sky—Ariana in his arms. Victoria reached over and shook Vance's arm. "It looks like your new friends are getting impatient."

Vance rubbed his temples with his eyes still squeezed tightly closed. "I'll be right out. It's so much harder finding an object I've never seen than it is locating someone I know."

Victoria slipped outside. "Hey, guys. What's up? How's the weather?"

Laughter erupted from Emma as she leaned against the hood of her car. "It looks like all three of these guys get nervous when they get close to what they're after."

Ariana took a spot beside Emma. "It's nice to know Adam's behaviors are *normal*."

Victoria laughed. "Yeah, *normal* for a superhero at least."

A squeak filled the air when Vance's door opened. "I found it. There's a big device right beneath the water's surface. I don't suppose any of us can breathe underwater?"

They shook their heads.

"Well, I also sense two humans. I don't know who they are, or if they have abilities, but it can't be a coincidence they're in the same place."

Adam shifted his weight. "I sense their minds. A man and a younger man...a child?"

"A child?" Estevan asked, but then his face went blank. A moment later, his eyebrows narrowed. "We don't have time!" His movements were fast and blurred as he pointed at Adam. "Stay low."

In a blur, Estevan rushed toward the boathouses along the water's edge.

"Something's gonna happen in ten seconds!" Emma yelled. "Eight seconds!"

Victoria's stomach tensed as she watched Vance run in the direction Estevan had taken off in. Adam lifted into the air and quickly passed him.

"Fly low!" Ariana yelled, clutching her hands to her chest.

"We should do something." Victoria bounced softly on her feet. "We can't sit here and watch."

Emma put her hand on Victoria's shoulder. "What can we do? We're here to guide them. To help them solve the mysteries. It's best if we let them use their skills. Have faith."

Victoria stopped bouncing when a thought knocked the air out of her lungs. She struggled for the words. "What if this was all a ploy get all the superheroes together before a big planned catastrophe? Some villain's way of—" Her words were cut off by a sudden shaking of the earth. The small vibrations quickly grew to a rumble beneath their feet.

ARIANA
in Shadow Town

"Earthquake!" Ariana yelled, desperately keeping her eyes on her husband flying toward the docks.

"It's not an earthquake." Victoria braced herself against the car. "It's different than last time—more mild."

Ariana tensed. Earthquake…superpower disruption. What would happen to Adam? With that thought, Ariana forced her body forward, toward her husband right as he began dropping out of the sky. "Oh, my god!" *Fly low.* It all made sense. She pumped her arms, needing to get to him.

'Ari, NO!' His words filled her head as he plummeted to the ground. *'Staaay awaaaay!'*

"Adam!" she yelled, pushing her legs faster. Her breaths came quick, yet didn't give her the air she needed.

From a drop of two stories high, her husband's curled up body hit the grass with a thud. She and Estevan had both told him to fly low. Why hadn't he listened?

A deafening boom filled the air as concrete broke off the old warehouse and tumbled to the ground. The resounding noise made it impossible to focus.

She rushed down the boat landing, between a string of weathered boathouses and toward her husband. Behind her, the other woman's footsteps crunched on the gravel.

Adam's motionless body caused her heart to stop. *Was he okay? He always said he'd be okay. Why had she wasted all this time being mad at him?* What had her stubbornness gotten her? How could she have ever compared Lenny to Adam? There was no contest. Through her tear-filled eyes, she saw Emma and Victoria rushing to their husbands' unmoving bodies as well.

The vibrating earth made it hard to focus. With all her might, she flipped Adam over, revealing his blood-covered face, Ariana's world stopped. *No. No. No.* Her hand wiped blood from his cheek as she pulled his mask away from a huge gash on his head.

"Adam?" She cringed when she realized she'd used his real name. There was so much noise, perhaps nobody heard...but at this point, she didn't care. She'd shout his name from the top of that warehouse if it meant he was okay.

Fury gathered and tensed her muscles when she heard a voice she recognized from TV—Mayor Payne. She spun around to stare down the barrel of some type of pistol.

"Tie them up," the mayor yelled over the noise, tossing some zip-ties to each of the women with his free hand.

The tears cleared from Ari's eyes. She needed to find a way out of this. Adam may be the superhero, but even someone with special powers needed help from time to time. She glanced up and caught Victoria's eye, feeling she was thinking the same.

Stall, Ariana, create a distraction.

Adam told her that one rule of being a superhero's wife was to always keep his identity a secret. And if there was a chance it'd get out, create a cover story—play whatever game you needed. "But he's The Kite!" she exclaimed. "We saw him fall from the sky and came rushing over to help."

The mayor stood away from them, swinging his gun between the three women. "It doesn't matter who they are. Tie them up."

Ariana shook as she slowly tied her husband's motionless hands together. Her eyes focused on the gold band around his finger as she tightened the ties. *Above all else...* She kept her eyes cast down, worried that her tears might tell the story of how they were connected.

"Hurry up," the mayor's voice boomed. "You'll be okay, since they're powerless. The earthquake's blocking their abilities."

Play the game, Ari. Play the game. "Blocking their abilities? They'll be okay? But they're the good guys. Shouldn't we be helping them?"

The mayor's body tensed. "There are a lot of good guys that don't have superpowers. Like, look at Shadow Town. Icy Tundra loses his powers and the city ends up in total chaos. New Shore has fully recovered. This will show the world not to rely on superpowers. We need to take back our cities and our country. Come on." He urged them with his gun. "Get going. Tie them up."

He knew the earthquake affected the superheroes...but Icy Tundra hadn't lost his powers. He had amnesia. Maybe there was hope for Adam. But the gash on his head...

Once Ariana had secured her husband's hands, Mayor Payne motioned toward a large boat tied up at the pier. "Get over there. Onto the boat."

Ariana breathed heavily with her eyes latched on her husband. The mayor waved his gun again, and his eyes focused on her like lasers.

He'll be okay. He's gotta be okay.

Prying herself from Adam's side, she joined the other two women shuffling their feet to the large charter boat. Each step cautious over the vibrating earth.

"What are we going to do?" Victoria whispered while they boarded the boat. The mayor was busy checking the zip-ties—tightening their purposefully poor attempts.

"He has no choice but to kill us. I wonder if he realizes that yet," Emma said. "We know he's behind this."

Ariana stepped to the front of boat. "Spread out as much as possible. He can't shoot all of us." Then a thought knocked the air from her lungs, and she searched her surroundings. "Adam said there were two people down here."

Before Victoria shuffled to the back of the boat, she whispered, "A kid like his nephew." She nodded at the mayor. "We have to deal with him first."

How? Ariana glanced around. *Know your surroundings.* Ariana's self-defense teacher's words came back. She couldn't forget about the boy.

With gun outstretched and sweeping between the woman, the mayor approached the boat. "What bad timing you ladies have. Quite unlucky."

Unlucky? I don't think so.

The fury Ariana felt during self-defense class returned. She pushed it down, staying in control. *Use that fury, Ari, but don't let it take over.* When the mayor was close enough to untie the boat, his eyes left the women for a moment, and Ariana seized her opportunity.

She launched herself at him, tackling him to the ground and recalling her self-defense teacher's training. She shoved her thumbs in his eyes, kicked between his legs, and twisted the gun from his hand. Mayor Payne screamed, but the other women were right there with her.

"What were your words, Mayor?" Ariana gritted her teeth, trying to get him in one of the lock-hold positions she had learned. "You don't need superpowers to be a hero."

In a move of sheer strength, the mayor threw Ariana off him. He twisted around to reach for his gun, which Emma scrambled to grab first, causing it to get knocked away instead...right over the edge into the water of the bay.

Ariana threw herself on top of the mayor again. "Get the zip-ties!"

Mayor Payne stumbled back, hitting his head against the post the boat was tied to.

With a look of horror, the mayor's eyes rolled back and closed.

Ariana was sure her face looked as terrible. "Oh no! Did I kill him?"

With the gun in one hand, Victoria leaned down and felt his neck. "No, he's got a pulse." She reached for the zip-ties Emma held. "Help tie him up quick." Her eyes glanced to Vance.

Ariana's eyes remained focused on the mayor. What had she done? *He's alive, Ari, and he's the bad guy.* Did Adam feel this way when he had to fight supervillains? *Note to self: console Adam more.*

Behind her, the boat's motor roared to life.

EMMA

in Shadow Town

Emma jolted back as water sprayed over the dock and the large charter boat tugged against the rope securing it to the dock. The engines revved, jetting water from the back of the boat. She whirled around, capturing a glimpse of the driver. A blond-haired, freckled boy wearing rather large earmuffs. She recognized him from the office at her sister's school—the mayor's nephew, Kyle Burg.

The boy rushed from the helm to the side of the boat. His arms and fingers stretched out to untie the rope.

"Oh no you don't!" Emma and Victoria both charged the boat, leaping onto the deck.

The boat swayed when they landed and Kyle stumbled back a step.

"Don't underestimate your opponent," Ariana yelled from the shore.

This kid was a supergenius. How did you compete with that? When the boy pulled a small device from his shirt pocket and smiled, Emma tensed.

A large hum filled the air that morphed into an ear-piercing screech. Emma attempted to cover her ears, but her muscles spasmed. The intense pain had her pulling herself into a ball and falling over onto the boat deck. Beside her, Victoria squirmed.

Kyle tapped his earmuffs and smiled. With quick movements, he untied the rope and headed to the boat's covered helm.

Emma's vision clouded. Her brain felt like sludge. What was going on?

Focus.

The noise drove her insane, and all she wanted to do was cover her ears, but her muscles were out of control. Random twitches and charley horses contorted her body.

She focused on a nearby tree, confirming they were moving. What would happen if he pushed them into the water like this? She'd surely drown.

This child…this supergenius must have figured out a way to disrupt muscle function, and perhaps thinking ability, with soundwaves.

Her larger muscles hurt the worst. Her hamstring, back, and abdomen spasmed. Tears rolled down her face, and all she could do was stare up at the sky. She tried to push the pain out of her mind enough to think, but everything was foggy.

She'd had muscle cramps once or twice in the middle of the night. She would spring out of bed and walk them off, despite the pain.

She forced herself to roll over, recoiling from the agony in every muscle of her body. She turned again, stretching out.

You have to stop the noise.

She pried her eyes open and tried to pinpoint the device causing the pain. From the helm to the fishing poles hanging off the back, she didn't see anything suspicious.

Maybe if you block the noise...

With another painful twist, her eyes focused on something bright orange. The noise made her jaw clench tighter.

Move. Push the pain aside.

Slowly and painfully, she crawled to the orange lifesaver. What was inside these? She picked at it with her fingernails until a piece of dense foam dislodged. Not the right size. She used her short fingernails to carve out a circular section. She rolled it between her fingers, then shoved it in her ear. She picked again, but another huge cramp shot up her back, making her body seize and her mind go blank. She collapsed against the deck.

Push forward.

This had to end.

She propped herself up on her elbows and reached a hand out for the life ring. Pulling out another piece of foam, she filled her other ear. Slowly, her spasms subsided. Her body was completely exhausted and soaked in sweat.

The only thing that kept her moving forward was the look of pure horror on Victoria's face as she clenched into a ball.

With a trembling hand, Emma pulled off more foam and crawled to her new friend, keeping out of sight as best she could.

Soon, both women lay on the boat deck with chunks of life preserver in their ears, catching their breath and stretching their heavy limbs.

Victoria turned toward Emma and whispered, "We need to turn the device off." She twisted her head, examining the boat deck.

Emma sat up. She spread her arms and mouthed back, "It's big." Again, she glanced around the vessel. Where could something that size be hidden? She then pointed down, remembering Vance's words. He had said it was underwater...or rather below the surface...like in the belly of a boat. Her eyes found a small metal handle on the deck, tucked away on the starboard side. "A trapdoor."

They pulled themselves over to the door and Victoria lifted the handle, revealing a dark cavern beneath.

"I'll turn it off," Victoria mouthed.

Emma nodded and pointed to Kyle. "And I got him." *But how?* He might be only twelve, but listening to all of Estevan's stories, she learned not underestimate anyone. An idea filled her mind, and she grabbed Victoria's arm. Estevan always said the easiest way to defeat a supervillain was to use their skills against them. "Don't turn it off yet. Back me up."

Emma motioned for Victoria to crawl after her. They made their way to the helm. Taking a deep breath, Emma crawled over the threshold.

Her elbow knocked an empty soda can to the ground. Emma cringed and flung her eyes to the boy. Her body stiffened as she waited for him to swing around, but he didn't budge. His earmuffs were still in place.

Sweat dripped into Emma's eye and she wiped it away. She pointed toward the boy and gave Victoria a nod. "Ready?" she whispered. When a nod came, she yelled, "Now!"

Both women flung themselves at the child. When the boy spun around, the look of horror on his face was something Emma knew she'd never forget, but she still pulled his earmuffs off.

His arms reached up to his ears, but midway, he dropped to the floor. Emma pointed to the steering wheel and Victoria took over.

Emma obtained the rope from the life preserver and tied the spasming boy up. Tears filled her vision. This wasn't something she ever thought she'd do. What if she had a child that turned out like this? That was a lot of responsibility.

She reached into his shirt pocket and pulled out the little remote control. She clicked a button...then another, until the noise and vibrations stopped. Her body tingled as she gingerly removed the foam from her ears. At least the boy had stopped spasming.

Victoria had turned the boat around. They weren't even out of the marina yet. What had felt like an eternity was probably only a few minutes.

When the boat bumped into the dock's buoys, Emma's chest constricted. How would they keep the superheroes' identities a secret? How much had Kyle already seen? She needed to get him out of here.

Emma ensured the squirming child's ties were tight, then positioned him so he couldn't see out the helm cabin. She needed to tie his feet as well as his body to the edge of the helm to keep him in position. He was yelling things, but

Emma had to tune them out, as they only upset her. The boat swayed a little when Victoria fled, rushing toward Vance laying on the shore.

She held her breath as she searched for Estevan, finally able to breathe when she saw him sitting up and shaking his head. Adam was doing the same, blood streaked across his unmasked face. Emma again looked down at Kyle.

When she returned her eyes to the scene on shore, she noticed that Vance still hadn't moved. Was it taking him longer to recover because this was the second time he'd felt the effects?

Way to the left, the mayor was also still motionless, hands zip-tied behind his back.

Well done, Ariana. He looks secure.

Estevan stumbled to his feet, still wearing his costume. He shuffled toward Emma. "Capitán Rápido, it's great to see you. Do you think you could escort our boat driver to the proper authorities?"

Estevan flashed her a bright smile and everything else around her dissolved, until Victoria's shrill voice pulled her attention away.

VICTORIA
in Shadow Town

"We need to get to the hospital!" Victoria yelled. It was all she could think of, seeing the wound in Vance's chest. The white fabric of his costume was soaked in blood. She pulled the fabric aside to reveal a bullet wound. Somehow, in the commotion, none of them had heard the shot ring out from the mayor's gun.

How had she not noticed this when she tied him up? She hadn't even thought to turn him over and examine him. Her lip quivered, and she tried to blink away her tears. He was invincible...at least he always had been before.

Victoria held her shaky hands to his bleeding chest wound. Blood oozed between her fingers, and her stomach threatened to spill its contents. "Vance? Can you hear me?"

He was still, yet a faint pulse was present when she laid her crimson fingers against his neck.

Time passed like a blur.

"I called 911," Emma said, laying a hand on Victoria's shoulder. "They're sending an ambulance. Estevan is already gone with Kyle and will catch up with the police."

"But his powers?"

"They're gone. But he's still a grown man against a tied up child. He'll be fine," Emma reassured.

"We need to get Vance out of costume." Ariana's eyes searched their surroundings.

"I can help." Adam's voice was hoarse and he looked like he had been hit by a bus as he stood over her other shoulder. He wiped the blood off his forehead.

"He always kept spare clothes in his car," Victoria wiped her tears on the back of her bloody hand.

Adam seemed to want to fly, but instead, took off in a jog, returning a few minutes later with his arms draped with clothing—enough for both of them to ditch their costumes.

When sirens filled the air, everyone pitched in to help Victoria finish changing Vance's clothes. When the first paramedic emerged from the ambulance, the two remaining men no longer looked like superheroes.

"I'll stay here and field questions." Emma rubbed her hands against her jeans.

"We'll bring your car to the hospital," Adam said. "I don't think I can do anything else...super right now."

The paramedics loaded Vance on a stretcher, and like a zombie, Victoria followed him into the ambulance, clutching his hand whenever she could.

Please be okay. Please. We have a lot of lost time to make up for.

He didn't stir as the paramedics switched out gauze pad after gauze pad. The medical lingo was like background noise that Victoria couldn't understand.

When they finally arrived at the hospital and doctors and nurses took over for the paramedics, Victoria couldn't take the suspense. "What's going on?" she demanded.

"His vitals are stable enough, but we need to get him to surgery. That bullet needs to come out," a woman wearing a white lab-coat assured her.

Minutes ticked by way too slowly—it was like the waiting room clock's batteries were dying. Victoria paced, double-checking the time on her phone. Her chest constricted and she felt like throwing up. All of her time with Vance ran through her mind. Images of the fun they used to have were shattered by the anger that developed between them. No more. If—*when*—he got out of this, there were no more games. No more pride. Life was too short for that.

Surgery took longer than expected, but finally the nurses brought Victoria to a room in the ICU.

Vance looked dead...all the color was drained from

his face. Her heart nearly stopped when he slowly turned his head.

"Hey, beautiful." His voice was weak. He opened his mouth to say more, but laid back and closed his eyes instead.

She wiped tears away and gripped his hand, squeezing it tightly.

A nurse held a stethoscope to Vance's chest. "It's lucky he made it here in time. If he arrived a minute or two later, he'd be dead."

Dead?

Surrounding Vance, the medical devices' steady beeping grew faster and louder and his eyes rolled back.

"Doctor!" the nurse yelled into the hallway.

Victoria's eyes followed the nurse before glancing back at an unconscious Vance. "What's going on?"

The nurse put her hand on Victoria's shoulder and gently pushed her into the hall. "Could you wait out here?"

A team of doctors and nurses rushed past Victoria, shoving her out of the way. They ripped Vance's gown aside. She heard the piercing sound of a machine, then someone called out, "Clear."

Behind the open door, Vance's body jolted on the table.

"Don't leave me now." Victoria couldn't breathe as she watched the crew work on the only man she ever truly loved.

Another piercing sound and another spasm from Vance's body.

Victoria held her breath.

Finally, a voice called, "There's his rhythm. I'll get the attending."

Victoria rubbed her temple and paced a tight line right outside his room. Two steps one way, then two the other.

When a nurse stepped out, Victoria stopped. "Okay,

ma'am. You can come back inside." The nurse guided Victoria up to Vance's still body. "Is he your husband?"

Victoria nodded, not even thinking to argue.

The nurse continued, "We'll be watching him closely." She pointed to some monitors hanging on the wall. "He's stable for now." When Victoria nodded again, the nurse left the room.

Sitting down beside Vance, Victoria held his heavy, calloused hand. Its warmth made her smile, despite her watery eyes.

He stirred. With a hoarse voice, he seemed to force out the word, "Victoria."

Her chest fluttered. "Shh. It's okay."

"Thank you."

Victoria squeezed his hand as he drifted off to sleep. She had spent all this time distancing herself from him, but now, she couldn't imagine being anywhere but at his side. Even if she lost him today, she'd be with him until his last breath. Somehow, she knew if the tables were turned, he'd do the same.

She pressed her forehead against their hands and whispered, "I love you."

Friday, April 23rd

EMMA

in Shadow Town

Emma held Estevan's hand as they pulled into the hospital parking lot. Yesterday, it had taken hours to explain to the police what all had happened, and she had been exhausted. Even after a semi-good night's sleep, she wasn't feeling much better.

Her husband looked as exhausted as she felt. She tugged him closer, wrapping her arm around his waist and leaning into his side. "I'm so happy you're okay. I don't tell you this enough, but you amaze me. The devotion you give me, the balance between your duty and your passion. I'm one lucky woman."

Estevan chuckled uncomfortably. "Come on, I have superpowers. It's me who is in awe of you. I think you're the brains behind this partnership."

Emma shook her head to deny it, but Estevan stopped her.

"Come on, *mi gatita*. Take a look at what just happened. You took care of everything without me. You found all the clues to figure this out, captured the mayor, and found evidence pinning him to his crimes. Also, you talked us out of any questioning by reporters and the police. Telling them you had come down to the docks to meet with the mayor about the high-speed train project was brilliant. And the way you explained Vance getting shot with a stray bullet when the mayor was knocked unconscious was clever."

Emma smiled. "How about the excuse that Victoria was searching the boat looking for a first aid kit when she stumbled upon the device instead?"

"Also brilliant." Estevan rubbed her shoulder. "I'm sorry Capitán Rápido got all the credit for the actual capture of the mayor and his nephew."

Emma laughed. "That never bothers me. We're kinda one and the same, anyway. I think we got lucky that the police already had evidence of Mayor Payne being the one orchestrating those earlier attempts on his own life. With the mayor in custody, his assistant--the one that looked like that reporter, Clark something-or-other, stepped forward and turned over the emails and data showing the mayor's campaign had been rigged." Emma thought back to Kyle Burg. "I feel bad about the boy, though. He's just a child that got mixed up in a bad situation."

"In cases like this, I have to keep reminding myself of the positives. Now that everything is in the open, Kyle will receive the help he needs. Imagine what good he could do if he grew up to use his brilliant mind to make this world a better place."

"It makes me question having children. What if they turn out like that?"

"But they might turn out like Samantha instead. All you can do is try your best to set an example and have a little faith in them."

"You have a point."

"Plus how many kids turn out bad, anyway? Very, very few." Estevan rubbed his cheek. "Do you think Mayor...um...ex-Mayor Payne will talk about who we are? Maybe Kyle saw something?"

"Your masks were all still on and as long as they don't connect us, everything should be fine. I don't think the boy saw anything from inside the boat, and when Ariana attacked the mayor, he hit his head pretty hard on one of the pillars. He's still saying he doesn't remember anything and has no idea how that sonic device got there. If more comes of it, we'll cross that bridge when we get to it."

Emma hoped they would never have to deal with that. It would put her husband at risk.

"Well, right now, we need your expert negotiations. You need to figure out how to get Vance out of the hospital. They're baffled about how he could have recovered overnight from a bullet wound."

Emma stopped and turned Estevan toward her. She stepped up on her tippy toes and gave him a tender kiss.

"What's that for, *mi gatita*?" Estevan asked with a smile.

"Do I need a reason to kiss my husband?" She laughed. "I think it's simply for you being you. I'm one of the luckiest women in the world."

"Because you're married to a superhero?"

"No. Because I'm married to you. My partner. A man who loves me for who I am. Someone I can be myself around and who supports me on whatever path my life takes me down."

Estevan wrapped his arm around her as they entered the hospital. He leaned down, while walking, and whispered, "That goes both ways."

Saturday, July 16th

3 MONTHS LATER

ARIANA

in Windy City

Adam took a step back, and his eyes roamed up and down Ariana's body. "Turn around."

"What?"

Adam twirled his finger. Ariana smiled as she spun in a circle, giving her hips a little extra sashay.

"Did you sit in a pile of sugar?"

Ariana twisted around to see her backside. "There's nothing there."

"Well, it's just that you have a pretty sweet ass."

Failing to hide a true laugh, Ariana picked a pillow up off their sofa and threw it at him, which he easily dodged. His words echoed in her mind. *'Oh, you're in so much trouble now.'*

Ariana backed up, giving him a seductive smile. *'Am I? Guess what underwear I'm wearing today?'*

Adam chuckled out loud. "I'm so happy to have my confident Ariana back. You are beautiful...and amazing."

"Seriously, now. Come on!" Ariana waved dismissively at him. "We have to get going."

Adam caught her hand and pulled her tightly against his body. "Don't dismiss what I said. I mean that. You're the most wonderful woman I've ever met. You have beauty on the inside as well as the outside. You stood by me, even though I was...well...a jerk."

"A jerk, huh?"

"An ass?"

"Perhaps. But I'm not innocent either. You stood by me through my crazy expectations...and my inability to even tell you what was wrong. I guess we're learning how to do this whole 'marriage' thing together."

Adam placed a passionate kiss on her lips. "Okay. We've got a wedding to get to, and it's going to be emotional."

"Why?" Ariana chuckled. "Will the cake be in *tiers*?"

A huge smile filled Adam's face and he pulled her into him, giving her another kiss. "I knew my jokes would rub off on you someday."

Ariana pulled back and snickered. "Or their wedding will be like TV antennas. You know, the service may be terrible, but the reception will be good."

"Are my jokes really that cheesy?"

"Yup."

"Maybe I'll have to work on them. Warning: you may be in for more of them. But seriously, I was thinking it'd be emotional because it's the first wedding we're attending since our own."

"You are a sweet guy, aren't you?" She traced a finger on the huge scar on Adam's forehead, not used to it yet.

"Sometimes, it's buried a little too deep. Luckily, I have you to help me find that part of myself."

A knock on the door interrupted them. Outside stood a beautiful, curvy redheaded woman with bright red lipstick. A red dress hugged all her curves. "Hello, Scarlet."

"You can call me Sarah."

Sarah, huh? "I'm glad you made it."

Ariana led Sarah down the hall and knocked on Lenny's door. He opened it, dressed in a pastel blue shirt and a dark tie.

Lenny smiled. "Is this the woman you told me about?"

"Lenny, meet your date, Sarah. You two can get to know each other during the three-hour car ride." At that moment, Sir Fluffypants scooted out of Lenny's apartment and headed down the hall.

Lenny and Sarah took off after the cat, but when Ariana tried to follow, Adam grabbed her hand and pulled her back. "Let them. I'm sure Sarah can handle a runaway feline."

Ariana chuckled, remembering Scarlet rescuing Sir Fluffypants last time from the tree outside. "Yeah, both Lenny and the cat are in good hands. Besides, it'll give them something to bond over."

"Playing matchmaker, huh?"

"I think you are, too." Ariana gave Adam's side a playful elbow. "The way I see it is if she's got a boyfriend, there's nothing for me to worry about."

"And if Lenny's occupied, I don't have to worry about him kissing you."

Ariana slapped his chest, playfully. "I told you that never happened. Why did I even tell you anything?"

Adam pulled her close. "Because I'm your husband and communication is one of the things that will keep us married for a long time."

With that, he kissed her, and she loved it.

VICTORIA
in Shadow Town

The sun shone brightly in the sky. It was a few hours after lunch and their shadows were beginning to grow long. Vance opened the car door and pulled Victoria out.

"Are you ready?" he said with an expectant nod.

Victoria smiled and leaned closer to him, white dress flowing behind.

Emma walked down the courthouse steps. "I thought it was bad luck for the groom to see the bride before their wedding."

Ariana giggled. "Adam saw me before our wedding too, since I had to save his naked ass. We've made it a whole three months now."

"It'll be fine!" Victoria waved her hand dismissively. "We did everything traditionally the first time and look where it got us. This time, we're doing whatever makes us happy. It's not about the wedding anyway."

She joined Vance as he walked her up to the wedding officiant. "We're ready."

The ceremony commenced, and eventually, "You may kiss the bride," was announced.

The smile on Vance's face made Victoria's heart flutter. When their lips met, she savored the feeling, reminding herself to never take it for granted.

Victoria pulled away and whispered, "I promise I'll never leave you again."

Vance chuckled. "Oh, don't worry. I won't let you even if you try. No matter where you run to, I'll be there, guiding you home or supporting you on your journey."

EMMA

in Shadow Town

It had been a long day. Emma stifled a yawn. She looked at Estevan, wondering if now was the time to tell him what had been eating at her for the past week.

She had waited for the perfect time to give him the news, but it never came. His week had been busy with helping Vance prepare for the wedding, taking care of crime in their city, and a big project at work.

Seeing the other happy couples around the table made her feel somehow complete. She looked over at her husband, devastatingly handsome in his tuxedo.

"What are you smiling at, *mi gatita*?"

"Just admiring how nice you look in black." She gave him a wink.

Estevan puffed out his chest.

Around them in the small banquet hall, servers began bringing out their meals. After their dinners were served, Vance raised his champagne glass to the room filled with about fifty guests. "I'd like to make a toast. Not many people have the chance to marry the woman of their dreams, and I'm lucky enough to have had that chance twice. This time, though, I'll never let her go. Here's to my wife, Victoria."

They all raised their glasses and took a sip… Well, everyone besides Emma.

Adam cleared his throat. "I think we should all celebrate the wonderful women we have in our lives. The ones that stand beside us, no matter what. The ones we tell all our secrets to—big and small."

Emma looked at her husband and gave him a seductive smile.

Estevan's eyes locked with hers. "And to our wives, who without them, we'd all have been lost so long ago. For having nothing to come home to makes you not want to come home."

Instead of another sip, Estevan gave Emma a kiss and whispered, "I love you."

"I love you, too."

Estevan nodded toward the champagne glasses. "Is there a reason you're not drinking tonight?"

Emma wanted to wait for the perfect moment, but she wouldn't keep this from her husband. She grabbed his tie and pulled him closer. Her lips to his ear. "I have a secret too."

Estevan stopped and whispered, "Hmmm... Is it something naughty? Tomorrow's Sunday and all."

Emma giggled. "Not at all. You ready?"

Estevan nodded, then his jaw fell open, seeing the future.

"That's not fair!" Emma exclaimed.

"Tell me your secret. I want to hear it from your lips."

She leaned closer, cupped her hand around his ear, and whispered, "You're going to be a father."

He turned to her, tears slowly welling in his eyes.

Emma nodded and jabbed an elbow into his ribs. "And you thought you couldn't do it. That our DNA wasn't compatible. Maybe some good came out of that sonar device the mayor and his nephew used."

Estevan didn't say anything, just pulled her in for a kiss more meaningful and passionate than anything Emma could remember. A new chapter of her life was about to start, and she couldn't wait to see what adventure it took them on...together.

THE END

If you enjoyed this novel, another superhero wife adventure can be found in the free short story, ***The Stellar Life of a Superhero Wife.***

You can download this collection free by signing up for Joynell Schultz's HIDDEN WORLDS Newsletter here: http://www.joynellschultz.com/subscribe

Also, if you have a moment and could leave a review on Amazon, that would be fantastic! A review to an author is like a $100 tip to a waiter/waitress. Sure, it can't be spent, but it is just as thrilling. A review can be super simple, just a sentence or two is plenty.

Want More?

If you enjoyed *The Secret Lives of Superhero Wives*, you may wish to check out these other novels by Joynell Schultz.

Love, Lies & Clones

June never asked to be cloned. She never asked for the faulty heart that beats inside her chest. But most of all, **she never asked for the chaos that would become her life.**

When her estranged father mysteriously appears at her doorstep to warn her of impending danger, she immediately dismisses him. But when he goes missing, his seemingly unbelievable claims prove to be true. **Not only is her life in danger**, but the lives of others like her are at stake.

As clues about a malicious conspiracy unfold, an AWOL soldier emerges insistent that he holds the missing link in this deadly puzzle, but **placing her trust in a stranger is the last thing June is willing to do.** With the clock ticking, *can June trust him with her secret... and her heart?*

For sale on Amazon here:

US: https://www.amazon.com/dp/B01MXTGIZL
UK: https://www.amazon.co.uk/dp/B01MXTGIZL

Blood & Holy Water

Ava is sick of mundane angel duties, and she wants a promotion to finally **earn her wings.** A promotion takes more than hard work; it takes a miracle--literally. Unfortunately, *her miracle's impossible,* because it involves a vampire.

Fin has no time for frivolous gestures. He's too busy avoiding his own kind to care what a naïve angel wants. But when the other **vampires uncover his deepest secret,** threatening what he cherishes most, nothing can help him...*except a miracle.* Too bad he chased the angel away.

For sale on Amazon here:

US: https://www.amazon.com/dp/B06XRN2NZ2
UK: https://www.amazon.co.uk/dp/B06XRN2NZ2

Hidden: A Pregnant Fairy Godmother's Journey...

Even being the best fairy godmother in all the land, Ciera's been hiding a secret. Not only is she pregnant, but she's magically pregnant with a human child.

Humans are not allowed in the fairy realm. Period. That includes half-fairy half-human babies. The only solution is to give the baby to its father before the Fairy Council finds out her secret. Finding the father should be easy, how many men named John could possibly live in this place called Chicago?

For sale on Amazon here:

US: https://www.amazon.com/dp/B074QQJ15B
UK: https://www.amazon.co.uk/dp/B074QQJ15B

About the Author

Joynell Schultz was raised at a zoo (yeah, bring on the jokes) which gave her a love of animals. She spends her days working as a veterinary pharmacist and spends her nights (cough, cough—very early mornings) creating imaginary worlds writing speculative fiction.

When she's not trying to put food on the table (takeout, of course) for her husband and two children (and keeping it away from her sneaky Great Dane), she spends her time reading, writing, enjoying the outdoors, and planning her next vacation.

Contact Info:
Email: joynells@gmail.com
Facebook: http://www.facebook.com/joynelljschultz
Twitter: http://www.twitter.com/JoynellJ
Blog: http://www.joynellschultz.com
Mailing List: http://www.joynellschultz.com/subscribe
　　Free short story collection (below) with sign up.

Quick Escape: Fantasy Tales — Enjoy a taste of another world with these three fantasy short stories.
Bitten: A desperate mother struggles to protect her son.
The Fairy Flu: A sick fairy confronts a childhood rival who threatens the kingdom.
The Enchanted Apothecary: A grieving shopkeeper becomes suspicious of a mysterious man who keeps visiting her apothecary shop.

84946093R00188

Made in the USA
Columbia, SC
19 December 2017